# THE MIDDLE EYE

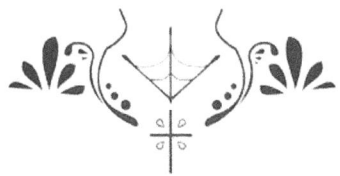

Rebecca Jean Downey

*The Middle Eye*
Copyright © 2013 by Rebecca Jean Downey. All rights reserved.

No part of this publication may be reproduced, stored in a retrieval system or transmitted in any way by any means, electronic, mechanical, photocopy, recording or otherwise without the prior permission of the author except as provided by USA copyright law.

This novel is a work of fiction. Names, descriptions, entities, and incidents included in the story are products of the author's imagination. Any resemblance to actual persons, events, and entities is entirely coincidental.

The opinions expressed by the author are not necessarily those of Creative Solutions Publishing.

Published by Creative Solutions Publishing
1911 SW Campus Drive, Suite 304
Federal Way, Washington 98023

*Cover design by Ronnel Luspoc*

*Interior design by Mary Jean Archival*

Published in the United States of America

Fiction / Thrillers / Crime

1. Fiction / Mystery & Detective / Women Sleuths

13.03.19

# ACKNOWLEDGMENTS

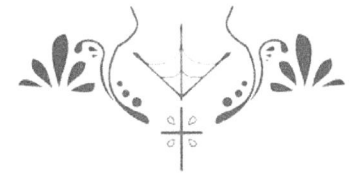

This work of fiction is dedicated to the memory of my mother, Norma Collings, who always insisted that I write something from my heart and not as a ghostwriter for someone else. Also, I want to thank my husband, James "Mike" Downey, for the freedom and the space to do so. I would like to express my thanks as well to my writing coach, Lucia Zimmitti, whose favorite saying, "that's too much on the nose," along with her incredible storytelling skills, helped me craft this novel. Most of my creative efforts were spent at the coffee shop in the library at the University of Texas at El Paso where manager Frances Luera encouraged me to complete this book. Thank you!

# INTRODUCTION

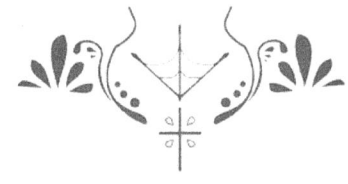

Since 2006, more than 211,000 people have been murdered by more than 200 Mexican cartels fighting for control of lucrative human and drug trafficking routes from Mexico to the United States, according to the U.S. Congressional Research Service. In 2013, when *The Middle Eye* was first published, Russian and Chinese human traffickers had a stake in Mexico's fragmented criminal justice system. Today, Mexican gangs and cartels have pushed the majority of those syndicates out of the country and ramped up the kidnapping of women and children for the lucrative sex trades and forced men to work as drug mules and coyotes. According to the Thomson Reuters Foundation, Central American immigrants hoping for a better life in the United States, are regularly forced into sexual encounters or required to carry contraband on them as they move north through Mexico. The Foundation reports that Mexico is an origin, transit and destination country for human trafficking, with an estimated business value of $150 billion a year. Unaccompanied children who appear at the U.S. Mexico border, are handled differently according to their country of origin. Children from any country other than Mexico or Canada are referred to the Office of Refugee Resettlement to be re-united with family members in the U.S. or placed in foster homes. Mexican and Canadian children are sent back to their homelands and placed at risk of further abuse.

Mexico is one of the world's most popular places for child abductions, mainly because crimes against children go unchecked. The United States 2020 Trafficking of Persons Report shows slight improvement in Mexican efforts to bring traffickers to justice, but local governments are rife with corruption. Four ongoing investigations into government employees engaging in human trafficking are underway.

Mexico continues to pose a risk to children's physical health and safety due to human rights violations committed against children, including child labor and a lack of child abuse laws.

Agencies don't agree on how many children are abducted in Mexico each year, but the number is in the many thousands. According to the National Foundation for Investigations of Stolen and Missing Children based in Mexico City, more than 20,000 Mexican children are abducted each year. The agency estimates that at least half of these children are snatched by one parent in domestic disputes. The other half run away because of family violence, go missing during illegal trips across the US border, or become victims of slave labor and sexual exploitation by traffickers. According to UNICEF, at least 16,000 children are victims of child trafficking for sexual purposes annually along the borders of the United States and Mexico. Regardless of the actual numbers of missing children, it is clear to this author that even one child harmed is too many. The vulnerability of Mexican children also attracts organized crime networks to Mexico, which draw upon their contacts across the globe to make money off the backs of children.

To further exacerbate the situation, Mexican families have a tradition of placing children as domestic workers in the house of an acquaintance or relative living in a bigger city. The parents hope that these children will have access to a better education and better job opportunities. Traffickers take advantage of this practice and try to gain the parents' confidence. Family members often discover too late that a child has gone off the radar.

This novel was written to raise awareness of the plight of children in Mexico, many of whom have no voice in their future. It is a work of fiction and in no way reflects actual places or circumstances where children might be at risk or in danger.

# PROLOGUE

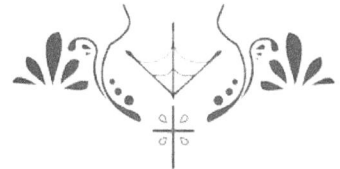

*The Middle Eye* introduces the reader to a psychic technique called controlled remote viewing, which was developed in the 1970s by the CIA when the agency suspected that the Soviet Union was conducting psychic spying on the United States. With the help of two scientists from the Stanford Research Institute, the United States established its own viewing program called Stargate. The US Army and the CIA utilized Stargate until the end of the Cold War when the US government declassified it.

This declassification provided those who had participated in Stargate the opportunity to help others with psychic abilities gain better control over their visions and dreams. A CRV specialist must follow a strict set of protocols in order to successfully tap into one's intuition and visual perceptions. Modern-day psychic viewers make themselves available to law enforcement agencies and individuals to help locate missing persons and solve cold cases.

# CHAPTER 1

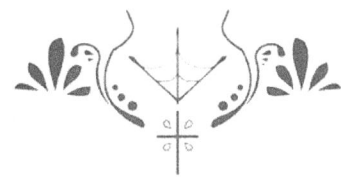

The light turns the indifferent wall into a ghostly theater of reflections.

I find myself in the middle of an eye, watching myself in its blank stare.

The moment scatters. Motionless, I stay and go: I am a pause.

—Octavio Paz (translated by Eliot Weinberger)

---

Penny Larkin focused, a blue cottage sitting in a field of green chili peppers. She rubbed her clammy hands on her jeans. Her damp blond hair lay flat against her neck, and the sweat poured down her spine. She opened and shut her eyes for the hundredth time.

*Still nothing*!

The pressure was mounting to pull the trigger and unleash her psychic will, yet she could see nothing beyond the home's weather-beaten front door. She knew enrolling in a class called controlled remote viewing had been a mistake. There was nothing in her life that was remotely close to being in control.

It was day four of the training; the classroom was hot, and her mind was still shooting blanks. The final exam required that she visualize the inside of the cottage and describe its contents. This was her last chance to redeem her failures of the past week. Today, she had at least managed to envision faint images within the house. Unfortunately, it was like trying to see through a gauzy sphere. Nothing came into focus no matter how hard she concentrated. Scared and disgusted, Penny threw up her hands and walked out of the classroom and into the New Mexico desert where the afternoon sun was baking the ground like shortbread in an oven.

Zarn Richter, the class instructor, followed her out the door. "Penny!" Zarn walked briskly toward her, smiling.

This irritated Penny further. It was no joke to fail. "For God's sake. You are giving up too soon!"

"Zarn, it's been four days. I'm a flop at this thing, and you know it!"

Penny looked up at Zarn, who was at least ten inches taller than her five-foot three-inch frame. The white golf shirt and khaki shorts were his uniform in class and in everyday life, Penny imagined.

Zarn refused to drop the big grin, his dark brown hair hanging in his eyes like a schoolboy. *Perhaps he found it amusing that in four days I have failed to view anything, except the insides of my eyeballs.* She was writhing in embarrassment.

"Penny, please, come back inside and try again. I told you not to try to predict an outcome with a viewing. Stop second-guessing yourself. You're making it too hard."

Penny stared straight ahead and caught sight of a small lizard tucked into the crevice of a rock wall.

"Please!" Zarn pointed to the door as if he could magically transport her back inside. "You don't understand, Zarn. There's more at risk here than my pride."

"Penny, I know this class is important to you, and that's why I keep insisting you take your time. You're trying to rush things." Apparently, it was hard work—harder than Penny had ever imagined connecting on demand with the unseen. Did she really have it in her to become a remote viewer? Her confidence was fading fast in spite of her instructor's encouragement. In the past, she had come by psychic information in her dreams. She was never in control of what she saw or when she saw it. This had interrupted her personal life and her career as a writer. Lately, it had brought her nothing but misery, having lost Porter Jenkins, her boyfriend of many years, after she had struck him in the head during one of her nightmares. He had stormed out of the house, swearing she had lost her mind, and declaring he would not return. He didn't. Penny had hoped this class would provide her with the tools she needed to gain control of her visions and, in turn, get her life, and Porter, back. It was looking more and more as though she was going to fall short of finding normalcy. She lifted her hands to the blue cloudless sky. "What am I doing here anyway?"

She squinted, trying unsuccessfully to filter out the sun's blinding rays. When she closed her eyes, little pinpricks of sunshine remained under her eyelids, bouncing around like Fourth of July sparklers. Finally, a fountainhead of tears forced her eyes wide open. She moaned as the tears tumbled on to her gray Henley shirt. Penny grabbed Zarn's shoulder and tried to steady herself. Whenever Penny faced a serious problem in her life, she usually solved it by running away. She pulled back from Zarn and tried to make a break for her car, parked in front of the classroom.

"It's time I got out of here!"

"You are not going anywhere, Penny!" Zarn held on tightly to her arm. "This class is way too expensive just to leave because things aren't going like you think they should."

Of course, Zarn made a great point. She had paid $3,000 for the class, and her checking account was bleeding red ink. Penny had hoped a remote viewing certification would provide her with a new more financially rewarding career, allowing her to back off from her job as a freelance writer. Most word jockeys she knew were starving, and she wasn't far behind.

"Okay. Just once more." Her body slumped forward in submission.

Zarn placed his arm on Penny's shoulder and guided her back to the classroom, which was located in an old hangar on land that had been abandoned years ago by Holloman Air Force Base. The room was pulsating with technology and stacked high with audiovisual equipment. Red, green, and yellow lights winked at her, but she ignored them. All of Penny's classmates had left, she figured, having successfully completed the exercise. The blue cottage was still there on the wide screen, just as it had been, waiting for her to return and get on with it.

Zarn stepped up to the television monitor and changed the videotape.

"Let's review yesterday's exercise first." "Do you have to rub it in?"

A video of her previous attempt at viewing flared to life. Penny became riveted to the screen. Yesterday, she had been asked to determine the location of a target simply by looking at a pencil sketch of an old metal building in some rocky foothills that led to a balding but formidable mountain peak. Penny observed herself studying the sketch that was lying on the classroom table. She rubbed her hands across the paper. Then she leaned back in her chair and scanned the drawing from an arm's length. She remembered thinking this was a ridiculous exercise because who could locate anything from just looking at one-dimensional lines made with a pencil on paper? Her doubt was apparent as the video showed Penny standing and walking over to Zarn.

"This is a joke, right?" She took the paper, tore it into confetti, and threw it in the air. She returned to her chair and rested her head on the table. As the video droned on, Penny looked over at Zarn, who appeared oblivious to her pain both on and off the screen.

"Take me out of my misery please!"

The television screen went fuzzy, just like Penny's thinking. "What do you see when you watch yourself on that tape?" Zarn asked.

"I see a self-absorbed loser whose impatience and lack of self-confidence are causing her to fail again and again."

"I am pretty certain you can pass this exam if you follow the steps I gave you to memorize. You're bright, and you have excellent potential for being a remote viewer."

Penny was surprised to hear Zarn's compliment, but she couldn't imagine why he thought that. As far as she knew, her classmates were passing with flying colors.

"This is something I just know, Penny. I've been teaching remote viewing for twenty years. However, if you are unwilling to embrace your skills, you will never become a viewer."

*Maybe I do have a chance at this!*

Penny stood, straightened her rumpled shirt, and ran her fingers through her hair. "Turn the television on, and bring forth the little blue cottage."

# CHAPTER 2

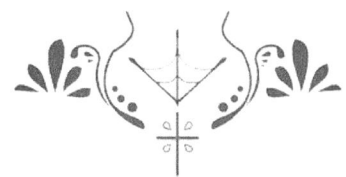

Penny followed the controlled remote viewing procedures to the letter. The CIA had, after all, developed them for the US military. In the past, she had just flirted with the protocols, and Zarn had warned her repeatedly that she would not be successful without using the remote viewing protocols in the exact manner they were prescribed.

Penny looked at Zarn, who was holding a sealed envelope. She knew it listed the contents inside the cottage. She also understood the rules required she do this alone, but he stood there anyway.

"Zarn, please step out of the room."

Penny turned back to the target, took a deep breath, and began. *Step 1: relax and clear your mind.* She tried to wipe her brain clean, as if she could completely dispel thirty-five years of memories in one fell swoop. She held her breath momentarily, trying to calm her rapid heartbeat. She saw Zarn looking at her from the hallway.

"Go away, Zarn! I can do this."

Once again, the fuzzy images began popping into her mind's eye. Instead of being encouraged, she knew this wasn't right. She had seen those before, and they had led her astray. She had to clear her thoughts completely. Penny began using the breathing exercises she had learned in yoga class. She placed both hands on her stomach and felt them rise and fall as her body accepted the rhythmic movements of deep breathing. Within a few moments, a blackout curtain dropped over her mind, and she was fully relaxed. Her breathing was almost imperceptible. Her hands felt warm and dry.

*Step 2: abandon all personal desires and wants in relation to the target.* Penny knew her previous fears of ultimately winding up alone in life had got her expectations in a jumble. Imagining the cottage was a place where two people loved each other and reared a family had killed the exercise for her. These assumptions had overridden her ability to concentrate.

*Step 3: be in harmony, in perfect balance with the void that is the exclusion of all other thought.* Penny imagined a key unlocking her head and allowing the contents to spill out on to the floor. She saw remnants of fear about the future, the grief over losing Porter and worry about her finances roll away. Images of her mother, lost in her nightly cocktails, faded from memory. The painful photos of her father's fatal accident, his prized racecar crumpled against an infield wall, dropped into nothingness. Only the cabin on the lake, her family's former summer home, hovered for a while before evaporating into a cloud of peace.

*Step 4: let your higher power take the lead.* Up until now, Penny had blown this step off completely. She pleaded for God's help. She was surprised at the immediate and commanding response. She felt as if she were shaking hands with the universe.

Penny knew she was now ready to view the inside of the little blue house. In her mind's eye, she saw the cottage in front of her. She began walking slowly toward it. The more steps she took, however, the farther away the house appeared. She picked up her pace, thinking she could outrun the tricks her mind was playing on her. The house got even smaller! Her eyes began to twitch and burn. She blinked back the tears. If she didn't do something soon, the house would be no bigger than a game piece on a Monopoly board.

"I can't fail now!" In a panic, she began to run, only to stumble over a large rock in her path, thrusting her forward onto her knees. Looking around, Penny tried to get her bearings. Her knees, though dirty, were unscathed. *Where in the world am I?*

Then, she saw a pair of eyeglasses lying in the grass, winking back at her in the sun's reflection. She picked them up, discovering they were bifocals. She tried the glasses on, not really knowing why, since she normally had perfect eyesight. As her eyes adjusted to them, she saw she was kneeling right in front of the little blue cottage. Penny jumped to her feet. She didn't have time to be amazed. She had to get inside that house!

She bounded up the three steps to the covered porch. The front door was ajar. Penny stepped inside the old house, which was surprisingly light and airy. She should have been choking from musty smells, she figured, but instead, the fragrance of lilacs hung in the air. *Where were they?*

Penny left the front door half open, hoping to leave by the same way she came in. Then she tiptoed through a small living room, following the perfumed air down a short hall and into a bedroom.

*There they are*! The purple lilacs were in a tall, clear vase filled with sparkling clean water. The flowers sat on a bedside table near a window that faced the rear of the house. The double bed was freshly made, and a white chenille coverlet fell gently over the sides of the mattress. The wood floor, painted gunmetal gray, had been scrubbed until it was spotless.

She backed out of the bedroom, retracing her steps. She moved into another bedroom down the hall. It was tiny, with just one window. The walls were covered with peeling pink paint. The room was adorned with only a twin bed and a bedside table. It seemed sparse and neglected—a total antiphony of the lilac-filled room. Penny didn't like how this room felt. She quickly left it and moved back down the hallway.

When she entered the kitchen, a coffeepot bubbled and purred on a gas stove. Coffee was on its way for some lucky duck. It smelled heavenly to her. A chipped porcelain cup—like the ones you find in a country café—sat on a 1940s-style metal table. Two straight-backed chairs joined it. Penny made a mental inventory of what she saw in the cottage, knowing she would be tested. She looked over at the stove. The gas flames were now licking around the sides of the pot. A boilover was imminent.

*Should I turn off the stove, or is that against the rules?*

Penny heard the front door squeaking on its hinges and then footsteps on the wood floor. Her eyes darted around the room, searching for a way out. There was a screen door leading to the backyard. She ran to the door and pushed it open. Her heart was pounding rapidly as she rushed out of the house. The spring banged the door shut behind her, causing a chill to shoot through her body.

Someone surely had heard the door, and she would be caught and punished! She darted across the decaying floorboards of the porch, tripped, and tumbled down the steps. She landed headfirst in the deep grass. Penny clawed her way across the yard, trying to get as far away from the cottage as possible before she was discovered nosing around where she did not belong. The screen door slammed again. Someone had followed her out the door! The sound of heavy boots—a man's boots—dragging across the porch drove Penny into a panic. Could he hear her heavy breathing? She did not move, hoping he would change his mind and return to the cottage. Instead, the brown leather boots came within inches of her head—so close she could smell the shoe polish. She opened her mouth to scream but soon understood the man could not see that she was lying right at his feet. To her relief, she realized she was not physically present and, therefore, not in danger. Penny took a deep breath, and when she released it, she found herself back in the classroom. The television screen was dark. She was alone.

# CHAPTER 3

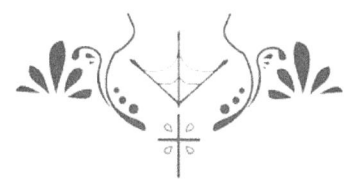

Penny's throat ached, and her tongue stuck to the roof of her mouth. She felt as if she had been running for miles, and yet she knew she had never left the classroom. Her hands flew to her eyes. *Where are those bifocals?*

She opened a metal folding chair and sat down at a nearby table. She picked up a pen and paper and started making notes about the things she recalled in the blue cottage. She was gushing with happiness and could hardly wait to tell Zarn about her experience. *Are all remote viewings this exhilarating?*

After several minutes, Zarn arrived and handed Penny a bottle of water. He returned her big smile but didn't say anything.

Penny chugged the entire bottle of chilled water. Her throat was still parched, but she was determined to tell her instructor the whole story. He was standing in front of her with his arms crossed and a look of satisfaction on his face.

"Ready to give me a report on what you saw in the blue cottage?" Zarn opened the envelope holding the mystery contents within the cottage. Even he did not know what was inside, for fear he might transmit it through his thoughts to his student. Every student had a different test. The targets ranged from airplanes to underground tunnels to outbuildings to houses similar to Penny's. "The experience was so real, I actually thought I was there," Penny said.

"Well, you were there, Penny. Your body wasn't there, but your spirit was, and that is a phenomenon that takes some getting used to. Some viewers can't or won't accept it."

"Well, I smelled those wonderful lilacs! They were heavenly."

Zarn perused the list.

"I don't see anything about lilacs, Penny."

"There has to be! They were hard to miss in the bedroom."
"Did you see the old beagle hound lying in the mudroom?" Zarn asked.

"What mudroom? I saw the kitchen and a coffeepot about to bubble over!"

"Sorry, Pen. No coffee."

"Then what in heaven's name did I see?" Her voice was pulsating with frustration.

"I am not sure. I've never had a student visit the wrong target. I've got to give this some thought."

"I've got no more time for thoughts! Thoughts are my enemy, and I am never going to get mine under control!" She jumped up and headed for the exit.

Zarn barked, "Don't move a muscle!" Then he ran out of the room. Penny plopped back down in the metal chair.

Zarn called the only world who would have the answer. Ingo Swann, the guru of controlled remote viewing, had developed the protocols Zarn used in his classes. Back in the 1970s, Ingo had been one of the founding fathers of the Army's psychic viewing program.

Luckily, he was in his office.

"Ingo, this is Zarn Richter. I'm fine. Yes, thank you. Sorry, I don't have much time to talk, but I've got a student in my classroom who just visited the wrong target. What in the world happened?"
"Zarn, although this is unusual, it is not a bad thing! You've got yourself an exceptional understudy who is picking up on a live target that has to be explored. There must be trouble brewing somewhere for your viewer to see it while concentrating on another target. You've got to help her locate it." "What should we do next?"

"Well, your student has got to revisit that target! And there is probably no time to waste. I'm dead serious. I wish I were there with you because I think something big is up. I only had one other experience with a viewer visiting the wrong target, and that ended with an Air Force pilot disappearing off the coast of the Philippines."

"I don't remember hearing about that."

"No, you wouldn't. He was on a secret mission. When one of our viewers saw the plane, he thought he had made a mistake because he was supposed to focus on a helicopter, not a fixed wing. He aborted his viewing and started again. By the time the viewer got ramped up again on the Air Force's orders, the pilot and the plane had disappeared. No amount of revisiting the target ever turned up a clue. And of course, the US government couldn't report it. The widow grieved in silence. Even though it wasn't our fault, we felt we had failed our country."

"Thanks, Ingo. I'll call you back with the outcome!"

"Don't be surprised if you've got a real barn burner on your hands. Good luck!"

# CHAPTER 4

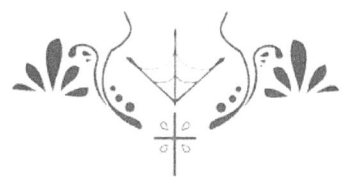

Penny drummed her fingertips on the table and tried to imagine what in the world would have caused her to be so far off the mark. *What kind of an idiot would visit the wrong target during a remote viewing test?*

Wrong turns and detours had been the story of Penny's life. Her mother, now dead, had always been the trailhead of most of her disappointments and wrong turns as a child, and today, here she was again, rising up in Penny's memory. Dorothy Larkin had regularly enjoyed stubbing out Penny's confidence like one of the half-smoked cigarettes she kept in a cocktail glass near her armchair. Drunk but determined, Penny's mother had loved sending Penny off on a wild goose chase as if it were some kind of cruel sport.

*Thanks, Mom. I think you're still at it!*

Zarn nearly galloped back into the classroom. "Penny, you won't believe this.

Ingo Swann is certain you have found a target that needs your help. He urged us to try to visit the cottage again as soon as possible and see if you can pick up on any clues that would lead us to the reason you got the viewing in the first place."

Stunned, Penny had a difficult time believing what Zarn had to say. How could she be focusing on one thing and visiting another? "Can you give it one more try?" Not waiting on her response,

Zarn ran over to the television and inserted the video.

"Zarn, I am confused. I can't see how it is possible for me to have gone into another cottage."

The blue cottage lit up the screen. Penny shook her head in disbelief. She stood and walked over to the television, totally unsure of what possible good this was going to do for her or anyone else. This time, Penny used the protocols like a pro and quickly found herself in a suspended state, somewhere between reality and the dream world. She wasn't quite sure where she was, but shadows were becoming definitive shapes, and the earth appeared to be rising up to meet her feet. The blue cottage flickered into her consciousness but failed to evolve fully. Instead, the image of a playground pushed the cottage out of her view. There were children everywhere. So many kids were running, shouting, and enjoying the sunny day that she couldn't begin to count them. Then Penny saw a small Hispanic girl, with dark, curly hair, playing by herself behind an ancient-looking cottonwood tree. She was loping her pink pony through the grass, up and over the tree's ropelike roots, which were spreading out aboveground in search of water. It was clear this little pony was something special to the child. Penny smiled, happy for her.

A dark blob with legs appeared from behind a hedge and crouched behind the little girl. Penny tried to shout out a warning to her because the shadowy figure looked foreboding. But Penny could not speak. It was only seconds before the girl was wrapped in a blanket and thrown over the man's shoulder. Penny burned the man's face in her memory as he looked back to see if he had gone undetected. His straggly brown hair stuck out of a navy blue baseball cap. His long, angular face had deep-set eyes, the nose of a prizefighter, and the stubble of a beard, which hid his poor excuse for a chin.

Breathless, Penny rushed forward in an effort to follow him. She arrived just in time to see the kidnapper climb into an old blue van. Penny tried to get a view of the license plate, but there was none. The engine roared to life, and the van rolled away from the curb. Penny turned back, hoping to find someone else who saw him. The children were still screaming and laughing, oblivious to the peril they might have experienced themselves. No other adult could be found. She tried to scream too, but nothing came out of her lungs but a gush of air.

"Hey, Penny, it's okay. Stop screaming!"

"Oh my God, Zarn! I have just seen the most horrible thing. A little girl has been kidnapped, and I couldn't even warn her. I was totally helpless to stop this god-awful man."

"Penny, you are helping her. You saw the kidnapping, and that's a start."

"I've got the man's face seared into my memory."

"I'm going to check with New Mexico and Texas authorities, since you're from El Paso, to see if any child is missing. I'll be right back!"

Penny felt sick to her stomach. Her face was hot, and her fingers tingled. Fear lodged in her throat like a dirty sock. She ran into the restroom and threw up. It didn't help. Her gag reflex remained. She hadn't counted on her horrific reaction to the kidnapping of a child, particularly a girl.

Penny met Zarn as she was leaving the restroom. Her blouse was soaked from cleaning herself up in the sink, and her face was damp with sweat. If he noticed her condition, he never showed it for which she was grateful.

"Penny, I am very sorry your first case as a viewer has to start like this, but you've got to get in your car and head back to El Paso. I just talked to the sheriff there, and sure enough, they've just lost a child in Alameda Park."

Penny was speechless. She wiped a damp paper towel across her brow.

"What's even crazier, Penny, is this is the second time this little girl has been kidnapped! Fortunately, the first time, a homeless man had mistaken her for his daughter who lives in Lawton, Oklahoma. They found her unharmed under the Stanton Street Bridge."

Penny stamped her feet, then grabbed her backpack and car keys.

"Can't you come with me, Zarn?"

"No, Penny. I've got another class starting in the morning. You can do this. I'll be available by phone. Call me day or night."

Penny threw her gear into a green Saab convertible and started the car. Never mind that the top was down, the air was cooling, and her damp shirt was clinging to her chest.

Zarn followed her to the car. His cell phone rang. "Yes, Sheriff, she's on her way. Her address is…"

"It's 2945 Loma de Brisa," Penny added.

"Okay. She'll meet you at her house in two hours. Got it. Thanks. Bye."

"The sheriff is coming to my house?"

"Yes. He wants to talk to you in a place where you are more comfortable instead of exposing you to his offices, which he says are in chaos, trying to find Rosa. Rosa Garcia. That's her name. She's eleven."

# CHAPTER 5

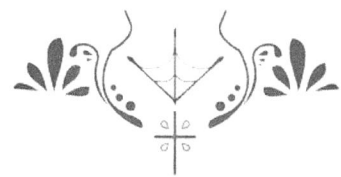

El Paso was normally a beautiful two-hour drive from the Air Force base housing where Penny and her classmates had bunked during the training. She would, however, have little time to enjoy the scenery. Somewhere, a pervert was holding a little girl against her will. Heaven only knows what he was doing to her. Penny knew she had to get back to El Paso, pronto, and that meant putting her foot down hard on the accelerator.

She hated driving fast, even though speed was a birthright from her father, Johnny Larkin, a racecar driver of international acclaim. Her father's untimely death in a road race in Southern California, at the age of forty, had always been enough to keep her within the boundaries of her own driving skills. But today, as she roared south on US Highway 54, the memories of driving her father's 1989 cherry red Pontiac Bonneville emboldened her.

Her dad had often let her drive his car down the rural roads of Indiana, churning up the dust and gravel as he yelled, "Faster, Penny! Faster!" Even though her feet could barely touch the pedals, she had always been happy to oblige, knowing her dad would never let her lose control. Today, however, it was just Penny behind the wheel of her convertible, enveloped by the broad expanse of sky.

At sixty-five miles an hour, the car seemed to crawl through the desert terrain. Penny took a deep breath and pressed even harder on the accelerator. The convertible's engine howled as the tachometer pushed toward the red zone. It was invigorating to feel the wind pounding against her face.

The road from the Air Force base to the Texas border took Penny through thirty miles of Northern Chihuahuan desert filled with flowering yucca, waving strands of ocotillo, patches of prickly pear, and an unrelenting growth of cholla trying to gain a chokehold on the desert floor. At speeds of eighty-plus mph, she crossed the Texas state line in no time. To her left, she saw a herd of bison, steam pouring from their nostrils, as they grazed on a patch of dry grass. The fleeting rays of sun crawled over their backs and up the eastern slopes of the Franklin Mountains. The heat was quickly losing its grip on the day and bringing a chill to the back of Penny's neck and arms. She wished she had donned her windbreaker before taking off.

Penny leaned back in the bucket seat and embraced the thrill of the throbbing pistons under the hood, the tires thumping against the road, and the wind whistling over the side mirrors. Her car radio was just a monotone in the symphony of speed that had always inspired her father to compete. Soon, she forgot the chill in the air.

Penny saw a sign for the turnoff to Transmountain Road. She needed to exit, but she was going too fast to do so safely. In her exuberance, she yanked the steering wheel to the right anyway, a foolish choice even for the most experienced driver. The Saab's wheels screamed. The car skidded out of control. Fifty feet ahead, a large palo verde tree loomed in her path. Suddenly, she was back in the Bonneville with her father who was yelling, "Speed up in the turn! Speed up!" It didn't make sense, but Penny pressed her foot even harder on the gas and tightened her grip on the steering wheel. Miraculously, the car began pulling out of its slide and correcting its trajectory. She came within inches of the arroyo where the palo verde stood, its arms open wide.

Dazed and winded, Penny released her death grip on the wheel and took her foot off the accelerator, allowing the convertible to slow on its own. Carefully, she guided the car to the side of the road and stopped. She rested her head on the steering wheel and tried to calm her breathing, which was near a pant. Her stomach ached. Her hands were shaking. She looked around to see if any other drivers had witnessed her foolishness. Thankfully, she was alone on the side of the road. Only the 7,000-foot Mount Franklin loomed before her.

Penny knew she would need good tires to climb the mile-high mountain pass. She got out of the car to check for damage to her tread and sidewalls. She tried walking, but her legs felt like deadweight. She was light-headed, and her toes were numb. She leaned into the front fender and flexed her fingers, then her toes. After several minutes, an urge to faint passed, and she stood upright and moved carefully around the car, checking each wheel for damage. Other than a few dings on the hubcaps, the tires appeared to have escaped any flat-spotting or gouges.

Penny got back in behind the wheel and revved the engine, which sounded solid and unharmed. She drove slowly up the winding road that would take her through an abandoned US Army munitions test site and higher still into the Franklin Mountains State Park. The convertible crested the mountain pass and followed the road into a downward grade, which would eventually lead her to El Paso's northwest side. To Penny, there was no more enjoyable experience than watching the sun setting behind the Portillo Mountains of New Mexico, seventy-five miles to the west. On this particular October afternoon, the sky's burnt orange haze was woven through with ribbons of pink, turquoise, and purple that seemed designed to outperform the cloudless sapphire sky in the remains of the day.

Scanning the horizon to the south, she could make out a sliver of the Rio Grande and a train heading west on the railroad tracks that ran along the US and Mexico border.

Penny would be home in ten minutes. She prepared mentally for her encounter with Sheriff Leo Tellez. She knew him by reputation only. At the age of forty-two, Tellez was something of a legend around El Paso County. In the past six years, he had cleaned up a sheriff's office that was scabbed over with dirty deputies and facing a financial crisis from mismanagement. He had also instituted a career track for correctional officers at the jail, bringing an air of respectability to an otherwise thankless job. It would be an honor for Penny to meet him at last, but she wished she were more prepared to do so. She had only one misdirected remote viewing under her belt. Would that be enough to find Rosa? She looked down at her shirt, which was stained with vomit, and gasped.

# CHAPTER 6

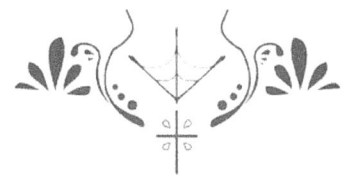

Penny pulled alongside the patrol car parked in her driveway. Sheriff Leo Tellez stood beside his vehicle, kicking rocks off the cement and back into her desert landscaping with his cowboy boots.

Penny got out of her car and shook the sheriff's hand. She saw an underlying sadness in his eyes.

"Thanks for seeing me so quickly." He appeared genuinely grateful for Penny's quick response to his request that she drive 100 miles in record time.

"I sure hope I can be of some assistance," Penny replied. "FBI Special Agent in Charge Peter Brooks believes Rosa Garcia may be a runaway. Rosa was kidnapped once before, and he thinks it is highly unlikely that she has been kidnapped again. His agency has chosen to stand aside until there is more proof she has been kidnapped. It's only been eighteen hours as we speak."

"It sounds a little crass coming from the FBI, "Penny said. "How can you ignore the fact that an eleven-year-old girl is missing?"

"Lately, we've had a number of kids around her age go missing for a couple days, and then they show back up at their parents' house. The FBI is tired of chasing its tail, only to find the child had an argument with a parent and hid out with friends or went to Juárez to stay with relatives who were willing to harbor them. I believe Rosa's case is different. But it's almost like she disappeared in midair."

"Nobody leaves us in midair," Penny said.

"It sounds crazy, but no one saw anything. And it doesn't look good for her, you understand. If she has been snatched by a pedophile, we may be hunting for a dead child."

Penny sucked air, ending in an embarrassing little hiccup. "Regardless, we have to find her," she said, trying to appear calm even though her insides were churning.

"Do you mind if we go inside, so I can run through the evidence we have so far and take notes on what you think you saw?"

Penny threw her backpack over her shoulder and escorted the sheriff into her house. The silence in the sprawling adobe-style home embraced them as she dumped her backpack on the dining room table.

"Coffee?" she asked. "I know I could sure use some."

"That would be terrific. I haven't eaten anything since yesterday." Penny went to the pantry and brought out a jar of peanut butter and a loaf of stale bread before hauling out the coffee beans. "It's not five-star, but it may help," she said. Then she headed to the coffeemaker and ground some beans.

The sheriff made a sandwich and offered to make one for Penny too. They sat at her circular oak kitchen table. Each gulped down the coffee in silence and finished off the sandwiches.

Finally, the sheriff took a deep breath and looked up in response to Penny, who was clearing her throat.

"I don't know if Zarn Richter told you, but the abduction I saw was the result of a mistake on my part. I was supposed to describe the contents of a cottage that was on a television screen in our classroom. Instead, I saw what may or may not have been the abduction of Rosa Garcia."

"We will take anything you can offer. Right now, we have absolutely nothing to go on."

"Zarn may have a little too much faith in me. I'm a novice at this, I must warn you."

"Zarn has helped the sheriff's office for many years, and he assured me you would be of tremendous help as well. He said you saw the kidnapper wrap Rosa in a blanket and put her in an old blue van. Knowing the make and model of the vehicle would be great."

"I'm not so good at telling one car from another." "Could you describe it?"

"It was pretty beat-up. The back bumper was crushed." "Did it have a license plate or other markings?"

"I think I saw the number 3500 on the rear door but no plates. The back was pretty dented up, though, for me to be sure."

"That would probably mean he was driving a Dodge Ram van, Penny. If that is the case, you've given us a tremendous break."

The sheriff stood and made a call to the station to alert his patrol units. When he returned, he continued asking Penny questions. He finally came to the inevitable one.

"Did you see the kidnapper's face?"

Penny let out a sigh. "Yes, I did. I'm still haunted by it."

"Do you think you saw enough of his face to give our sketch artist something to work with? I mean, it was, after all, just a dream."

"It may sound like just a dream to you but seeing things like this scare me! And what's worse, I couldn't speak or interfere with the kidnapping. I had to just stand there and watch it. It was horrible."

"Penny, if you can give our artist something to go on, we may actually have this guy in our database of sex offenders."

Penny groaned.

"Almost forgot." Leo pulled a plastic bag out of his jacket pocket. It held what appeared to be small pink cotton top. "Take a look at this while we ride downtown. It's Rosa's."

"You're going to drive me to the sheriff's office?"

"It'll save us time. And time is pretty precious right now. I'll have one of my officers bring you right back home."

The top seemed very tiny. "Could it be for a doll? Are you sure this is hers?" She pulled it out of the plastic bag and checked the size. It was a child's size 6.

"How could an eleven-year-old squeeze into such a small top?" "Her mother said it was one of Rosa's favorites and that she wore it all the time."

"I hope we're not looking for a girl who is being starved to death. No one should be that size at eleven years old!" Penny tried to remember just how big Rosa had appeared in her viewing. Now that she thought about it, she had figured Rosa to be around five or six. Penny's gut instinct told her that there was perhaps more to this story than the fact that Rosa had gone missing. She did not yet know what was going on in this tiny young life, but she was determined to find Rosa and rescue her from more than her kidnapper.

# CHAPTER 7

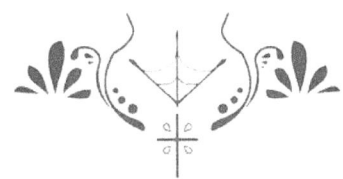

Deputy José Gómez, the department's witness identification specialist, was much younger than Penny expected. He looked as though he were right out of high school. His dark hair complemented his brown eyes. His face was full but not fat, and his nose was short. His efforts to grow a beard were going nowhere. Penny was nervous to be there. She hated it, but she had grudgingly agreed to the sheriff's request to give the sketch artist a description of the kidnapper. Hopefully, what she gave him would help to move the case forward.

The office was small, holding only a computer and a filing cabinet, so there was barely room for both of them to sit side-by- side at the long, narrow folding table the deputy used as a desk.

Penny didn't see any paper or pencils. "Where will you be doing the sketch?"

"We don't actually do sketching any more. We gotta computer program that has specific facial characteristics, and we put 'em together to create a composite." The deputy threw some files on the table and pulled a chair out for Penny, indicating she should sit.

Gómez sat next to Penny, so close she could smell his breath, a mixture of tobacco and breath mints. His nicotine-stained fingers began shifting back and forth among the on-screen icons, each holding what appeared to Penny to be a pocketful of facial characteristics such as noses, chins, lips, and foreheads. When the software program fully opened, it revealed a single oval shape—a clean slate, ready for Penny to fill in the blanks.

The deputy pushed back from the table a little and rubbed his hands across his face.

"Is there a problem, Deputy Gómez?"

He rolled his eyes. "It's nothin' I can't handle."

Penny felt uneasy, and she wasn't exactly sure why. "Have I done something wrong?"

"No, miss. It's just—I think this is a waste of my time and yours."

"Don't you think I can help?"

"I don't believe in your kind of thing—psychic stuff." He looked up at Penny. She knew he could see the concern on her face. "But just wait until my friends hear I was working today with a lady who sees dead people!" He pushed his chair back against the wall and laughed.

"I'm not a psychic," Penny answered in defense of her new profession. "And I don't see dead people. Controlled remote viewing is just tapping into a skill we all have if we would embrace it."

"Yeah. Right. And my mama's a fortuneteller! Didn't the sheriff tell you? We all know Rosa is dead. The kidnapper hasn't offered up a ransom, and it's been nineteen hours since she went missing."

Penny stood up and began maneuvering her way toward the door. She was confused and felt disoriented. *Has the sheriff been keeping information from me?*

"Hold on now!" Deputy Gómez yelled. "My orders are to get a composite from you, and by God, I'm gonna do it." He acted as though he was actually going to force her back to the table.

Penny was a person of her word, and she had agreed to help the sheriff, so she reluctantly returned and sat back down beside the deputy. The odor of smoked cigarettes broke over her again as she watched his fingers tap the keys to bring the oval back on the screen.

"Let's start by determining the shape of the face," he said. Penny told Gómez that the suspect had a long, narrow face, a punched-in chin, and dirty brown hair. It was hard to tell how much hair he had because he was wearing a blue baseball cap. Gómez added a cap.

Next, they dropped in exaggerated arched eyebrows and small gray-brown eyes. Then came a stubby, broken nose and a brown mustache that did a poor job of covering a crooked upper lip and cowardly-looking chin.

"I remember his cheeks were sagging a bit," Penny added.

The deputy responded by rolling his eyes and clearing his throat. "My, you do have an active imagination!"

"I am doing my best to find Rosa, regardless of your beliefs. I saw the kidnapper take her, and I am determined to get her back." Penny tried to push away the memory of the kidnapper throwing Rosa over his shoulder as if she were nothing more than a bag of trash. She sniffed as her nose began to run, which probably meant she was going to cry. She knew she shouldn't let the deputy get to her, but he was tiresome. She trembled as she tried to ramp up her courage to continue. She wiped the tears from her eyes and looked in amazement at the very likeness of the suspect, who was now peering out at her from the computer screen. Her skin itched, and she instinctively moved her right hand over her left arm to check for bug bites. There were none. "Deputy, I believe you've pegged him," Penny said, trying to ignore his ugly attitude.

"I'm just doing my job," Gómez grumbled. "There's one more step. You need to take a look at some known sex offenders to see if the photos match up with our composite."

Penny dreaded the thought of looking at a gallery of sexual perverts.

"Of course, I'll do it, if you think it will help catch this guy." "I can't see how this imaginary character of yours is going to do us any good, but my orders are my orders."

The deputy pushed a few keys on the computer, and a bunch of thumbnail photos popped up. "If one looks familiar, just double-click on it, and that will enlarge the photo. In the meantime, I'm going to run this composite to dispatch, which I hope doesn't send our staff on a wild goose chase."

Penny was glad to be alone. She didn't want the deputy witnessing her reactions to what appeared to be hundreds of sex offenders living in El Paso. How many were in her neighborhood? She was afraid even to find that out.

In spite of the agony of having to look through these photos, she knew, from personal experience, that any one of these guys could do considerable damage to Rosa's psyche if she did live through this ordeal. *Rosa, this is for you.*

Penny began the laborious process of scrolling down and dipping into photo after photo. The task certainly began to put a face on sex crimes against children. Each name listed the man's or woman's height, weight, and even shoe size. It gave the specific year of the crime, its nature, and the likelihood of the predator committing another assault. The list rated the offenders as *moderate*, *high*, and *unlikely*. Before she knew it, an hour had passed, and Penny was beginning to think it was a pointless exercise. The men had all started to look the same: flecks of gray in a head of black hair; long, short, and scruffy mustaches; balding guys with bad comb-overs and bad teeth. Her back ached from leaning forward in a tense position, and her eyes were tired. *Maybe the deputy was right*, she thought. *I am wasting everyone's time*. It was embarrassing, but Penny figured if she left right now, the sheriff eventually would forget she ever existed, and his deputies like Gómez would stop making fun of his decision to ask for her help. She reached for her cell phone with every intention of calling a cab.

Her eyes, which were stinging and probably bloodshot, rolled over the blur of photographs one last time. As she leaned in to shut off the computer, she saw him in the lower right-hand corner of the screen. Penny reared back in her chair, trying to get as far away from the kidnapper as possible. Even in one dimension, he seemed to be taunting her. But the fascination with this horrid man, as if she were a bystander staring at a fatal accident, made her finally double-click on his picture. Immediately, his ominous and all-too-familiar face began filling the blue screen and sucking the air out of the small room. Penny's silent screams, which had previously failed to save Rosa, reignited in her throat. As hard as she tried, however, she still couldn't make a sound nor could she catch her breath. Her hands flew to her neck. She tried to dislodge the scream that was now strangling her. Finally, she coaxed out a soulful moan, which also allowed her a precious gasp of air.

"Any luck?" the deputy asked from where he stood in the doorway.

Penny began coughing and could not stop. She turned to the computer screen and jabbed a finger at the photo of the man named Donnie Harper. She desperately needed to be freed from this stifling room.

The deputy looked at her in disbelief. When he saw the suspect that Penny had singled out, he just laughed and shook his head. "You can't mean Donnie Harper? He's a harmless old dude."

Finally, she recovered enough to speak. "Unless we can find Rosa soon, Harper will not let Rosa live through this. He has never requested a ransom because he wasn't after money."

"As I said before, you've got the wrong guy. You saw it. He is listed as unlikely to commit another assault. We can't pick this man up. He's had a clean record for forty years."

The deputy shook his head and slapped the side of the monitor to emphasize his point.

Instinctively, Penny jerked her head back, repulsed by his behavior, and hit her head on the wall. She felt as if Gómez had slapped her too. He was angry and felt imposed upon. She could appreciate that. But there was no excuse to laugh at her. She was just trying to find Rosa, and that should count for something. Penny looked at the deputy's eyes. He showed no sign of backing down from his opinion that she was a charlatan trying to make a buck off the county. She gently rubbed the back of her head where a large bump had formed. Penny hadn't meant to waste anyone's time, but maybe he was right. She felt cold and drained in spite of her certainty that Donnie Harper was their man. But being certain about Harper could only carry her so far if everyone else doubted her opinion.

Penny wrapped her arms around her shoulders, holding on to herself for dear life. Thoroughly disgusted with Deputy Gómez, she stood, stepped around him, and opened the door. "If Rosa is dead, then I'm done here. Remember, I told you, I don't see dead people."

# CHAPTER 8

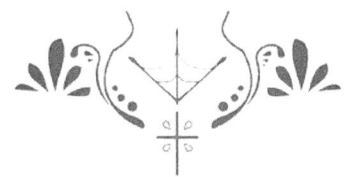

It was Tuesday, and that meant that Dr. Jonathon Márquez would be spending the day at the Vista Nueva Rehabilitation Center in Ciudad Juárez. He had three patients in residence who were trying to kick the plague of drug addiction. Overcoming a drug habit in Mexico was exceptionally difficult. A few years before, Mexico had decriminalized the possession of small amounts of marijuana, cocaine, heroin, and methamphetamines. Although the new law was good for his wallet, it was often deadly to his patients. The doctor had tried to get lawmakers to rescind it, but to no avail. Warring drug cartels that permeated the country often recruited their young workers by dangling drugs as well as *dineros* in front of them.

Dr. Márquez was known in Juárez as an expert in treating heroin addiction. Today, he was studying the blood work of Martín Ladera, a young heroin addict who was barely out of high school. He was treating Martín at the request of his mother, who had begged him for help. Márquez often placed his patients under anesthesia and administered medications to accelerate the withdrawal process. He had just completed rapid withdrawal procedures on Martín and had left him in the recovery room under the careful eye of his registered nurse, Frances González, while he checked his blood work. If everything looked good, he would order daily shots of methadone for him.

Dr. Márquez liked working alone in the center's medical laboratory, hidden behind a wall of metal storage cabinets and discarded lab equipment. Other doctors who visited their patients seldom used the lab to confirm their diagnoses, preferring to guess on their patients' progress in kicking their drug addictions. Two physicians, Enrique Ramírez and Rogelio Domínguez, had stopped by a few minutes before to say hello and to challenge Márquez to a game of pool. He had waved them off, and now he could hear them standing just outside the lab, talking soccer and American football. They were commiserating about the Dallas Cowboys and its useless quarterback.

"Maybe next year!" Rogelio said. Enrique laughed. "It's always next year!"

Márquez opened a tube of another patient's blood, scoping sections of it and recording markers, which would show him how serious his patient was about recovery. Blood tests didn't lie.

It was stifling in the back of the room. Márquez rolled up the sleeves of his lab coat, took out his handkerchief, and wiped his forehead. Maybe he needed to take a break and walk over to the recreation room where most of the residents hung out. It was always good to observe how his patients interacted with the other residents anyway. Music was usually blaring from a boom box there, and the young men, most of them teenagers, hovered over the pool table or talked on their cell phones to their girlfriends or their mothers.

The doctor packed up his microscope and placed it carefully in his medical bag for transport back to his office. While he was leaning over to snap his bag closed, he thought he heard a crash, as if the boom box had been thrown against the wall. The music stopped. He couldn't hear anyone laughing as the teens were prone to do, even in their misery. A strange hissing sound penetrated the rehab center, followed by what Márquez imagined was a kind of supersonic crack, a repeated release of air, and more hissing.

Rogelio began shouting, "No, por favor. ¡No me maten!" This was followed by a blast of what Márquez now recognized as gunfire. The continued *rat-tat-tat* of automatic weapons brought more agonizing moans throughout the substantial cement building. Márquez knew he had to hide. These were no doubt drug cartel hit men coming in to settle a score. Chances were they would check the lab next. He found a large metal cabinet and squeezed his lanky body inside. There was barely room to breathe. He latched the door and waited. Then he remembered his medical case, which was sitting just to the right of the cabinet. He had to retrieve it before anyone came in the lab. It had his name on it, and he was well-known at the rehab center.

Márquez held his breath, trying to calm his rapid breathing. He slowly opened the door and leaned forward, trying to grab his bag. His legs and feet were numb, but he knew he had to get his bag out of sight before the gunmen arrived. His fingertips were almost touching the handles, but he needed to lean out farther to grab it. He fell forward, bruising his elbows on the floor and banging the cabinet door against a filing cabinet.

*My God, they are bound to hear that!*

The pain of being bent like a pretzel, even for a few minutes, had all but paralyzed him. It took every ounce of his strength to pull his deadweight back into the cabinet. He lugged the bag inside and tucked it under his head like a pillow. He was just closing the cabinet door when he heard the clicking of boot heels on the cement floor of the laboratory. His fingers were damp and cold as he placed them over his mouth, trying to contain any sound of his breathing or the possibility of choking on his own fear.

The killer came so close to his hiding place that he could hear him chewing his gum. Stabbing pains now pulsed through his legs, and his left foot went into a muscle spasm. It was all he could do to keep from crying out. He could hear the clink of the glass tubes holding the warm vials of blood he had just placed in a disposable tray. He braced for what he thought was his inevitable fate. The door to the metal cabinet would be torn from its hinges, exposing him to the barrel of an automatic rifle. Márquez was thankful that at such close quarters, death would come quickly.

*Please, God! Help me!*

"¡Nadie está en el laboratorio!" the gunman shouted. The sound of his footsteps faded as he ran out of the lab. When Márquez heard the slamming of the center's front door, he let out a long, slow, agonizing breath and wiped his fingers across his face. Tears had pooled beneath his nose. The saltwater fell over his lips and into his parched mouth. He wanted to get out of the cabinet but thought better of it. He would be wise to wait another ten minutes. He checked his watch every minute, and when he thought he couldn't stand it any longer, he opened the cabinet door. He listened for any sound of movement in the center, but it was so quiet, he could actually hear the clock ticking on the laboratory wall. Márquez rolled out of the cabinet and pulled himself to a standing position by hanging on to the legs of the lab table. A stabbing pain shot through his chest.

"Aghhh!" he cried out. Márquez reached into his right front pocket, fumbling for a small sleeve of nitroglycerin. His hands trembled as he tucked one under his tongue. This was the second angina attack in the last month. If he didn't do something soon, this city was going to kill him.

When the pain had eased, he picked up his bag and began walking slowly toward the operating room to check on Martín and his nurse. Márquez figured someone in the neighborhood had heard the gunfire and had called the police, but that didn't mean they were going to show up anytime soon. Waiting for the police to arrive in Juárez could take hours. No one wanted to respond and risk getting killed too. He knew the cartels often left the *sicarios* at the scene for a while to knock off anyone who came by to help.

Márquez trudged through the laboratory. His legs felt like lead, and it took a great effort just to walk. He stumbled over his colleagues who were both lying in the dimly lit corridor. Enrique had slid down the wall, a scar of dark brown tracking his descent to the floor. Rogelio was lying facedown. His back was peppered with holes, although there was surprisingly little blood. He checked for a pulse on each, but he knew they were both gone.

He dreaded heading into the operating room where he had left Martín and Frances. The perspiration was now soaking the sleeves of his lab coat, and he could smell his own sweat. He threw open the door and looked around the room. A single light bulb, dangling from the ceiling, was still swinging back and forth. Martín was lying on the gurney, though his body was now riddled with bullets. His arms were hanging on either side of the bed, and blood was oozing from his mouth and dropping onto the white sheet. The doctor lifted Martin's arms and rested them at his sides. He took a closer look at the tattoo on Martín's right bicep. He had meant to ask him why he had chosen this cult, which was growing in popularity across Mexico. The tattoo was a drawing of a skeleton with an amber-colored hood. The name "La Santa Muerta" was inscribed on a medallion that hung from her neck. He had seen these tattoos before on young, unemployed men who loitered on the streets of Juárez. He shook his head in sorrow. No one should pray to a saint of death to save him.

Frances was on the floor, her arms folded across her abdomen, where she had apparently tried to stop her own bleeding. He closed her eyes, which were wide with fear. Her face was streaked with blood and tears. Márquez leaned against the wall, trying to gain his composure. He had paid for Frances to complete nursing school. She was the niece of a good friend, and she'd turned out to be one of the finest nurses at the hospital. Now she was dead, and he was responsible.

Márquez felt helpless. Was this the life he had dreamed of when he'd attended medical school? Only God held the answers, and He didn't seem to be talking these days. Reluctantly, he left his patient and nurse and moved toward the recreation room. The fading rays of sunlight accentuated the frenetic details of the bodies lying in front of him. He moved around the room checking for a pulse on each young man. He found his two other patients, Juan and Robert, lying near one another. Juan had his right arm slung over Robert's body as if he had tried to protect him. But automatic rifles left few survivors, and Robert was clearly dead too. The smell of the blood, a metallic stench, was overwhelming. Márquez pulled his handkerchief from his pocket and covered his nose.

There were body parts and intestines everywhere—not that he wasn't used to them, but he preferred them orderly and fully functioning. He was a healer, and this was a crushing blow to his sense of calling. He sniffed, wiped his forehead again, and rushed out of the room. He followed a path of bloody footprints down the hallway, but he stopped abruptly at the front door, realizing that to leave this way might be a death wish. His legs shook, and he felt light-headed. He turned around and walked to the back door where the medical staff could access the ambulances that transported their patients to the clinic. The wide oak door, which was large enough for stretchers, opened onto a narrow flagstone alley. Cautiously, Márquez unbolted the door and looked out. A couple pushing a stroller walked toward him, oblivious to the massacre, followed by two boys on skateboards who were shouting and laughing at one another.

Márquez grabbed his bag, gingerly moved out the door, and fell in behind the couple, who turned and smiled at him. The baby in the stroller began to cry. A jolt of fear rattled his confidence. Would the noise draw the attention of the gunmen, if they were still there? His knees banged against each other as he tried to maintain his composure.

"*Con permiso,*" Márquez said as he walked around the baby's parents.

"*De nada,*" they replied, still suspecting nothing out of the ordinary.

He waved them good-bye and ventured onto a tiny brick pathway between two homes. The bricks led to the street where he had parked his car.

Within twenty feet of his Jeep Cherokee, Márquez could see that something was terribly wrong. The windshield had been broken, and a brick was resting on the car's hood. He walked around the car to the driver's side, where a message was scrawled in blood on his window: "¡*Que esto sirva de advertencia!*"

*Now they're targeting me!* Márquez had lost several doctor friends from the hospital where he worked. They had been shot multiple times in the parking lot or in front of their homes. Now, it appeared, was his turn. The message warned him to stop treating drug addicts or else. The last thing a drug runner needed was a doctor trying to cure a customer. Márquez grabbed his chest, fully expecting a full-blown attack of angina. The pain, thankfully, did not come. He breathed in deeply and wiped his runny nose with the bottom of his lab coat. He left his SUV behind and walked as casually as possible back to the sidewalk, trying not to draw the attention of neighbors who were already scared to death. He would continue walking for a couple of blocks and then call his wife to pick him up.

The doctor's cell phone rang, sending excruciating shock waves through his body. He looked around to see if anyone heard the ring. The street was empty.

"Hello," he whispered.

"Doc, where are you? Did you forget you were to meet me at El Patio at seven?"

It was Sergei Andulov, the Russian mobster he had met a few months ago. Andulov had been trying to convince Márquez to join him in his child-trafficking ring. It was repugnant to him as a physician, but very lucrative, a sure ticket out of the growing madness of Juárez.

"Sergei! Don't leave the bar until I get there!" Márquez shoved his medical bag under his arm. He saw that his lab coat and his hands were streaked with blood. He removed his coat and threw it in the gutter. He didn't stop running until he reached the tavern. He was out of breath when he walked in the door of El Patio.

Andulov had already downed several shots of tequila, and his lips were loose. He babbled on about how much money the doctor was going to make.

"I have an excellent opportunity for you!"

"I told you, I can arrange for the kidnapping of three or four teenage girls, but you have to give me time."

"Yes, yes. But I have something else!" Andulov took another shot and wiped his mouth on his sleeve. "You know of Guapo Chavez?"

"You mean the head of the Baja cartel? Chavez is a mortal enemy of my wife's family."

"Your father-in-law doesn't have to know we have business with Chavez."

"Chavez is a very dangerous man. It's insane to tie in with him."
"He asked a big favor of me, and it has nothing to do with drugs."

"I don't think I can help you."

Márquez pulled out his handkerchief and blew his nose. How ridiculous was Andulov's request? The Chihuahua cartel considered him and his wife, Genie, a protected family, thanks to his father-in-law's position as the cartel's head of transportation for major shipments of drugs into the United States. There was no way he wanted any of these men turning on him. It was bad enough now to have the Betas cartel after him. He was pretty sure it was the Betas who had attacked the rehab center. Everybody knew they used violence to protect their own drug-smuggling routes, and they controlled most of the automatic weapons moving from the United States to Mexico.

Márquez shook his head and threw back a shot of tequila. "You don't understand. This is your chance to get out of Mexico permanently and live where you would like. Chavez will pay you one million dollars to help him."

"I got a warning tonight at the rehab center from the Betas.

They said they are going to kill me next."

"Chavez has deep connections. He can fix that."

"What in the world would I have to do for that amount of money?"

"Someone is really sick and needs your help." "Who?"

"I can't tell you yet."

Márquez twisted on the barstool. Having anything to do with Guapo Chavez was a deadly choice. "My father-in-law misses nothing. He would find out for certain, and he wouldn't hesitate to take me out."

"What if I could guarantee that he would never know?"

Márquez shoved his medical bag under his feet and cleared his throat. "How can you guarantee it?"

"No one will know about this except you and me. This is a big, big favor for Chavez, and he does not even want his own men to know."

Márquez ordered a beer and a tequila chaser. The cold, dewy glass felt good against his fingers. He looked at his hands and noticed that they were still covered with blood. He wiped them with a cocktail napkin. "What do I have to do?"

# CHAPTER 9

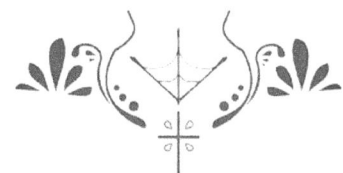

In her home office, Penny had Rosa Garcia's pink top spread out on the desk near her laptop. It was pitch-black outside. There was no moon, and the stars seemed listless and subdued, much like Penny's mood. By now, Penny figured, everyone in the sheriff's office was getting a good chuckle out of her insistence that Donnie Harper was the sex offender who had kidnapped Rosa. When Penny learned more about Harper, she couldn't blame the department for being hesitant to bring him in. At the age of sixteen, Harper had attacked his thirteen-year-old next-door neighbor and had taken her behind his family's tool shed where he'd tried to molest her. She'd been able to tear away from him before he could consummate his intentions. This little episode had landed him a year in juvey, but since then, he had had a clean record and was not considered a sexual predator, even though he had to register as such. Now, at the age of fifty-five,

Harper lived in his deceased parents' house in the Lower Valley and worked for a rancher along the Rio Grande.

Even Penny began to have doubts, and yet his face was still hardwired into her brain. It made her crazy, but she wasn't giving up on him yet. She had shared with the sheriff the deputy's conjecture that Rosa was dead. Leo continued to insist that Penny go on with her viewing. "We owe Rosa that much."

Leo said he would order a broader background check to see if Donnie Harper was still behaving himself. It was all Leo could promise her as they had little reason to detain him, even for questioning.

Now, Penny sat in her black leather desk chair and stared at the teeny-tiny blouse. Two buttons were missing from it, and a patch of green slimy stuff was stuck to the hem. There was a black check mark on the clothing tag at the back of the blouse, indicating to Penny that it probably came from a used clothing store. Penny examined the top from all angles and took a whiff. It smelled of tortillas and refried beans. Rosa's parents were no doubt extremely poor, Penny surmised. That meant there would be no available funds for a ransom, even if the kidnapper asked.

Her hair kept falling in her eyes and distracting her. She looked for a rubber band in her desk drawer to put her hair in a ponytail. When she pulled her hair back, she was surprised to find tiny beads of sweat on her forehead. The sheriff had placed some unreasonable expectations on her, and it didn't seem fair. Penny was in some kind of race, and she didn't even know where the starting blocks were. All he had given her was a pink top no bigger than a doll's. That was enough to make anybody sweat!

She remembered Zarn had cautioned her about not overpromising the capabilities of remote viewing. "If someone is relying on you to save a life, you and they may be sorely disappointed because the missing person may not live through the ordeal. You must be prepared to fail."

She looked at the clock. It was 7:45 p.m. She dialed Zarn's office number, but it rang and rang. Finally, the answering machine clicked on. "Hi, Zarn. I am trying to do my best to help the sheriff, but I only have a piece of Rosa Garcia's clothing. It doesn't seem like enough to go on. Call me, please!"

Penny ran to the living room and got her backpack, which still held her notes from class and the textbook Zarn had used, *Remote Viewing from the Inside Out*. Penny flipped through her notes, looking for answers. She had written in the margins, "Do not get emotionally involved with the target!" Zarn had repeated this frequently throughout the training, and now Penny understood why. Every time she thought of Rosa as the victim of a sexual predator, she began to personalize it. *What if it had been me?* As a teenager, she had been fast enough to escape her foster father's grasp, but Rosa had been caught off guard. *What is he doing to her? Where would he take her? Is he going to kill her? Is she already dead?* Penny's mind swirled out of control. She grabbed her textbook and staggered down the hallway and back to her office. She stared at Rosa's pink shirt, which she had tossed on top of her laptop. Penny shook her head in frustration and threw the textbook on her desk. Her cell phone rang, and she jumped. *Did they find her?* She wrenched her phone from her jeans pocket, and it fell through her shaking fingers. She was perspiring, and the sweat made her hands clammy. She dropped to her knees and reached for the phone. It tumbled forward and skidded over the tile floor. Finally, she scooped up the phone and clutched it tightly. "Hello."

"Penny, it's Zarn."

"Why am I trying to find this little girl?" Penny yelled into the phone. "You sent me on an assignment I can't handle!"

"Settle down! You can do this. I would have never suggested you help the sheriff if I didn't think you could."

"But the only target I have is her shirt. I need more!"

"Have you looked at the television news? They are running a school photo of her."

Penny turned on the TV as Zarn continued to reassure her. Sure enough, Rosa's photo came up on the local news channel. She checked with two other stations, and each had the same picture. It seemed all the stations were following the case closely. "Yes, I see her."

"Go to the Internet, and pull the photo of her off one of the news stations' Web sites. Then go to Google Earth and download the home address the sheriff gave you. You can pull up a view of her house and her neighborhood."

Penny pulled Rosa's school photo off the Internet, then found her house on Google Earth. The tiny house was stuffed between two others that looked about the same size and same condition—*deplorable*!

These two tools gave her new targets. "Thank you. I think these will help me a lot. But I'm still not sure I can do this. Remember, I've not had any experience with targets like these."

"Call me in the morning, and we can review what you've found. My class doesn't start until nine."

Penny leaned back in her chair and studied the photo of Rosa, which she had printed out in color. She wanted to make sure she didn't make any mistakes with these two new targets. She turned to her textbook to review the viewing protocols. Her eyes brushed over a sentence where the author warned that public scrutiny and failure to achieve a successful outcome could wear down a remote viewer. "It is important," the author wrote, "that remote viewers have a strong personal support system to catch them when they fail."

The word, Penny noted, was *when*, not *if* a remote viewer failed. Penny's own support system was negligible. Four months ago, Porter had moved to China to work as an engineering manager. For eight years, they had shared a loving relationship and household expenses. Penny believed she had only herself to blame for the breakup. She had kept Porter awake night after night with her dreams—nightmares, really. She could never control them and had spent most of her time in front of her computer, trying to decipher the clues to messages from the likes of Middle Eastern terrorists and other criminal types. Her sleepless nights had also made it tough to meet her writing deadlines; she'd often delivered her work product at the last possible moment. This was not the best impression for her valued clients, she knew. Even their closest friends didn't fault Porter for taking a hike and winding up as far away from Penny as possible. Now that Porter was gone, her finances were stretched to the breaking point, and this had driven her to find an alternate source of income.

Penny had hoped the controlled remote viewing class would actually give her life some order, and the word would get back to Porter that she now had her act together. So far, nothing had gone as planned. She was as confused and as freaked out as ever. She could not afford to fail, not just because of the money, but because her failure would become known not only to Porter but also to their friends, and this would shove her down the road to more personal humiliation.

Her problems, of course, hadn't just begun while living with Porter. She had loved her father dearly, but he was never home when she was growing up. The Indy car circuit had kept him on the road eight or nine months a year. She had been left at home with a mother who drank too much and criticized Penny's every move. Her mother's alcoholism left Penny with lots of time by herself. That was when the dreams started. They would appear in her mind like movie trailers and sometimes repeat themselves until she was physically ill. Most of the time, she never found out what the dreams meant, but occasionally, she would discover what they came to be within a week or two. This was a lot for a child to absorb. And her father's death while doing what he loved still made her angry. He had deserted her and left her to care for an alcoholic mother. When her mom had died eighteen months after her dad, Penny had felt guilty for being happy to be out from under her critical eyes.

Little did she realize that foster care wasn't a picnic. When she was sixteen, her foster father, Richard Mahlback, had tried to rape her. Penny had been strong enough to escape his clutches, and she'd run from the home. She'd been scared and bruised when she'd been found two days later, hiding in an old barn. She'd had to spend several weeks in a mental health clinic until she could feel comfortable in a new foster home. That Rosa might be suffering at the hands of a sexual predator made Penny wonder if she could actually handle this assignment objectively. She didn't want the sheriff to know how it made her stomach churn and her hands tremble. She needed to make a go of this assignment if she were to tackle her finances. She would just have to buck up and do her best.

Penny clicked on the Google Earth Web site and looked at Rosa's neighborhood again. She tried to imagine herself walking up and down the unpaved road in front of her house and meeting the neighbors who lived on either side of the Garcias. She pictured a blue cloudless sky, the sounds of barking dogs, and children playing ball in the street. She shut her eyes and leaned back in her chair. As her breathing mellowed, a strand of tiny houses appeared in her mind. The homes were tightly packed together, and the desert landscape had a gridlock on the front yards.

As her viewing became clearer, Penny saw an old woman with a broom, sweeping a dirt floor, a small window covered with plastic to keep the dust at bay, and a good-sized backyard with a garden brimming with vegetables. She breathed in deeply as heavenly smells wafted from the window of the tiny kitchen. Inside the home, the aroma of cinnamon rose from the oven. Apple empanadas were browning beautifully there. A mother carried a baby on her hip as she checked on the oven, then moved effortlessly around the kitchen. The woman lightly kissed her baby on its bare chest and laughed.

*That can't be Rosa's house. Rosa's mother would not be laughing.*

Penny moved her viewing out of that house and on down the same street, which had no sidewalk, only a dusty trail running in front of each home. On the front porch of the next house, a small boy was sitting on the crumbling steps, crying. Dirt streaked across his face like rubber marks from a screeching tire. His hands were very small and dirty. His feet were bare, and he looked as if he hadn't had a bath in several days.

The boy has to be related to Rosa.

Penny tried to imagine how both children could be so small, so stunted. Could it be malnutrition? *Is it some sort of genetic disorder?* Penny was jolted back to her office by a ringing sound. She sat straight up, blinking at the bright lights in her room. She stared at the telephone on her desk, but it was not ringing. When the sound came again, she realized it was her doorbell. She looked at her watch.

*Who could be at my door at eight at night?*

The FedEx gal had her sign for a small package and apologized for coming so late. It had been a long day, she told Penny.

"Yeah, that makes two of us!"

As Penny shut the door, she saw the funny Chinese characters on the box. "Porter!" she shouted as she rushed to the kitchen for a paring knife. The package revealed the most beautiful pearl necklace Penny had ever seen. The insert called them Chinese Akoya pearls, cultured off the coast of the South China Sea near Hepu. "Wow, they're huge!"

Penny ran to the bathroom and fastened the pearls around her throat. They were stunning even on her gray shirt. She strutted through the hall to the kitchen where she grabbed a bottle of water from the refrigerator. "Yes, yes, yes!"

The phone rang, cutting off her celebration. It was the sheriff checking on her progress. It had been five hours since Penny had left the sheriff's office.

"What do you have for me?" "I think I'm making headway."

"Penny, every minute counts with these kids!" he was shouting. "I know that, Leo. I know. Give me thirty minutes. I'll call you soon. I promise."

"It's too late! I need to know where Rosa is now!" "Please give me just a little more time."

"You're off the case, Penny. I made a mistake hiring someone who had no experience in controlled viewing. Zarn vouched for you, but I don't have the luxury of testing your skills against Rosa's life. I'm sorry. I'll send you a check for your time."

Penny heard the phone slam in her ear.

# CHAPTER 10

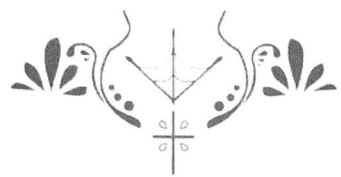

Leo Tellez was furious at his stupidity. He couldn't just sit there and wait for Penny. Maybe she would never call, and then what? His deputies were already mumbling under their breaths about the department using a psychic who made a crazy claim about Donnie Harper. Now, he would really look stupid, and stupid would not get him reelected next fall. Being sheriff was all he had left. Leo jumped to his feet and left the building. He steered his patrol car onto Montana Street with no particular destination in mind. He was hoping that time on the road might help him get his anger under control. He was mad at just about everybody. He was angry that the world had perverts who preyed on children. He was mad at his deputies who made fun of his decision to ask Penny for help. He was mad at himself for being so gullible. Why couldn't Zarn cancel his class and come down here? It was an emergency!

Leo had to admit he had no right to be angry with Penny, even though he was disappointed in her. She was a novice after all. But when Zarn had worked with him, Leo could rely on him for a response quickly. Leo was sure Penny was begging for more time because she had nothing more to offer. Sure, Penny had provided them with a description of the would-be pervert and the old blue van. But how reliable was she? No blue van had turned up on the streets of south El Paso, and his officers had shown the computer-generated sketch to hundreds of Rosa's neighbors, resulting in absolutely no clues. And as for Penny fingering Donnie Harper, Leo was worried he would hear soon from his detectives that Harper was not a suspect.

It had now been at least twenty-four hours since Rosa had gone missing, and the FBI still had a "wait and see" attitude toward her case. Although Leo didn't fully understand why the FBI was dragging its feet about helping find Rosa, he didn't mind its reluctance to get involved. He had hoped to be a hero and find her first. He had, after all, found her once before. Leo recalled the frosty November evening when he'd received the tip as to Rosa's location. He'd discovered her fast asleep in the cardboard box under the bridge, just as the anonymous caller had described. She wasn't far from the community campfire that had warmed the crew of people who called the bridge home. The vagrant who had snatched her sat near the box, singing Rosa a lullaby.

Dug Warner turned out to be a confused, troubled soul who was taken to a mental health unit for evaluation. He kept telling the sheriff he was waiting on someone to take her, but someone never came. He was tired, he told Leo, and happy to have her out of his way. Though he was later charged with kidnapping, Warner would never serve a day in jail. He was just too sick for that.

Delivering Rosa into the arms of her parents had been one of the proudest moments in his career. Manuel and Marvela Garcia were both profusely grateful and choked out a humble *gracias. Those were the gravy days*, Leo thought, the days before his own personal life had collapsed.

Leo had been so deep in thought that he was surprised when he found himself heading north on Highway 54. It frightened him that he had been a victim of mindless driving—something he preached about in public forums. He took the Fred Wilson Road exit just ahead. He had made this trip many times but was stunned to realize he had done so tonight in a trance.

The cemetery where his wife, Alejandra, and his infant daughter, Marta, were buried was just a block away. Leo always found the Morning Meadow Memorial Park to be a good place to think. He liked to imagine that his wife served as inspiration when he had a particularly troubling case. He just needed to be here, he guessed, and was thankful his subconscious had obliged.

The night enveloped Leo in an icy stillness. It was too dark to read the names on the tombstones, but he knew exactly where he was and whose names were there. He moved his cold hands across their chiseled letters and was reminded of the finality of it all; death had taken the dearest person in the world from him two years ago, and his newborn daughter had not stayed around long enough for him even to see her smile.

When Alejandra was six months pregnant, she had begun having seizures. Her obstetrician, Alberto Gonzalez, diagnosed her with eclampsia. Hypoxia, blood pressure spikes, and changes in blood flow to the Tellez's baby began to plague Alejandra's pregnancy. She was hospitalized. She refused to have a C-section immediately despite her doctor's urging. She hoped to hang on for the baby's sake. Doses of magnesium sulfate did not control Alejandra's seizures; it was agonizing for Leo to watch her suffer. At twenty-five weeks, Alejandra's blood pressure spiraled out of control. Dr. Gonzalez demanded Alejandra agree to a C-section. She was rushed to the delivery room, and Leo, who had originally been scheduled to be there at the birth, was barred from entering.

As sheriff, Leo Tellez was used to calling the shots, and now all he could do was pace up and down in front of the swinging doors to the delivery room. After several minutes, he'd begun stamping his feet because his toes were going numb. Sweat poured down his arms and legs and rolled into his socks and leather boots. Not being there for Alejandra was paralyzing him. He leaned against the hospital's white walls for support and arched his body far enough forward to look into the windows of the delivery room. The doctor and nurses were frantically working on his wife. Then, in an erratic movement, he saw a nurse wrap their baby in a receiving blanket and rush out another door, probably on her way to ICU. He wasn't sure whether he was the new father of a daughter or son. It didn't really matter to Leo and Alejandra. They would welcome either with open arms.

After ten minutes, the hurried tempo in the delivery room changed. To Leo, it seemed as if the operating room personnel were moving in slow motion. The looks on their faces became clouded with concern. Something wasn't right. He shoved his way into the room just in time to see the doctor tear off his surgical gloves and throw them on the floor. The doctor looked up and saw Leo standing inside the double doors. The words tumbled out of Dr. Gonzalez's mouth as he rushed over to Leo: "I am so sorry, Sheriff. We've lost her."

The doctor's voice brought the blood rushing back to Leo's hands and feet, but his body was damp from sweat, and he was chilled to the bone. He began to shake. He was a pro at telling family members about the death of a loved one, but now it was he who must absorb the blow. He fought the urge to remain suspended in a state of denial; in fractured time, he could hover somewhere between life and death. In this place of solace, the hurt could not touch him. But finally, death wrapped its icy fingers around his throat. Alejandra was gone.

He couldn't lose her. *No! Absolutely not!*

The fabric of Leo's life had begun to unravel right before his eyes. He saw the medics covering Alejandra's body and preparing to transport her to the morgue. The last thread holding his world together snapped, and he stumbled forward, his legs like jelly. Dr. Gonzalez caught the sheriff in mid-fall.

"The good news is that the baby is still alive," the doctor said, trying to lift Leo to his feet. Dr. Gonzalez, who was at least twenty years Leo's senior, draped his arm around Leo's shoulders and escorted him into the Pediatric ICU.

The neonatal nurse handed them both paper masks and led them to a tiny incubator. The nurse seemed to understand her mission of mercy and did so silently. Her thin fingers pointed the way to a small pink ribbon tied to the rail of the bed where the baby's footprints hung on a card and the name "Tellez" was printed in magic marker. It was only then that Leo knew he had a daughter and that he would call her Marta. That was the name Leo and Alejandra had agreed upon months earlier.

He leaned over the small, frail body whose heartbeat echoed in a monitor beeping near her crib. He wasn't able to touch her because of the bubble that encased her to protect her from the evils of the world. That was all right with Leo. There were a couple of tubes running from Marta's body, one of which led from her tiny nose and the other from her leg. Leo didn't want to know why. He hurt too much to have the details. He would leave Marta's care to the experts.

For the next four days, Leo camped out in the waiting room near the ICU. Marta Tellez was a fighter, but the poor supply of oxygen and the fact that she hadn't received all of the essential nutrients from Alejandra's placenta had left her in a brittle state. Her chances of surviving seemed less and less likely as the hours wore on. At 5:36 p.m., seventy-two hours after Marta Tellez was born, she went to heaven to join her mother. Leo didn't blame Marta for leaving too. It was going to be a lonely world without Alejandra in their lives.

---

The headlights of a car driving down the cemetery road blinded Leo and jolted him back to the present. He saw Lt. Pancho Ontiveros carefully making his way down the stone path toward him, a small shaft of light guiding his steps.

"Sheriff, we need you back at the station. Reporters are demanding we make a statement about whether we think Rosa was kidnapped or if she's just a runaway."

Leo realized his regular visits to the cemetery must have been well-known to his staff, and this was certainly going to be seen as a sign of weakness on his part. He could barely make out the eyes of the lieutenant, who was not only one of his officers but also a friend. It sickened Leo to realize he found greater companionship among the dead than the living and that his own friends knew it too. He released his grip on Alejandra's tombstone and stood upright. This habit would have to stop, he told himself. Alejandra and Marta were dead, but he was not. He would have to find a way to go on living without them.

# CHAPTER 11

Rosa Garcia wiggled her toes under the cool sheets on the twin-sized bed that was pushed next to a wall of peeling pink paint. She had just opened her eyes after what seemed like a long, long sleep. Her stuffed pink pony lay clutched in her right hand.

*Where am I? Where's Mamá?*

She wondered these things, but she did not feel afraid. She was too tired to be afraid. As she rolled over, she saw the sun streaming through the small window across the room. She was hot, and the room was small. Maybe she could raise the window for some air.

Before she could get up, the door to the room opened, and a short, skinny man entered with a tray of food. He was followed by a taller man carrying a black leather bag.

Rosa was puzzled, but she was feeling so relaxed that she thought she would just wait and see who these men were before moving from her comfy bed.

"Good morning, Rosa. This is just for you," the shorter man said. "I brought you a burrito and even a chocolate shake. Your mother tells me it is your favorite!"

"You know my mother?" Rosa asked.

"Of course, Rosa," he replied. "Your mother is a very kind woman. She has asked me to care for you and to help you grow stronger."

"I am already strong," Rosa answered. "I can outrun my best friend at school!"

"Yes, yes, my dear Rosa. But you want to be even stronger, don't you? I will help you grow into a beautiful woman."

"I am too young to be a woman yet," Rosa said with some apprehension. Ignoring her comments, the stranger placed the tray of food on her bedside table. When Rosa saw the plate and smelled the burrito steaming fresh from the skillet, she overcame her questions about what she was doing there. She sat up and tore at the food. She ate like an animal, even though the burrito was burning her mouth. She didn't stop until she had devoured it and sucked down almost all of her shake. Rosa licked her lips, tasting something chalky on her tongue.

"Now, that's a good girl!" the man said. "I will feed you well."

Rosa nodded her approval. "My brother, Pedro, and I don't get to eat at home sometimes—just at school."

"Well, from now on, you are going to eat every day, three times a day," the man replied. "And you can have all of the cookies you want. Would you like one?" The man handed Rosa a cookie, which she eagerly took from his hand.

She munched on the cookie, savoring a chocolate chip as it melted on her tongue. Rosa couldn't help but smile. Her mother never bought cookies for her. Wherever this was, it wasn't so bad. She fell back into her bed, her belly full. She was curious about the two men but figured if they were feeding her, they wouldn't hurt her. Her mother had told her to be careful of strangers, but these men seemed very nice.

"What is your name?" she asked her waiter, smiling. "Call me Diego," he said.

"Okay, Diego. Thank you for my food. It was *delicioso*!" "Who is your friend?" Rosa asked, still smiling.

"You can call me Dr. John, Rosa. You have a fever, and I want to make you well."

The doctor leaned over Rosa, his stethoscope hanging from his neck, and brushed her hair away from her eyes. He lay his hand on her arms and then on her forehead. "You see, you are very hot, and we must give you some medicine to bring down your fever."

Rosa rubbed her tiny fingers across her face. It was hot to the touch.

"You will make me feel better? I am very tired."

"Yes, I will make you feel much better, but you must get your rest," Dr. John said. "I will leave you a big glass of water, and whenever you are awake, you must drink from it."

Rosa felt reassured she would be okay under the care of her new friends. She would think about where her mama and papa were later. Rosa yawned. She stretched out her pencil-thin arms, pulled up the blanket, and burrowed deep into her pillow. Her eyes fluttered shut.

# CHAPTER 12

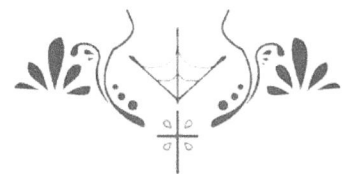

Penny was devastated. Being fired from the sheriff's office was career suicide for a controlled remote viewer. She might as well start perusing the Sunday classifieds for a job. Word would spread quickly among law enforcement agencies that the sheriff had tried a new psychic viewer, and she had flopped. With Porter's income gone, she was barely covering her mortgage and was behind one month on the electric bill. She had begged the electric company to give her time to make it up, and they had thankfully agreed. The handful of clients she had left was not enough to keep going. She would have to sell her house and move back to Indiana. At that thought, Penny stood, turned off the lights in her office, and sat back down in the dark.

She hadn't anticipated the tremendous pressure involved in finding a missing child or locating anyone for that matter. Zarn had tried to warn her, but she had blindly raced back from Alamogordo, ready to conquer the world. She had liked Leo Tellez immediately and thought they could work well together. He had innately unhappy eyes, but he was so committed to his job that she couldn't help but admire him. The thought of disappointing him brought a lump to her throat. She swallowed hard, choking off the tears. Here she was, a thirty-five-year-old single woman with no friends and no one special in her life. She was overcome by the emptiness that now embraced her. She took a few breaths, trying to calm her anxiety. She didn't like the feeling of hopelessness that was encircling her now. Where would she go? She had no one to turn to now that Porter was gone. She had always shunned friends, not wanting them to know how much she struggled with her nightmares. Now, she was totally alone. No one would know for days if she died right here, tonight, sitting in the luxurious black leather chair she had purchased a few years ago when the economy had been good.

Penny flipped on the small television in her office and searched for the eleven o'clock news. An anorexic-looking female reporter and a scruffy old man stood in front of a mural painted on a building located in south El Paso. Penny recognized the spot. The mural depicted Spanish soldiers from the sixteenth century on their northward route from Mexico. The TV crew's lighting cast dark shadows on the Castilians' helmets, creating an ominous backdrop for presenting the news.

"We now have a comment from one of Rosa's neighbors," the reporter said as she turned to the old man standing at her side.

"We all know *que esta muerta*," he shouted. "Some *hombre's* got her, and she's not coming back!"

The reporter threw her left hand over her mouth and then made a slashing motion with it, across her neck, indicating the cameraman should end the interview.

The next thing Penny saw was the newsroom where a thirty-something anchor, sporting a head of brown, thinning hair, a gray suit, and green silk tie, sat at a desk with the badge of a national news affiliate behind it. "We are interrupting our on-the-scene coverage because the sheriff is now holding a press conference."

Penny became engrossed in the television, wondering what Leo had found out that she didn't know. Had the sheriff been holding out on her?

Leo stood behind a podium with the logo of the El Paso County Sheriff's Department prominently attached. He looked distinguished and in control, Penny thought. His eyes were now determined and focused. His angular cheekbones were rigid, and strong, giving the impression of someone with a fierce resolve to succeed. She wondered what had changed him.

"The El Paso County Sheriff's Office believes that Rosa Garcia has been abducted and that there is a very good chance she is still alive. We have no indication to tell us otherwise, and we are proceeding with our investigation as if she is. We are pursuing some very good leads and will not rest until she is found."

A reporter asked a question about the FBI, but Leo ignored it, ended the questioning and walked off the platform.

Penny noticed, much to her relief, an officer handing the media copies of the composite Penny had created with Deputy Gómez. The sheriff turned back to address the reporters. "This man is only a person of interest as this point. We have not been able to locate him. If you see him, please call our office. Do not attempt to apprehend him."

The news conference ended, and Penny shut off the TV and picked up the pink top. She rubbed the fabric between her fingers. A thorn pricked her index finger. "Ouch!" She rolled back the hem of the blouse and saw what appeared to be a remnant from a soaptree yucca. Penny had taken a desert survival class at El Paso Community College and knew the soaptree derived its name from the material that once made it a popular substitute for soap and was often used as cattle feed by Texas ranchers in times of drought. The yellowish, leathery leaves, with their fine white threads, ended in a protective sharp spine. It was a piece of a spine that had punctured Penny's finger. What was it doing in Rosa's clothing?

Penny fingered her new pearls and leaned back in her chair. She tried to picture Rosa running through a desert landscape. Had she carelessly fallen into a yucca? That would really hurt and could cause her considerable injury or even a serious infection.

Encouraged by the added clues and the advice from Zarn, Penny made up her mind to hunt for Rosa on her own. She knew she could find her as long as she kept her emotions in check. *To hell with the sheriff and his deputies! I'll show them!*

Penny headed to a bookshelf in her office, which held her prized collection on southwestern history. She pulled out a book on El Paso and paged through it until she found a photo of the mural she had just seen on TV. The fresco was included in a walking tour of five murals painted by local artists and scattered across several blocks in the Lower Valley. She checked out the address of the mural and wrote down the cross streets. Then she went to her computer to map the location, which she discovered was just around the corner from the Garcia home.

She would use the mural as inspiration to help guide her visually to the street where Rosa lived. Rosa's shirt, her photo, and the Google images of Rosa's house could only carry her so far. The mural would add another dimension to the target, and she hoped it would strengthen her viewing, and perhaps allow her to see something that would help her find Rosa. Using this technique of giving more context to the target reminded Penny of when she found the bifocals.

Penny placed her hands on the photo of the mural and leaned forward, relaxing her back muscles, which had grown tense during the sheriff's press conference. She stared intently at the painting and watched as the colors in the mural melted into a wall of purple and black. She tapped into the now well-practiced protocols for viewing and embraced the inner space of discovery now awaiting her. She could see a pinpoint of light widening before her like the lens on a camera. Her first vision was that of a dust devil, stirring up the sandy soil along a pathway that fronted a series of similar clapboard homes. The dust made it hard to distinguish one from the other, but eventually, Penny found what she was sure was the Garcias' home.

The little boy Penny had seen in her earlier visit was gone from the crumbling steps that led to the front door. The sides of the house looked as if they had been painted brown with a broom. The wood around the windows was rotting from the relentless rays of the desert sun. The screen in the front door was torn and ragged, and a gap between the door and the threshold was at least two inches wide. No doubt, the home was as dusty inside as out.

As Penny moved her viewing up the steps and through the rickety front door, she saw, just as she had guessed, that the interior of the home was full of dust and dirt. The small boy she had once seen on the steps was now sound asleep on a small, faded green sofa. He was clutching a baby blanket that had seen better days. The ragged, silky binding of an unknown color was tucked up near his small innocent face, and his thumb rested inside his mouth.

Penny looked around the living room and found it void of anything homey. There was no television or even a radio. Two scatter rugs were tossed carelessly around the rough-hewn wooden floors whose finish had long ago disappeared. A single end table was the only other piece of furniture.

Her ears picked up the sound of dishes rattling in the next room. Penny's eyes traveled on into the kitchen where a woman around her own age gathered glasses and plates and sat them in a scarred porcelain sink. If this were Rosa's mother, she did not appear sad or mad. In fact, she seemed to be feeling nothing. The was about five feet four and wore a plain shirtwaist dress about the color of khaki, although it was difficult to tell because to Penny it looked as though it had been laundered a zillion times. The woman was washing some Mexican pottery—cups, saucers, and plates—and placing them on a shelf above the sink. Penny was impressed by the care with which the woman handled the pottery, as if they were precious to her.

Penny's eyes followed the woman as she dried her hands on a tattered tea towel and left the kitchen. She walked down the hall toward the bedrooms. There did not seem to be a bathroom. *Oh, wait a minute. There* is *a bathroom.* It was a toilet in what looked like a closet about three-foot square. There was no bathroom sink, just the stool, and a couple of rolls of toilet paper on the back of the tank.

Penny caught up with the woman, who was now in what was obviously her bedroom. There were two framed photos on the dresser where she stopped. One was of the boy who slept in the living room. The other was of Rosa. The woman, who Penny now assumed was Rosa's mother, picked up the photo of Rosa, wiped the dust from the glass with her fingertips, and stared at it for a long time. Finally, she turned the frame over and reached into the pocket of her dress, pulling out a big wad of bills. She opened a dresser drawer and carefully tucked the money and the photo of Rosa beneath some old socks and yellowing underwear.

Rosa's mother turned and looked squarely at Penny, even though Penny knew she couldn't see her. Penny's feet began to retreat even before her mind wrapped itself around the travesty she had just seen. She rushed from the room, leaving Rosa's mother alone with her thoughts.

Penny shook herself out of her viewing and found herself safely back in her own house. Rosa's disappearance was getting more and more confusing. Penny's hand trembled as she reached for her phone. Her fingers shook so hard she had trouble touching the numbers. At last, the receiver was ringing in her ear. Hopefully, the sheriff would answer his phone.

# CHAPTER 13

Leo plopped down in his office chair when he heard Penny's voice on his cell. He didn't want to talk with her because he was still upset. "What do you want, Penny?"

"I want to help, even if I'm not on the clock."

"Look, the information you gave us has hit a dead end." Leo had tried to appease her and had distributed her composite around to the media either to shake out Donnie Harper or uncover another suspect who looked like him. It wouldn't be the first time a witness had created a composite that turned out to be close but not quite what the perpetrator looked like.

"Leo, I don't know where Rosa is, but I think I have an idea of why she disappeared."

"What do you mean?"

"I think Rosa's mother got a lot of cash for her," Penny said. "If you could, get into the Garcias' home and check out the top drawer of her bedroom dresser."

"I don't think I could justify a warrant for searching the Garcia home, Penny. I have no proof."

"Well, aren't family members the first in the line of suspects in such crimes?"

"It would be a stretch to follow that road—parents actually selling their child to human traffickers. This goes way beyond kidnapping."

"I saw what I saw!"

"The Garcias appear to be very dedicated to their family. Why would they sell Rosa?"

Leo was finding this phone conversation tiresome. He had work to do, and Penny was delaying it.

"I've got to disagree with you. The Garcias don't seem to take very good care of their kids. The parents don't look malnourished, but their kids sure do. I guess none of that makes any difference, now that I'm no longer working with you. And anyway, Rosa is probably in Mexico by now."

"Who said she went south? Most human trafficking cases head for large US cities. I have already put an all-points bulletin out across the nation and with Interpol."

"Interpol?"

"Interpol is the world's policing agency. Right now, they are working hard to stop online child pornography," the sheriff explained. "It's a worldwide problem. But as for human trafficking in Texas, I just don't know."

"Will Mexico help us, just in case somebody took her to Juárez?"

"We don't get much cooperation from Mexico. We might get lucky, though, being that Rosa's so young. I'll try to make contact with the Juárez chief of police."

"Could you ask him about any human trafficking rings he's heard of that might be operating in Mexico?" Penny was pleading now. "What other options do you have?"

Leo knew Penny was right. *What were his options?* Twenty-seven hours had already passed, and his department had little or nothing concrete to go on. Canvassing the Garcias' neighborhood with Penny's composite had resulted in only one woman thinking she had seen a man similar to his description visiting the Garcias' home last week, but she couldn't be sure.

Leo saw a deputy standing at his office door. He signaled to him that he would just be a few more minutes. He watched as the deputy paced in the hall. Leo felt bad about what he was going to say, but perhaps the officer would overhear him and get the drift that he was done with Penny.

"I can't put you back on my payroll, Penny. I appreciate your ideas, but I have no need of your services now." Leo thought he could hear Penny exhale. "I've got to go now. Someone's waiting for me outside in the hall."

Penny was not hanging up. Leo tapped his foot impatiently. "What happened with Donnie Harper?" she asked.

Leo shook his head at the officer and turned his chair away from the door so he wouldn't hear anything more of their conversation. "Harper did not answer his door when a deputy made a routine visit. His parole officer said he had not heard from him in two weeks, which was unusual, because Harper was always religious about reporting in."

"Doesn't that sound suspicious?"

"We can't go arresting someone simply because he doesn't answer his door!" He hadn't told Penny, but Leo had insisted that his deputies continue to hunt for Harper. It had angered his department, but Leo had refused to budge on his orders to find Harper and bring him in for questioning.

"I don't care if you hire me back or not. I'm going to find Rosa by myself."

"Penny, I am begging you to lay off. Go back up to Alamogordo and check in with Zarn. Take a refresher or something." He knew blowing Penny off was not a good idea, but he had to make her mad enough to quit searching. He was relieved when he finally got Penny to hang up.

---

After ten minutes of poor phone connections, Leo finally made contact with the Ciudad Juárez Police Department and talked with Chief Raúl Morales. Leo told Morales that his deputies were looking for a missing eleven-year-old girl. "By any chance, do you have any missing children?"

"Sheriff, we have more than 20,000 children missing in Mexico, especially in Acapulco and Cancún, but we can't be sure if they ran away or were the object of foul play."

"Then you haven't had any problems in Juárez?"

"In the past six months, we have been seeing a spike in kidnappings in Tijuana and Ciudad Juárez, but mostly it has been executives from factories being held for ransom. As for missing females, they are mostly women in their twenties and thirties. The chief in Palomas did call me yesterday about two fourteen- year-old girls who have disappeared. He wanted to know if I had any kids missing in here."

"What is your best guess?" Leo asked.

"We are literally buried here with killings, day and night. I have not had time to even think about human smuggling. I could only wish some of our citizens would go away!"

Chief Morales laughed and then took a deep breath. Leo thought perhaps the chief was smoking because there was a long pause before Morales spoke again.

"*Amigo*, I must give you a heads-up. I don't like to speak of this because our *federales* want to keep it quiet, but there are rumors that kidnappers in interior Mexico have Russian mob connections. If you have had a little girl disappear in the States, perhaps they have moved north of the border. Maybe it is getting a little too dangerous in Mexico, even for the Russians."

"Could you fax me over any information on the Russian connection?" Leo was intrigued with this new twist in the case. "There's an outside chance that they are involved in this kidnapping, but I need to consider everything."

"I will, but you must promise not to say I was the one who provided you with the information."

"Of course not! Perhaps I can return the favor someday."

"I will share this with you because our hands are tied in Mexico. We know about the human smuggling across our borders, but we are understaffed. We have a new federal anti-trafficking law, but there have been no convictions or sentences of offenders yet. We have so many other problems with the narco-wars that human trafficking is not a priority."

Leo thought Morales sounded sincerely sorry he couldn't help. This call to Juárez left him with even more questions. Was there a possibility that Rosa's kidnapping was more than an isolated event?

Could a ring of human smugglers from Russia be taking up residence in El Paso? The possibility intrigued him. Should he contact the FBI with this information? Leo decided he would wait. But one thing he was going to do immediately was wake up his good friend, Judge John Barton. He was Leo's best chance of getting a search warrant at this time of night.

# CHAPTER 14

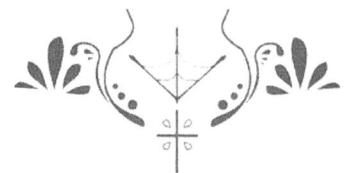

When Leo's Crown Victoria rolled into Penny's driveway at 7:02 a.m., she was pacing back and forth on the sidewalk. Penny's skin was crawling with the anticipation of finally proving her worth to the sheriff's office. When Leo had called her at 1:30 a.m., telling her he was headed to a judge for a signed warrant, she had begged him to let her go with him to the Garcias' home.

There was no way she was going to miss this.

Leo said she would not be able to be in the house during the actual search because of legalities, but she could search the neighborhood for clues to Rosa's location. Penny had told Leo she would settle for that, although she secretly had plans to circumvent the legalities and see inside the Garcia home for herself.

The sound of the Ford's tires rolling along Alameda Avenue, combined with a good set of shocks and Penny's lack of sleep, gently rocked her back and forth into a shallow slumber. Penny dreamed she was hiking through the desert. She came upon a forest of cacti and yucca. She tried to avoid the thousands of spikes and thorns protruding from each of them as she walked cautiously across the desert floor. No amount of tiptoeing around kept her from piercing the soles of her tennis shoes. She cried out. "Ouch. That really hurts." She woke up when she leaned forward and grabbed her foot.

"You okay? We are almost there, Penny." Leo was talking to her. She tried her best to focus, although she was still groggy. "And before we arrive, I want to remind you not to interfere with our search by trying to enter the house. You will contaminate the scene, and anything we find will not be admissible in court. But looking around the neighborhood could prove to be valuable to us. See if you pick up on anything out-of-step with the norm."

Penny rubbed her foot, trying to get her brain working. "Can I ask questions of folks?"

"My officers have canvassed up and down the street, but you never know—some of these neighbors may have been approached about selling their own kids, and our officers never asked about that."

Leo didn't say anything else until the Crown Vic pulled up in front of the house. The dusty road had several other cars leaning into the sloping, grassless yard.

"The Garcias appear to have company," Leo noted.

At that moment, a woman stepped out of the home holding a wicker basket and a faded kitchen towel. It was evident she had delivered food.

"Are you going to talk to her?" Penny asked.

Without answering, Leo got out of the car and headed over to the woman who was now on the verge of reaching her old blue Pontiac. To Penny, she looked like one whose life had been hard. She had many creases and frown lines on her brown face; it was hard to tell her age. Perhaps she had worked in the cotton fields along the Rio Grande or picked vegetables on the farms near Fabens, Texas, Penny thought. Her faded, flowered dress was on the brink of losing its hem, but it appeared clean and pressed. Her white shoes were scuffed, and the heels were worn down.

The woman saw the sheriff advancing on her and reacted with a look of fear.

Penny saw him hold out his hand to her as if to reassure her that there was nothing to worry about. At once, her demeanor relaxed, but she still had an uncertain look in her eyes.

Penny couldn't hear the conversation. She lowered the automatic window to see if she could glean some details. The morning breeze was surprisingly refreshing as it moved across Penny's face, but it wasn't strong enough to carry the voices. The woman shook her head *no* and then *yes*. Penny watched intently as Leo placed his hand gently on the woman's arm and helped her into her car.

He smiled, waved her good-bye, and walked back toward the Crown Vic.

Just as Leo arrived at Penny's car window, another patrol car pulled up behind them and parked. Two uniformed officers got out and walked over to their boss. They looked alarmed when they saw Penny in the car, but Leo appeared to be unfazed by their reaction.

The woman pulled away from the home, her eyes still centered on the sheriff. She drove slowly down the road, perhaps not wanting to stir up any dust, as if that might stir up trouble for her too.

"Let's do this thing," Leo said to his men. Then he turned to Penny and said, "I'll catch up with you when the search has ended." The three men walked slowly up the crumbling steps. Penny watched Leo knock on the door. Mrs. Garcia greeted the officers and motioned for them to come inside.

---

Penny hopped out of the Crown Vic and began strolling down the road. Once she was certain no one was looking, she made a U-turn and hurried back toward the house. She figured the sheriff and his deputies would be busy talking with Manuel and Marvela Garcia before beginning the search. They would not notice if she peeked in a window, just to confirm her suspicions.

As she tiptoed behind the house on target for the bedroom window, which she believed belonged to Rosa's parents, she saw a small, fragile-looking boy turning the corner and running straight for her. She froze in place and tried to calm her racing heart. This was indeed the boy she had seen crying on the porch and then later sucking his thumb on the sofa!

"Who are you?" he asked Penny. His slender arms were crossed defensively over his chest. He wore a Spiderman T-shirt and a pair of torn jeans.

Penny chose her words carefully, trying not to frighten the boy, who looked perilously close to starvation. She had to restrain herself from offering to take him to McDonald's.

"Well, hi there!" Penny said, all smiles. "My name is Penny, and I am with the police. We are at your house looking for clues as to where Rosa might have gone."

"There aren't any clues back here, just dirt and weeds!"

"Well, thank you for telling me. That's good to know. I'll move on down the road and see what else I can find." The boy appeared satisfied with her answer. He turned and ran up the steps and inside the back door, which slammed behind him.

Penny moved cautiously toward the bedroom window, knowing that the boy might tell on her. She would just have to take the chance that he would not. She had to see what was going on inside. There were only two windows on the side of the house, and Penny was certain the window closest to the road belonged to Rosa's parents. To her dismay, she was too short to look in the window. She found a large rock, which she rolled toward the wall. Perching precariously on the stone, she waited for the deputies to find the cash, thereby proving to her and to the world that she was, indeed, a competent remote viewer.

# CHAPTER 15

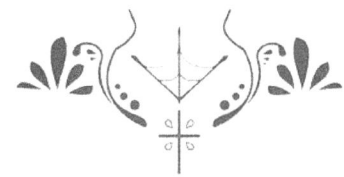

When the front door opened, Manuel Garcia was standing behind his wife. To Leo, the couple did not appear at all alarmed at seeing the three officers standing on their porch at 7:45 a.m. Leo took a deep breath and wished he could turn around and head back to the office. Penny had probably called this wrong, and his department would be embarrassed by the gaffe of ordering a search warrant on a grieving family. It was too late now. Leo introduced his officers, Sergeant Richard Clark and Lieutenant Ontiveros, as they stepped into the small living room. Mrs. Garcia invited the officers to sit down. Leo cleared his throat, as if the words he dreaded to say were stuck there. "Mr. and Mrs. Garcia, we have a warrant to search your home."

"A warrant?" Mr. Garcia asked. "Are you here to arrest us?" His arms, which had been stretched out in a welcome, fell to his sides. His wife remained standing behind her husband, making it difficult for Leo to read her reaction.

Leo wanted this to go as smoothly as it possibly could. He spoke in a gentle tone. "The court has given us permission to examine your home and its contents."

When Mr. Garcia turned and looked at his wife, Leo could see that her face was turning from brown to gray. Her eyes were vacant and showed no hint that she had anything to hide. He was going to kill Penny if she was making this stuff up! Leo was hoping to keep things relaxed as his officers looked around the tiny home. "I will remain with you both while the officers do their jobs."

Mr. Garcia guided his wife to the sofa. They sank into the sofa almost simultaneously. The sheriff heard the back door bang shut, and the Garcias' five-year-old son came in the room, presumably from the backyard. "Mommy, the police are here," he said. "Have they found Rosa?"

Leo tried not to gasp when he saw the young boy's legs, which were not much bigger than the legs of the end table at the edge of the couch. His ankles looked as if they would snap in half if he jumped off a curb.

"Pedro, the police have not found Rosa, but they are looking around our house perhaps hoping to find clues as to where she has gone," his father answered.

All three members of the family watched as the two deputies walked down the short hall and entered the first of two bedrooms. The sound of drawers opening and closing carried into the living room. Mrs. Garcia brought her hand to her face, hiding her displeasure. Pedro climbed into her arms. Then she looked up, as if she remembered her manners. "Would you like some food? We have so much. The neighbors and friends from church have been very kind."

"No, thank you. We will be out of your hair very soon." Leo liked the family and didn't want them to be found culpable, but he was fond of Penny in spite of her rocky start and wanted to believe her.

---

Penny was sure her hair was about to burst into flames. Why hadn't she worn a cap? She felt the top of her head and winced. It was going to be a brutally hot day. The sun burned into her scalp as she hung around the Garcias' bedroom window. The officers had yet to reach the master bedroom, where she hoped Mrs. Garcia had hidden the cash.

Penny's wobbly perch began to make the arches in her feet ache. She leaned into the window frame again, just in time to see the two deputies walking into the master bedroom. Sergeant Clark stopped in front of the couple's dresser and began pulling out the drawers and stacking them on the floor. One drawer fell to pieces as he yanked it out, dropping socks and T-shirts around the deputy's feet. Penny ducked from the window in case Leo, hearing the commotion, would make an appearance. When she looked in the window again, the deputies were still alone. Sergeant Clark was pulling out the top drawer of the chest, this time with more care. He carried it to the bed and dumped the contents. Penny's stomach had butterflies. Would he find the money Marvela Garcia had hidden there? Or was Penny sending them on a pointless quest as Deputy Gómez had claimed? Penny held her breath when Clark found the framed photo of Rosa in the drawer. He laid it carefully on the bed and then he continued his search. He jumped away from the dresser as if he had seen a snake. Penny could see Clark motioning for Ontiveros to join him. He held up a roll of cash that was secured with a rubber band. Penny watched as the sergeant began to count it. When he had completed the count of the bills, Clark shook his head and then shoved the cash into his lieutenant's hands. She watched the sergeant plop down on the bed and cover his face with his hands. Penny had seen enough. She hopped down from the boulder and ran across the front yard and on down the road. The sand invaded her mules and soiled her white socks, but she no longer cared. She felt vindicated now. She would walk a couple of blocks, just to clear her head, and then return to the sheriff's car and wait for him to give her the good news.

---

When Lieutenant Ontiveros returned to the living room and asked the sheriff to follow him, Leo was relieved that his men had at least found something of interest. He was hopeful they were about to have a real break in the case, even if it wasn't what Penny had predicted. He looked at the Garcias and spoke softly, "Please wait here until we return."

"But, Sheriff, I need to help you!" Marvela cried.

"We must do this ourselves, Mrs. Garcia. It is the law."

As Leo walked down the hall with his lieutenant, he could hear Marvela sobbing and Manuel trying to console her. The officers entered the small room with the scuffed pine floors and dreary gray walls. Leo's stomach churned. It would be profoundly painful if he found out that the Garcias' greed had actually led to Rosa being sold into slavery. The sheriff looked at the picture of the Virgin of Guadalupe at the head of the double bed and shook his head. Then he turned to Clark, who was standing now and waiting for them.

The sergeant showed him the dresser's top drawer, which was now upended on the bed. He handed Leo the framed photo of Rosa and a very large wad of cash.

"Have you counted it?" Leo asked.

"Yes," replied Clark. "What are the Garcias doing with $50,000?"

Just then, a large wailing sound came from the living room. The sheriff ran to see what had happened. Mrs. Garcia was resting her head in her husband's lap. Her tears were flowing so heavily that her husband's khaki work pants were stained as if he had wet himself. Pedro was gripping his mother's back. He looked scared and confused. *As well he should be*, the sheriff thought.

Ontiveros stepped into the living room and held out his hands, which were clutching the cash. Mrs. Garcia responded with more crying, and little Pedro joined the chorus.

"What is going on here?" Manuel asked. "Where did you find that money?"

Sheriff Tellez got down on his knees to get at eye level with Mrs. Garcia. "Mrs. Garcia, do you know what has happened to Rosa?" he asked.

Mrs. Garcia caught her breath as if to protest. Another gust of tears burst forth as if cleansing her from her sin. Mr. Garcia looked confused, but gently, he helped his wife into a sitting position. The husband looked grimly at the sheriff and then at his wife. *"Debe decirles lo que le pasó."*

*"Ahorita no,"* she pleaded.

"It is necessary for you to tell them, and me also, the truth," the husband pleaded.

"Mrs. Garcia, the quicker we know what happened, the better chance we can find Rosa," the sheriff interrupted, sensing her reluctance to come to grips with her own guilt. Slowly, the sheriff stood, his knees aching. He realized Mr. Garcia had probably been kept in the dark. He leaned carefully over Mrs. Garcia. "Por favor, señora." His voice reflected his frustration and anger.

Mrs. Garcia wiped the tears from her face, her hands shaking. "Okay, okay. I tell you everything. Diego, your friend, Manuel, you know him—he came to the house and said a family in California wanted to hire Rosa for $50,000 a year as a housekeeper. If she doesn't like it there, he said, she can come home. This is a *gran familia,* and they live in a beautiful home with a swimming pool. I saw the picture! And if she does good, they will hire her for another year."

"Marvela, that is ridiculous!" her husband protested.

"They promise to send her to college if she stays with them for four years," she continued, ignoring him. "Her teachers always tell us how smart she is, you know. I thought it would be good for Rosa, and the money would help my mother with her cancer treatments."

Manuel looked at his wife in disbelief. "Why? Why would you do such a thing? Our Rosa is very dear to us. She is not for sale!" Manuel threw up his hands and started walking down the hall to their bedroom. Marvela called after her husband who turned back and looked at his wife. "Manny, please believe me. I am very upset about *Mamá*. I don't want her to die. I kept thinking Rosa would have a chance to go to college. That is not something we will be able to give her."

Manny turned back and looked at his wife, whose tears were flowing nonstop. She was wringing her hands and moving into a fetal position on the sofa.

"Please, *Papá*, help *Mamá*," Pedro yelled. "She is very sad, and she says she is sorry."

Manny walked back to the sofa and addressed both his wife and his son. "We must do everything to help the sheriff find Rosa." "Maybe you bring my Rosa back?" Marvela said, looking up at Leo. Her face was streaked with tears, and she looked drained and lifeless. "I make a big mistake. Please help us!"

# CHAPTER 16

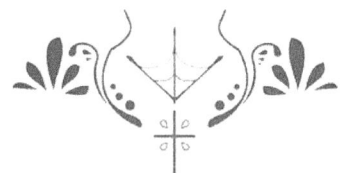

Penny had walked down the dusty lane for several minutes. Her arms were hot to the touch. She was overheated and likely sunburned. Why hadn't she brought a bottle of water? She decided to stop and rest before heading back to the car. The sun had totally drained her energy. Even at this early hour, it had to be well over 80 degrees, she thought. She was dizzy, and her throat was dry. She licked her lips, trying to generate some moisture in her mouth. On the side of the road, she found a mesquite tree with several large rocks circling it. There was enough shade to allow her to sit down until she felt better. She leaned back against the trunk of the tree. The grooves in the bark cut into her back, but she didn't care. A merciful breeze slipped over her face, bringing her a little relief.

She promised herself she would shut her eyes for just a little while and then return to find Leo, who would be looking for her very soon. Within a few minutes, her mind grew increasingly confused. Maybe it was the heat, but she felt something pulling her away from the comfort of her shady tree. She reluctantly accepted the mysterious force pushing her onward through a field of desert plants, most bearing thorns. The sun was again beating down on her head, and the sweat was stinging her eyes. She could barely see where she was going and longed to return to the shade of the mesquite tree. She looked down and realized she was not wearing shoes! Certainly, this was a dream. She would never walk through the desert without protection for her feet. Penny walked as carefully as she could in her white socks. Soon, her destination became clearer. She saw a boy and a girl running and playing in the midst of a virtual forest of cacti and soaptree yuccas. There were no swing sets or monkey bars, just well-worn paths in and around the vegetation. She waved hello. If the children thought she looked weird standing in the desert without shoes, they did not say so. They merely slowed down and waved back. As she walked toward them, she stepped on a cactus, causing her to stumble. When Penny hit the ground, she woke up. She was still sitting under the mesquite tree. There were no children around. When she tried to stand, she saw that several thorns from a nearby barrel cactus were jammed into her right foot. She was afraid if she took her sock off too quickly, she would tear the sole of her foot to shreds. She carefully removed her sock, pulling the thorns out of her foot one at a time. Each thorn was like a tiny fishhook and left small spots of blood on her skin. She rubbed her hand across the bottom of her foot, assuring herself the damage was minimal. She adjusted her socks and slipped on her shoes, but when she tried to stand, she was a bit wobbly and unsure of her ability to walk back to the Garcia home. She gingerly limped into the center of the road. She had left her cell phone back in Leo's car, so she couldn't even call him. She would just make it on her own as slow as that might be.

As her eyes adjusted to the searing sunlight, she thought she really could hear children laughing. She moved toward the sound. On the left side of the road, she saw a field brimming with soaptree yuccas. She heard the children screaming at one another before she actually saw them. A boy and girl were running and dodging the yucca in a daredevil manner. Penny rubbed the finger that had been pierced by the thorn on Rosa's top.

*Rosa played here too! This place must make the children feel safe,* Penny thought. Certainly, no sane adult would venture in there. She waded deeper into the sea of desert plants. Since when was she sane?

The boy and a girl, both about Rosa's age, stopped abruptly when they saw Penny. "Hi, guys," Penny said.

"Hello," answered the young boy whose hair was the color of midnight. "My name is Helio, and this is my friend, Ana. Are you lost?"

"No, no. A friend of mine is visiting the Garcias. I am waiting for him," Penny said. "Do you know Rosa?"

This time, Ana chimed in. "Of course, we know Rosa! She is my best friend. We walk to school every day." Ana was slightly smaller than Helio. Her face was round and her skin was dark brown.

"Were you playing with her when she disappeared at the park?" Penny asked Ana.

"I did not go to school that day. My grandmother kept me home to keep an eye on her baby because she had to go to the doctor."

"How old are you, Ana?" Penny continued.

"I am eleven, just like Rosa," she replied. "But I'm taller." Ana started to move away from Penny.

"Don't go," Penny said. "I want to ask you some questions about Rosa."

"I have to go home. I need to do my homework." Ana ran out of the park before Penny could say anything more. If Helio was not helpful, she would have to find where Ana lived.

She knew she had to act quickly or she would lose Helio too. "Helio, were you at the park with Rosa?" Penny asked.

"Yes, I was there, but I didn't see where she went!" he answered, his young shoulders rising in defense.

"What were you doing when Rosa got lost?" Penny pressed. "I was playing with some friends at the swing set, trying to see which one of us could swing the highest." "Did you see anything out of the ordinary?" "No, everybody was just having fun."

"Do you play in the park every day?" Penny asked. Maybe something had happened on an earlier day that Helio might have noticed.

"Pretty much, we come to the park every day after school." "Have you ever seen anyone hanging around the park who looked like they didn't belong?"

Helio considered Penny's question for some time.

"On Wednesday, there was a man who stopped by the park to get directions to the nearest auto parts store," Helio recalled. "His van was not running good, and he needed a place close. And I was lucky. He gave me a dollar for my help!"

"Can you remember what he looked like?" Penny asked, trying not to show her excitement.

Helio looked thoughtful and remained quiet for a few seconds. "I can remember some things about him. But can you give me a dollar too?"

"Perhaps, if your description can help us find Rosa," Penny said.

"Well, I wasn't the only one who saw him!" Helio was shouting now as if he needed to weasel out of his earlier confession. "Ask somebody else then!"

"Please, Helio, your description might help us find Rosa!" Penny waved a five-dollar bill, and his eyes widened.

"The whole park of kids was standing around him. He promised a dollar to the first person who could tell him where the nearest car parts store was. Of course, I won because my dad is always at *Autocamiones Reparar* at the corner of Rojas and Chelsea."

"Was Rosa with you?" Penny asked.

"I don't remember if she was or not," Helio answered. "I would guess not, though, 'cause her family doesn't know anything about cars. Her dad always takes the bus to work."

"What kind of car did the man have?" Penny continued.

"It was an old green van—no, it was blue! Something like they drive in Juárez, I think," Helio said. "You know, something right out of the *yonke* (junkyard)!" The boy laughed and then became quiet. Penny could see his mind thrashing through his memory bank. "I know it had Juárez plates because they look like my uncle's."

"Did the sheriff's deputies ask you about this man?" Penny continued.

"No, the cops don't know anything about him," Helio said.

"Was he short or tall?" Penny asked.

Helio stood in front of Penny, shuffling his tennies back and forth; he seemed to be deep in thought. "Well, I can't remember everything, but I remember he was skinny and short. In fact, he was not much taller than I am! I kept thinking, *how does he get his feet to touch the pedals?* I know I can't drive my dad's car yet. Give me another year though!"

"So he was *corto*. What else can you remember?"

"He smelled bad. And he was wearing a blue baseball cap."

"What color was his hair?" Penny asked.

"It was light brown. I noticed that right away because everyone I know has dark brown or black hair." Helio laughed.

"Did he have a mustache?" Penny said.

"Yes," Helio added. "But his lips looked funny. They were very thin, and his teeth were kinda brown like he didn't have a mother telling him to brush them every day!"

"What color were his eyes?" Penny continued.

"I don't remember that," Helio laughed again. "I was too busy trying to earn that dollar!"

He leaned in and grabbed the five dollars out of Penny's hand. Penny reached in her blue jeans pocket and pulled out a folded piece of paper. She had not looked at it since Deputy Gómez had given it to her, but now, she reluctantly unfolded it and showed it to Helio.

"Is this the man you saw?"

Helio leaned forward and looked carefully at the composite. "It sure is!"

"Thank you, Helio. You are helping us find Rosa." "I'm a hero then?"

"Yes, you are a hero to me, and you will be to Rosa and her parents when we find her. If the sheriff's deputies have more questions, where can we find you?"

"I live at 2346 Camino Agua, just three doors from Rosa." "Thanks again, Helio!"

"No, thank *you, señorita*!"

As Penny left Helio, she saw Leo's car approaching. She climbed in the car, happy to be free of sunshine and thorns. Leo stared at her glumly, but she returned his sad look with a great big grin. Penny fell back into the broad leather seat and buckled up for what would be a very interesting ride back home.

# CHAPTER 17

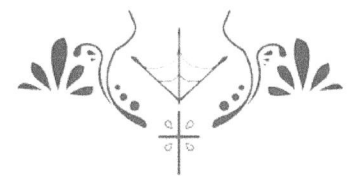

"Tell me again, why you aren't arresting Marvela Garcia?" Penny asked as they pulled into her driveway.

"I don't want to alert the kidnapper that we are onto him, for starters," Leo said. "And second, what good would it do to take Mrs. Garcia out of her home and place her behind bars? She has enough to worry about."

"But she has broken the law!" Penny said. "And what if she tries to hide in Mexico?"

"I am willing to take that chance right now," Leo said. "Like I said, the kidnapper may be watching to see if Mrs. Garcia spills her guts to the police."

"You mean like kill Rosa, if he hasn't already done so?" "Precisely. We will deal with Mrs. Garcia later when we've sorted this all out and have Rosa back safely at home. Marvela Garcia is not going anywhere."

"I can imagine that Marvela is very sad about not having the money to help her mother with her cancer."

"No doubt, but she realizes she made a very big mistake." "Maybe or maybe not. It might be tough having to choose between your mother and your daughter, I guess. Although, not having kids, it would be hard for me to appreciate Marvela's choice to abandon her own child."

The whole way home, they exchanged information on what both had found. Penny never confessed to peeking in the Garcias' bedroom window, but Leo gave a detailed description of what had happened during the search.

"Marvela collapsed under the weight of her guilt," Leo said.

Penny told him about meeting up with Helio and Ana and how Helio had described the man who had visited Alameda Park the day before Rosa had been taken.

"The icing on the cake is that he identified the kidnapper as the man in our composite drawing!"

Leo looked over at Penny and smiled. "Thank you, Penny."

Penny's cell phone beeped. She pulled her phone out of her jeans pocket and opened her text messages. "I've got to go. It may be Porter, sending me a message from China!" She jumped out of the car and ran toward her front door.

Leo caught up with her as she was rummaging through her purse for her keys. "Penny, thank you again." He pulled her hand out of her bag and held it. "I'm sorry. I truly am."

Penny pulled her hand back and dug back into her purse. She dangled her keys at Leo and then leaned forward and gave him a quick hug. "I'm really exhausted. I want to take a shower and climb into bed."

Penny shut the door and left Leo alone with his thoughts.

---

Penny crawled into bed, her filthy shoes still on her feet. She rolled toward the bedside table to check the phone for messages. The cell phone text had been a false alarm—an ad for car insurance. She picked up the receiver and heard the welcome triple tone signaling that someone had left a message. When she heard Porter's voice, her heart jumped into her throat. His usual voice of authority was soft and humble. "Honey, where are you? I'm missing you. I'm sorry I left when I did. I'll try to call you on Sunday. Bye."

Penny kicked her shoes off the bed, took off her socks and dug a deep hole under her down comforter and crisp sheets. She was much too tired to think about Porter now. She stretched her legs across the width of the king-size bed, and flexed her toes. It felt so good to be helping Leo find Rosa. Making a difference in the world was all she ever wanted, and that hadn't happened until Porter left her. Penny yawned, and dropped her right arm over her eyes. She'd have a much better grip on what she would say to him when he called back. Right now she needed a little shuteye.

# CHAPTER 18

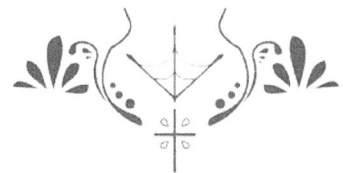

Penny slept in fits and spurts, like an engine without oil. She was exhausted and determined not to move from her bed; therefore, she lay suspended in a fog of nothingness or so it seemed. It was in this state that Penny became mindful of a two-lane roadway filled with bumper-to-bumper traffic. She was driving one of the cars, a nondescript gray sedan with a manual transmission. Penny hated driving a stick, though she had reluctantly accepted her father's instruction as a teenager. She was in heavy traffic and had to shift gears continually to keep from running into the cars ahead. She tried to keep a safe distance, but drivers still nudged their way into the lane in front of her. Exasperated, she pressed her foot harder on the accelerator, hoping to close the gap; a van muscled its way into the space ahead of her anyway. She couldn't stop in time, so she swerved into the right-hand lane, causing a driver in a red sports car to blow his horn. Penny roared up alongside of the van, waving her left hand in the air and trying to get his attention. She wanted to give the driver a piece of her mind. When the man looked over at her, she tried to yell at him, but no sound came out of her mouth. It was then that Penny knew this was no ordinary traffic jam, and that the driver in the van was no ordinary man. She knew him. It was the kidnapper, and furthermore, she was certain this was Donnie Harper!

Her mind was turning faster than the revolutions of the cranky motor under her hood, and her hands and arms were covered with sweat. It was tough keeping her grip on the steering wheel. As the traffic lightened, the van picked up speed, and in response, Penny tried to shift into fourth gear. Her clammy fingers bungled the move, and her body fell forward into the steering wheel, causing her car horn to go off. She had to veer left, but not before she creased the van's passenger door with her bumper. Harper turned sharply into her car, knocking her into the guardrail. Luckily, Penny's vehicle bounced back into the stream of traffic with little more than a buckled right fender. She was feeling more like a jockey than a driver. She leaned into the steering wheel, and had she possessed a crop for the flank of her lumbering car, she would have whipped it into a gallop. Instead, she fought with her weary four cylinders, which moved only at a trot. Undaunted, she kept pumping the accelerator and experimenting with different gears in an effort to fool the car into gaining speed.

Consumed with chasing the kidnapper, Penny failed to see a semi in her rearview mirror. Its foghorn bellowed out a warning for her to get out of the way. She squeezed her car into a narrow opening between the blue van and a bright yellow pickup truck. The truck gave her the space she needed to stay in pursuit of Harper. Her hands were clamped around the steering wheel with such force that the muscles in her arms began to ache. Perspiration poured off her face as Penny steadied her eyes on the van's smashed bumper and its silver 3500 ID plate. The silver medallion reflecting against the afternoon sun convinced her that this was the same blue van that had carried Rosa away. The only difference now was that it had Juárez plates, just as little Helio had told her. The realization that the kidnapper was within reach propelled her forward. She leaned her head down and wiped her forehead on the sleeve of her T-shirt. She was tired and wanted to return to the comfort of her cool sheets and down pillow, but she persevered.

Her remote viewing training had been designed around a stationery target, and now, flashes of light and dark began intercepting her view of the van as it charged down the highway.

She had to return to her protocols again and again in order to remain centered. Her brain was exhausted from all of her mental gymnastics. Sweat was now stinging her eyes and causing her to squint in order to stay in pursuit.

Harper took a sudden turn to the right and exited the highway. Caught off guard, Penny had to exit quickly and barely kept from sideswiping the guardrail again. She followed the van into a residential area, holding back behind another car. She wasn't sure he could really see her, in that this was not a physical pursuit, but she was taking no chances. Penny scanned the unfamiliar street signs for an intersection she knew. Finally, Harper stopped at the Gas-n-Go corner store. She thought she had been to this store because she recognized the sign over the door that read, "Owned and operated by Celia and Armando Marín," but she still couldn't determine its exact location. She watched Harper buy chips, dip, and a six-pack of beer. Then, strangely enough, he drove to a florist and purchased a bouquet of flowers. He hopped back in his van and drove away. Penny was still uncertain of where she was, but she was happy to know she could remain in tune with her target, and that might mean eventually providing the sheriff's office with the kidnapper's exact location. She glanced at her knuckles, which were white from gripping the wheel so tightly. She relaxed a little. Thankfully, the van never got above thirty miles per hour. Perhaps he was driving the speed limit, hoping not to draw attention to himself.

Harper drove by the Bonita Bakery, one of Penny's favorite haunts, and made a left onto Niño Aguilera Street. She was thrilled to see the bakery. She let out a big sigh. *Yes!* She slapped the steering wheel with her hand. *Now we are getting somewhere!* Harper traveled to the end of Niño Aguilera and turned right.

The sun was setting, and the glare on her car window made it difficult for Penny to tell where he was headed. She shaded her eyes for a better look and wished she had sunglasses. He was not driving down another city street at all; it was more like a dirt lane, similar to those used by ranchers and farmers. His van stirred up dust, which mixed with the last rays of the sun, creating the illusion of a sunset right in the middle of the road. Penny watched Harper park his van and walk with his purchases to a small blue cottage, which was set in a field of green chilies. In the distance, she could see farm workers harvesting the chilies and dumping them into large burlap bags. She turned her eyes back to Harper, who was entering the house by the back door. With his hands full, the screen door slammed behind him.

Penny was stunned by the realization that she had already seen this cottage during her viewing in Alamogordo. But she had to hurry.

He was already inside. The fact that Donnie Harper was not in his own home confused her. Had he killed Rosa, and was he now in hiding from the sheriff? Or was Rosa still alive and stashed away in this house? *I have to find out for sure!*

As she followed Harper into the cottage, she was surprised to find the simple act of walking took more concentration than following him in his van had. Fuzzy images were swirling in front of her. She felt dizzy and befuddled. She knew from past experiences that these kinds of images were only a subterfuge created by her mind as a defense mechanism. After all, who wants to be face-to-face with a sex offender? But Penny was determined to find out what happened to Rosa, and that meant overcoming even her own terror.

She eventually wiped her mind clean of everything but the sight of Donnie Harper putting away the groceries. A closer look revealed the kidnapper to be a scrawny man who looked as though his brown sweatshirt and pants would just drop off his body if he inhaled. His tennis shoes were one or two sizes larger than his feet. Were these his clothes? Penny could only surmise they were borrowed or, at the very least, thrift-store purchases. She could understand why the deputies didn't think he was capable of kidnapping Rosa. He looked pathetic.

Harper returned to the van for the bouquet of flowers. In the kitchen, Penny watched him fill a clear glass vase with water and arrange what turned out to be lilacs in the container. Harper carried the lilacs into a bedroom, placed them on a bedside table, and left the room. For a second or two, Penny actually thought she could smell the flowers, but this sensory perception soon dissolved. She took a quick look around the room. The white chenille bedspread and the gray wood floors sent an eerie chill through her body. She wanted to escape, but her feet felt as though they were glued to the floor. She was stuck in Harper's bedroom! The room felt as if it was getting smaller and smaller, and she feared she would soon suffocate if she remained in there any longer. She heard footsteps in the hall. Harper was on his way back to his bedroom! She stepped out of her shoes and left them by the window. Trying to get back to her own house was like pulling her body through a keyhole. Pain shot through her arms and legs as she forced her spirit to remove itself from the blue cottage. She traveled through a long tunnel of gray that seemed to go on forever. Finally, her eyes fluttered open. She was home, but she awoke with a pounding headache. Her body felt heavy with exhaustion, even though her pillow-top mattress enveloped her. She took a deep breath, and her lungs begged for more air. She panted and coughed for several minutes until she managed to fill her lungs.

Moving from one dimension to another after such a long viewing was apparently as difficult to achieve physically as it was spiritually. Penny would have to work on her recovery techniques. If she were ever to get another job in law enforcement, she wouldn't have all day to pursue criminals. She pulled herself into a sitting position and leaned over the side of the bed, still light-headed. The floor swirled before her, but she kept scanning her bedroom until she found what she needed to see. Her dusty brown mules had returned home as well. They weren't still sitting by the window in Harper's bedroom!

It had been exhilarating to follow the van and to find the blue cottage, but Penny knew she couldn't capture the kidnapper with only her mind. She had to be there, and that meant getting in her car and driving to the blue cottage. She took a deep breath and for a moment considered if she were, indeed, up to the task. Was this yet another miscue that would bring her ridicule by the sheriff's department? But the sheriff's department was no longer her employer. She could do whatever she felt like doing, and this felt right. But what did she hope to accomplish by finding the blue cottage? Could she confront Donnie Harper all by herself? Would she be prepared for bad news if she found that Rosa had been killed?

When Penny had signed up for the controlled remote viewing class, she'd known full well what might ensue. She had read about successful graduates finding lost children and even solving cold cases law enforcement had abandoned. But reading about solving a crime and really doing it were not the same thing. Fear welled up in her throat. She grabbed a bottle of water from her nightstand and gulped it down. She would have time to answer these questions on the road, she thought. Something told her she needed to act now. She walked into the dining room, scooped her car keys off the table, and ran out the front door.

# CHAPTER 19

Penny wheeled out of her driveway in a flurry, screeching her tires as she raced toward the interstate. Her heart was pumping fast, providing her with the adrenaline to keep going. To prevent herself from being totally consumed by fear, she would use the driving time to formulate a plan. She would call Leo once she had found Niño Aguilera Street and the blue cottage. She wouldn't waste his time until she was sure what she'd seen today was the same place she'd visited during the first remote viewing in Alamogordo. And though she wanted to prove herself, she had no plans to become a hero.

She drove more than twenty miles before reaching the I-10/Paisano Street exit, which took her to the Lower Valley. Penny used her GPS to guide her to Niño Aguilera Street, which was only three blocks long, with a couple dozen houses. She figured, *how difficult could it be to find the blue cottage on such a short street?* But cars were parked close together on both sides of the road, making it tough to see the homes without driving slowly. She drove up and down the street, looking for the blue van, but it was nowhere to be found. Surely, she had not beaten Harper home? Penny pulled to the side of the road and reached for her purse, which held her phone. In her rush to leave the house, she had left both her bag and her phone behind. She couldn't believe she had been so stupid to forget them both. She rummaged through her car for spare change, but turned up only a nickel and a few pennies. Even a pay phone was out of the question. It was time for plan B. Penny remembered the Bonita Bakery. Hopefully, someone was still in the store. She had to call Leo.

It was dusk when she arrived at the bakery. She pulled in front to see if anyone had started the night shift. She hopped out of her car and looked in the window. The shelves held only a few loaves of bread. There was no one around. She was returning to her car when she saw smoke rising from behind the building. Penny found the baker puffing on a cigarette in the alley. Cigarette butts lay at his feet. His white uniform was covered in flour, and there were streaks of colored icing on his apron where he must have wiped his hands. The baker looked surprised and a little fearful when he saw her. He took a few steps back. His lips quivered, and his brown wrinkled face showed his displeasure at being caught off guard.

"Please help me! Can I use your phone?"

"*Señorita*, we're closed. You can call from the gas station down the street."

"I need to use the phone please! I am on the trail of the kidnapper of Rosa Garcia, and I have to call the sheriff now!"

"You mean the little girl that went missing in Alameda Park?"
"Yes! Please let me call for help!"

The baker threw his cigarette down, leaving it to smolder among the others, and led her through the kitchen and into a small office near the ovens. It was hot in there and pungent with the aroma of freshly baking bread. Penny wiped her fingers across her face, which was damp with sweat. She tried to dial the phone, but her fingers kept shaking. Her mind went blank. *What is Leo's cell phone number?*

The baker was staring at her, perhaps wondering if he had made the right decision to give her access to his phone. Penny gave the baker a pleading look. She held the receiver in her hand but had yet to dial. *For God's sake, get a grip!*

Finally, she punched in the number and let out a breath when she heard it ringing. Leo was good about picking up his phone, and Penny hoped he was not on the other line. The cell phone went to his message service. "Leo, this is Penny. I'm at the Bonita Bakery on Wayland Avenue, but I am searching for the little blue cottage on Niño Aguilera Street. I'll be waiting for you in front of the cottage. I found Harper during a remote viewing, and I followed him. I am sure he is the kidnapper. I don't know if Rosa is still alive, but I want to try to save her. Look for my car parked on the street."

Penny thanked the baker profusely and ran back to her car. Hopefully, Leo would pick up the message and either come or send a patrol car immediately.

On Penny's third time down the street, she noticed a dusty lane, hidden by live oaks whose branches dipped precariously across the driveway. She had a hard time containing her excitement because she felt sure this was the lane that she had seen Harper take to the blue cottage. It was now dark, and in the distance, she could see a flashing light emanating from the front window. She drove slowly down the lane until she could see the house more clearly. In the starless night, she couldn't confirm the color, but it looked familiar. There was no sign of Harper or his van. *Where in the world is he?*

Penny thought this might be the perfect opportunity to check out the blue cottage before Harper returned, if he returned at all. She backed her car out of the lane, drove down the street a half a block, and eased her convertible into a ditch. She got out and opened her trunk. She grabbed a windbreaker and a tire iron. Then she remembered her pepper spray in the glove compartment that Porter had always insisted she carry. She opened the passenger door and retrieved the spray, a pad of sticky notes, a pen, and a wrench, tucking them in the pockets of her coat. Then she raised the hood and wrote a note to Leo indicating she thought she had found the little blue cottage where she had seen Rosa. "The cottage is half-a-block north of my car on the same side of the street. I've gone to check the house. It looks empty. Don't worry, Leo, I won't try to do your job! Ha! Ha!" Penny stuck the note on the air cleaner and hoped Leo would find it. Then she headed out on foot, and when she got closer to the drive leading to the cottage, she got down on her knees and began crawling through the field that surrounded the home. She could smell the peppers crushing under her fingers as she made progress. She would have to remember to keep her hands away from her face or the stain from the chilies could set her eyes on fire.

Penny counted on the cloud-covered sky to move toward the house undetected. It looked deserted, but she couldn't know that for sure. She progressed slowly and deliberately. When she got near the house, she waited for several minutes, watching the front window for any sign of movement. When she was certain no one was home, she went up on the front porch and braved a look in the window. She saw nothing but furniture and a wide-screen television that flickered on the wall. This startled Penny; thinking certainly, there was someone inside. Who would leave the house with the TV still on?

Penny moved carefully around the house to the backyard, a grassless area with two large trees and a rickety back porch. A light in the kitchen window was casting creepy shadows across the yard and exposing a detached garage and an old Silver Stream trailer.

She was certain she had seen Donnie Harper arrive at this very spot. *Where did he go?*

Penny walked closer to the house and peered in another window, and what she saw made her gasp. On a bedside table was a vase of lilacs. Penny wasn't sure how the house had played a role in Rosa's disappearance, but she knew it had. *I've seen enough! This cottage has to be involved in the kidnapping.*

She decided to return to her car and wait for Leo. Before she could make a move, headlights illuminated the driveway, followed by a second set. People were arriving at the house, and Penny had been too slow to get out of there in time. She was furious with herself. How many mistakes could a remote viewer make and still survive?

She ran to the opposite side of the backyard, only to be thwarted by a tall wooden fence, which was so full of decay it would never hold her weight should she try to climb it. *Where can I hide?* Penny was frantic. She tightened her grip on the tire iron and scanned the yard for cover. She raced to the farthest reaches of the backyard where she had seen the Silver Stream RV peeking out from behind the garage. The trailer looked unstable and neglected; Penny guessed it was a derelict sent out to the backyard before being hauled to the junkyard. That was good. No one would be the wiser if she hid there.

The trailer door was unlocked, and as she stepped inside, she met an odor of cigarettes and mildew. *Does someone really live here?* She found it unlikely since it was so small. She knelt down and parted the dusty venetian blinds covering the trailer window. Sure enough, the blue van had arrived, and behind it was a large black SUV. The SUV was a big surprise to Penny, and not one she relished.

In the dim light shining from the kitchen windows, Penny saw Donnie Harper get out of his van and wait for two men who followed him to the back of the house. This made Penny's hands tremble as she tried to tighten her grip on the tire iron. Her hands were slick and cold. She fumbled for the pepper spray in her windbreaker pocket.

Penny felt a sense of relief as she watched the three men enter the cottage through the kitchen door where she had been standing just a few minutes before. She had to act quickly to get past the van and the SUV to find help. She'd opened the trailer door and had her right foot on the trailer's steps when the cottage's back porch light went on. Its dim yellow bulb cast a ghostlike halo over a man's bulky features. Penny saw the glow of a lit cigarette as he moved his arm to and from his face. Perhaps his size was exaggerated by the shadows and the ugly angle of the lighting, but she thought he was much bigger than most men she knew. She backed away from the trailer door, closing it as quietly as she could. Hopefully, she would not have to find a place to hide here because she saw her options were few. She opened a tall cupboard, but it was jammed with spices and bottles of liquor. She headed to the only bedroom, a space about as big as her walk-in closet, and looked around for a place to hide. She had no time to deal with the smell of old tennis shoes and motor oil. Was he a mechanic? She knelt on the far side of a double bed, ready to lay low, should the man enter the trailer. Several minutes passed, and Penny heard nothing. The silence was reassuring. She sat up, trying not to touch the floor, which felt grimy. Perhaps the man was done with his cigarette and had gone back into the house. But then, was she imagining it or did she smell cigarette smoke? *Could the man be heading for the trailer?*

Penny shivered as she flattened her body against the cold linoleum floor. She could not stop shaking, and now, her teeth were chattering. She tried not to breathe through her nose; the smell of filth was everywhere. The grip on her tire iron made her hands numb. She released her hold and began to massage her fingers with her other hand.

The thud of heavy footsteps was followed by the squeaking of the trailer door. She shoved her face into the pile of a shaggy throw rug that gave off putrid smells. The man cleared his throat, and Penny thought she heard him spit phlegm. The rattle of the aluminum door slamming behind him set Penny's spine on fire. Her back felt hot and exposed. Now, she was hearing his feet, probably in boots, stomping around the trailer. Smoke rolled into the bedroom; he was that close.

She saw a light go on, but it was near the floor and very dim. Penny heard bottles clanking together and realized he had opened the small refrigerator in the galley kitchen. She listened to the twist and pop of a bottle cap, perhaps a beer. *Now, please go away!* No such luck. The man lumbered toward the bedroom. Penny couldn't lie any lower. She pulled her windbreaker over her head to hide her blond hair, hoping to blend in with the dark floor.

The mattress took the full force of the huge man as he dropped onto the bed. He growled like a bear. Then Penny heard him guzzling his beverage, followed by a loud burp. She could hear him take a deep breath and draw in on his cigarette. Then he coughed and threw his stubbed out smoke over the side of the bed. It bounced off Penny's back. What would happen if her clothes went up in flames?

About ten minutes passed, and Penny could hear the man snoring. On occasion, he would startle himself awake, then groan as he fell back asleep. One time, he threw his right arm over the edge of the bed. His fingers were dangling precariously close to Penny's legs. Penny had one option, and that was to do a snake crawl around the bed and out the door of the bedroom. She hoped the squeaky trailer door would not awaken him, but if it did, by then she would have a head start and would run like hell. Penny wriggled herself around the back end of the double bed and was just about to exit the bedroom, when a foot on her backside shoved her flat, knocking the wind out of her.

Helpless and in intense pain, Penny could not move. She tried to take a breath but simply could not. The man pulled her into a sitting position. She could tell he was puzzled, but he said nothing. He waited until he saw that her breathing was returning to normal before questioning her. "Who are you?"

With what little energy she had left, she flung the tire iron at his head. He reacted by picking it up and yanking her to her feet. He spun her around so that her back was against his body and then he shoved the tire iron under her chin, causing her head to sink into his chest. He smelled of whiskey and sweat and a just-smoked cigarette.

"I don't know why you are here, but we will find out soon enough."

He grunted and pushed her out of the trailer. In the dark, he stumbled, and Penny fell too, a few feet away from him. She tried to reach into her zipped pockets for her wrench or her pepper spray but couldn't get to either one before he was all over her again. He gathered her up like a rag doll. The beast was considerably taller than she, perhaps six-foot-two and almost 300 pounds. Penny knew that at 126 pounds, she would be no match in hand-to-hand combat. She tried wriggling free of his hold, but he only tightened his grip, and she was sure he was bruising her chest and arms. He carried her the rest of the way to the house, holding the tire iron against her chest so firmly she could hardly catch a breath.

The muted porch light did not prepare her for the bright lights of the kitchen. Her assailant pushed her through the screen door, and she fell against the legs of the table. Their entrance caught Donnie Harper off guard. He jerked his head around, dropping his metal spatula on the floor.

Another man, who was standing at the kitchen sink, turned quickly, drawing his gun and pointing it at the door. "What's going on, Petya?" the man yelled.

"I found her in my trailer, hiding. She had this tire iron." Petya pointed to Penny's weapon. He leaned over and yanked her to a standing position.

"You don't fool me, Petya. You been doing too many women, and finally, some little lady came back to make you pay!" The man laughed.

Penny was totally confused. Who were these guys? She thought only Donnie Harper was involved in Rosa's kidnapping. *What have I done to myself?*

The man, who was wearing what looked like a chef's coat, walked over to Petya and Penny, with his gun pointed directly at her. In spite of the steamy kitchen, Penny was suddenly chilled, and she began to shake. The chef's coat had an embroidered restaurant logo with the word "Andy's." Under that was the name "Sergei Andulov." *Is he a professional chef?* His name meant nothing to her, and she was addicted to cooking shows.

Penny had never seen this coming. No amount of remote viewing had shown her that others were involved in Rosa's kidnapping. Except for a little training from her dad, she had never been around guns, and now one was aimed squarely at her. Her stomach was queasy as if she might vomit. She took small, short breaths, trying to keep from puking on the man's shoes. Her eyes fluttered, and the kitchen lights became a kaleidoscope of swirling colors. Penny slid down Petya's legs. The pain of the tire iron jerking on her neck brought her back to consciousness. She tried to push the iron away, but the man only pressed harder against her throat. She was choking to death! She held her hands up in despair, hoping he would let go, but he did not care if she lived or died. Desperately, she turned and wrapped her arms around Petya's legs, trying to pull herself to a standing position. He kneed her chest, and she fell onto the floor again. This time, she did not move. *God, don't let me die like this!*

The chef's fingers were hot to the touch as he pulled Penny off the floor. She could feel the oxygen rushing into her body as she became vertical, but she was dizzy and wasn't sure if she could stand. He leaned in close to her, and the odor of alcohol stung her nostrils. Repulsed by a smell she had grown to hate as a child, Penny stepped back. Petya responded and shoved her into Andulov again. This time, Andulov drilled the barrel of the gun into the nape of her neck. The pain was intense. He threw his head back and laughed at her.

Penny blinked, hoping to keep away the tears. She now knew these men, whoever they were, played for keeps. She looked around the kitchen, perhaps taking in her last glimpse of earthly things. A half-empty vodka bottle sat on the kitchen table, and several empty bottles were scattered around the kitchen floor. *How fitting*, Penny thought, *to die by the hands of an alcoholic*. Sweat poured down her face and arms. *I'm sorry, Dad, for being a screw-up!* She fought the urge to faint again. She would at least give herself the dignity of being conscious when Andulov shot her.

"Andy, what do you want me to do with her?" Petya asked.

Andulov pulled the gun away from her neck. He looked disgusted, but he put his gun in his shoulder holster and turned back to the kitchen sink. He picked up a chef's knife in his right hand and began chopping a block of frozen spinach with the precision of a pro. The force of the blade echoed off the wooden block. Penny could feel the perspiration dropping in between her fingers. She wiped her hands against her jeans.

"Bring her to me, so we can talk while I work." Petya pushed Penny toward the cutting board. Andulov held the knife and rubbed his fingers over the edge of the blade. A small bubble of blood formed on his index finger.

His eyes met Penny's, and then he grimaced, as if the prick had caused him pain. "It is deadly sharp."

Penny tried not to react when he wiped the blood on his white coat. His eyes were as black as his curly head of hair and his thick beard. He turned and stared intently at Petya.

"Where did you find her?"

"I found her hiding in my bedroom."

"I can't believe a word you are saying, Petya. That is ridiculous." "What were you doing in the trailer?" Andulov asked Penny.

She did not answer. Her teeth were chattering, and she thought any words would come out like gibberish. Andulov moved in closer to her, the blade of his chef's knife now pressing against her cheek. She could feel his steamy breath spreading across her cheeks. "You answer me, now!"

Penny's eyes watered. She tried to remain calm. Any quick move and the sharp knife could slice her face to ribbons. Her main focus now was remaining alive. Penny's eyes widened. "I was looking for my boyfriend, Frederico. I thought he lived somewhere around here with his cousin."

"You expect us to believe that?" He pulled the knife away, gazing at her in disbelief. "You are a stupid bitch and a liar!" Andulov turned toward the kitchen counter and drove the knife into the middle of the wooden cutting surface.

Penny jumped, but she was determined to maintain her argument of innocence. She knew she couldn't back away now. "Isn't this Federico's house? He cheated on me! I came by to pay him back for going out with my sister, Lucy."

"Look, lady, I am busy here, making chicken Florentine for me and my pals. I don't have time to argue about what you are doing on my property. But I will find out!" He yanked the knife out of the wood and returned to his food preparation. "Petya, tie her up in the living room, and join us for dinner in fifteen minutes. Don't touch her. I will deal with her later!"

Petya shoved Penny out of the kitchen and threw her onto a threadbare floral sofa. Andulov called after Petya. "I said, don't do anything stupid. She's mine!"

Andulov's warning distracted Petya long enough for Penny to wrestle out of his grip. "Stop it, lady!" He lunged for her, but she continued to fight him off. He yanked a rope from a hook on his leather belt and wrapped it around her legs. She kicked him in the shins with both feet, making him furious. Petya slapped Penny with the back of his hand, his gold nugget ring gouging a place in her cheek. She cried out in pain.

"You cannot mess with Petya!" He pressed his face against hers, scratching her with his beard. Penny's face burned, and his body odor sickened her. She leaned as far away from him as she could and rubbed her fingers across his face, hoping the green chilies staining her hands would sting his eyes. It worked!

"Damn it!" he yelled and punched Penny in the stomach. She doubled over, falling on the dingy sofa. He wedged her head between two cushions and stomped off.

*Now was a good time to get away*, Penny thought, but as she pulled her head out from between the sofa cushions, her eyes felt grainy and pinched. Every bone in her body cried out for aspirin. She lifted her head and strained to focus on the front door. The room looked hazy and overcast with a heavy layer of dust that hung in the air. Her hands were still free, and that meant she could make a break, even if she had to hop.

Before she could make a move, Andulov, who had apparently heard the ruckus, came into the room, trailed by Donnie Harper. He laughed at his bodyguard, who was just coming out of the restroom, water dripping from his face and shirt. Andulov pounded Petya on the back. "Cut this shit out! You letting a woman beat you up?" He and Harper turned and left the room.

Petya slugged Penny in her pelvis and bound her hands with the tie, which he'd stripped off his thick neck.

"Aghhh!" Penny could not help but cry out again. Her despair seemed to please Petya, who stood over her smiling. His eyes were red; he wiped his hands across his face, coughed, and spit on the floor, remembering the damage the chilies had already done. She knew their sting would not go away anytime soon.

The muted television was flashing football scores across the murky room and creating a light show that danced around them. She turned her head away, focusing her attention on the sofa's floral pattern. He leaned in closer, but she refused to turn her head toward his. His breath was now warming the back of her neck. The flowers on the sofa began swirling into a ring of bright colors. Pictures of Penny's life began floating by and bringing some relief from the sheer terror of the moment. She was dipping her toes in the chilly water at her parents' lake home. She was waving good-bye to Porter, suitcases in tow. She was sorting through her dead father's personal effects, finding a sweet photo of them both on a boat. For a fleeting moment, Penny thought she saw Leo running down the street, calling to her. But this filament of light faded into a cacophony of dark, snarling images, and she was drawn back into the reality of the challenge before her.

She turned and stared into Petya's playful eyes. She would show no fear. In response, he drove her body into the sofa and shoved his hands between her legs. He forced them as far apart as they would go, with her ankles bound. She felt him lay the full weight of his body on hers, driving the wind out of her lungs. He began moving up and down on her. Thankfully, she was still fully clothed. He reached under her buttocks and jammed her body into his. Penny began to wheeze. With her hands tied, she was helpless to do anything but push them against his waist, hoping to grab an occasional gasp of air. She found it impossible to speak or even plead with him to stop. She could only moan.

"You like Petya? That is good. I try to keep you alive, if you give me what I want."

It was too painful to keep trying to force air into her lungs. Her hands ached, and she thought she had jammed her finger from pressing so hard against Petya's unforgiving frame. She was too exhausted to care what happened now. She felt the darkness closing in.

"Petya, dinner is ready!" Andulov shouted from the kitchen. "Damn it!" Petya growled.

"Get in here now! And leave that woman be. I have my own plans for her."

As Petya lifted himself off Penny, he punched her in the sternum, causing her lungs to engage. She managed a few gasps of air. Tears streamed down her face and onto her neck. He stood and adjusted his slacks, tucked in his shirt, and then as an afterthought, rammed his right hand into her blouse, tearing off two buttons and cupping one of her breasts in his fingers. He squeezed hard.

Penny stuffed the pain, refusing to let Petya know how bad it hurt.

He snickered, yanked his hand out of her shirt, and sauntered into the kitchen.

Penny wanted to bawl her eyes out, but there was no time for hysteria. She was grateful to be breathing. While Petya was in the kitchen, she frantically tried to form a plan to get out of there alive. How long did she have? Her first thought was to come up with a way to distract him when he returned and hit him with the pepper spray, which was miraculously still in the pocket of her windbreaker. But both of her hands were tied, so that option was out.

The second choice for Penny was to try and cajole Petya into liking her. It might delay things long enough for Leo to arrive. She would just have to grit her teeth and bear any sexual advances he might employ. Flirting with Petya was a disgusting thought, but her desire to live made it seem like a small sacrifice.

Penny's third plan was tricking Petya into untying her hands, then using the wrench and the pepper spray in a double whammy. *It just might work!*

The house was small, and the living room was next to the kitchen, separated by a wall and an archway. That made it easier for Penny to hear the men making toasts from the bottle of vodka she had seen on the kitchen table.

"Harper, do you know this woman?" Andulov asked.

"No, I have never seen her before. I have no idea where she came from or why she is here."

"I am thinking that the gods have given us a little bonus, eh? Maybe I give her to Rosa's buyer as a gift."

Penny's mind went haywire upon hearing Andulov's plans to include her along with Rosa to human traffickers. But that meant Rosa was still alive! There was still time to save her. This sliver of hope made her wild with joy. Perspiration ran between her breasts and onto her belly. She was surely bruised and swollen, but with this news about Rosa, she would fight on undeterred. Petya may have brawn, but she had her brains! She sat up on the sofa and tried to maneuver her feet. Her ankles were tied so tightly she couldn't even shuffle. Penny thought she heard Andulov on his cell phone. She rolled off the sofa and continuing rolling toward the entrance to the kitchen.

In between the banging of pans, Penny missed much of his conversation, but when the dish washing stopped, she was able to hear the last bit of his phone call. What she learned threw a wrench into the gears of her battle plans. "My pilot says there is room for one more on our flight to San Diego. Excellent!"

Penny's heart raced, and her armpits were wet with sheer panic. She would have to take desperate measures to keep from getting on that plane. *When are they flying to San Diego? Tomorrow?* The good news was that she now figured she was more valuable to them alive than dead. She had to keep them thinking that way. If she screwed up, she was only one blink away from a bullet.

# CHAPTER 20

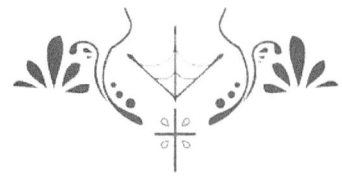

Thankfully, Petya's silk tie had enough give that she could bend her elbows and lay them against her windbreaker. Penny unzipped both of her coat pockets. She could hear the scraping of plates and the running of water in the sink. The men were apparently nearly finished with the dishes. Penny braced herself for what she had to do to survive. She heard Andulov, who was now yelling at Harper. "Diego, you have done a good job caring for our dear Rosa. I want to give you a share of my profit from selling this new young woman. You like? I have a client in Romania who prefers blondes, and she will bring us good money.

Not giving her away, after all. Nobody gets something for nothing from me!"

Penny heard the men drinking a celebratory shot of vodka. "¡Salud!"Then they all broke out in laughter. She wasn't sure what was so funny, but they couldn't stop laughing. Finally, she heard Donnie Harper's voice.

"It is time to feed Rosa."

Penny rolled herself back toward the sofa, not wanting them to know she had eavesdropped on their dinner conversation. She watched as Harper carried a tray of food through the living room and down the hall. She heard a knock on a door and then heard muffled voices and the door open and shut. *Is that Rosa's bedroom?*

To carry out her escape, Penny decided she needed to be aware of the exact location of each man at all times. She watched as Petya headed into the bathroom. But where was Andulov? Penny swore she could hear footsteps creaking on wooden stairs, giving her the creeps. Unless there was someone else in the house, it had to be Andulov heading down to the basement. She imagined him leaning over a greasy tool bench, a single light bulb dangling from the ceiling, while he mixed up some strange concoction he would force her to drink before transporting her to his private plane. Penny shuddered at the image of being drugged and carried off while unconscious. She would not let that happen!

Petya came back into the living room, wiping his hands with a bathroom towel, which he threw on the floor. He dropped into an armchair near the sofa and looked over at Penny. "Now, where were we?" He rubbed his damp hands on his pants and then reached for her.

Penny took a deep breath, trying to keep her world from flying apart. Petya must have noticed the color draining from her face. He pulled her close and whispered, "You are a beautiful woman. Why don't you just relax and let me make you happy?"

Penny's body went limp at the realization that mighty as her plans were, they were unrealistic. Her eyes filled with tears. "Please don't!"

Petya covered her mouth and nose with his massive hand, once again blocking her airway. "Keep quiet! This is between you and me."

Penny tried to move out of his grasp. It was impossible, and finally, she shook her head, indicating she would not yell again.

He removed his hand from her mouth, and she took a big breath, getting as much oxygen into her lungs as possible. It sickened her to do so, but she gave him a weak smile and looked directly into his eyes. He loosened his hold on her, allowing her to fall back into the depths of the sofa. Penny was relieved to know Petya could be managed somewhat, just by changing her attitude. Though she was exhausted, she was determined to find out what Andulov was doing in his basement. She was hoping there were no other captives scheduled for the trip to San Diego besides Rosa and her. She cleared her throat, desperate to find her voice.

"Is there someone in the basement?" She began to cough. Her throat was really aching now, and she could barely swallow.

"No. No more women. If I tell you what is down there, I have to kill you!" Petya laughed at his own joke.

She faked a laugh, hoping to encourage Petya to keep talking and kill time. Her green eyes focused on the lights from the television.

"It is too bad you are flying to San Diego tonight," Petya said. "You could stay here with me. I have to guard the house until Andy returns." He rubbed her arm and squeezed her gently.

Penny tried not to react with alarm, but she pressed her fingers tightly into her thighs in an effort to keep them from shaking. *The plane is leaving tonight?*

"Why do you have to stay behind?" Penny asked.

"I told you, I have to kill you if I tell you why!" Petya laughed heartily again at his own bad joke. "Andy runs his vodka business in the basement. Don't worry, there are no women down there!"

Penny was totally perplexed at hearing about the vodka. How many things was Andulov into?

Petya pulled Penny off the sofa and forced her down on the floor. The linoleum was old and bumpy, and Penny tried to wiggle away from him. Petya said nothing but lay down on the floor beside her. His body was so huge, she swore it took up much of the small living room. His thick chest was heaving, and she could hear his lungs rattling as he embraced her. Penny thought he was too young to have a heart attack, but she could hope.

"We could have a good time, drinking shots of vodka and listening to music in my trailer, if you weren't going away."

Penny turned on her side with her eyes on the front door. Petya rolled her back toward him like a Tinkertoy. "Don't look away from me!" He ran his stubby fingers through Penny's hair. He was panting now, and small beads of sweat dotted his upper lip. Sensing the perspiration on his face, Petya used his tongue to clean his lips. Then he noticed the two buttons missing on her blouse, realizing perhaps that he had done this damage earlier.

He placed his hand inside her bra. This time he did not squeeze her breast, but only stroked it gently.

Penny's stomach churned. She would rather be kicking Petya than playing him, but her survival skills convinced her to go along. Besides, he was so strong that with one snap of her neck, she would be dead.

As Petya unbuttoned her shirt, Penny tried to divert her mind from the inevitable. Her thoughts went to Leo. She sighed. Would he even bother looking for her? Why should he? She'd gone rogue, and now, she had to pay the price for her desperate desire to succeed without him. Too late, she realized Rosa's kidnapping wasn't an isolated act but an organized crime—a cruel game in which she was now a pawn, a game piece to be played again and again. Petya, apparently, was making the first move.

He drove his mouth into hers with such force that it cut her lips. She felt the blood trickling down her throat, and it caused her to gag. She tried to turn her head away, but Petya held her neck in a vice-like grip. She began to feel light-headed, then oddly free, liberated from what she had for a lifetime feared—the loss of herself. Her eyes glazed over, and her mind traveled to another time and place. She dreamed about her high school prom, where she had arrived at the dance too late. All the couples had been paired, and she was forced to dance alone to a slow, melancholy song. Penny Larkin had not seen her foster father lurking in the wings, nor had she realized that he would soon sweep her into the dark, the darkest night of her soul.

# CHAPTER 21

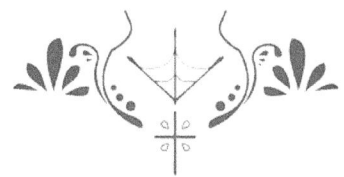

Sheriff Leo Tellez received the call from his dispatcher that a man at the Bonita Bakery had called in at 6:35 p.m. to report an emergency. The baker had been practically incoherent, speaking in both Spanish and English, until he'd finally made it clear that Penny Larkin needed backup. He had told the dispatcher that Ms. Larkin had left a message with Sheriff Tellez that she was at the Bonita Bakery and needed help immediately. The baker was worried because it had been thirty minutes, and no help had arrived. Leo had jumped in an unmarked gray Ford Mustang and ordered two other patrol cars to meet him at the bakery. He barged through red lights at busy intersections, determined to find Penny before she did something foolish.

The sheriff beat both patrol cars to the scene. He was now standing behind the bakery, where he had found the baker, Simeon Ramírez, pacing back and forth. Cigarette butts were strewn across the alley. Ramírez was kicking the cigs with his feet. The sheriff tried to understand him, but he was almost in tears. "*Ella quería usar mi teléfono. Y le dije sí*, I say, 'yes, yes!'"

Leo was puzzled. Why hadn't Penny used her cell phone to call him?

"*Ella te llamó desde la panadería.*"

When Ramirez told the sheriff Penny had called him from the bakery, he opened his cell phone to check his recent calls. He saw there was a number he did not recognize, and then he remembered that in all the confusion at the office with the press conference, he had seen the call come in and chosen to listen to it later. He'd forgotten. *How stupid!* Leo turned away from the baker to listen to the message. He heard Penny trying to explain how she had seen the location of the blue cottage in a dream and that she was going there to check it out. She sounded agitated.

"I'm not going to try and do your job, Leo. I promise. I just have to follow up on my viewing in case Rosa is there. Every second counts. You told me that, remember? Look for my car parked somewhere on Niño Aguilera. Thanks."

The urgency in her voice reverberated in his head like a bell in a tower. What in the world had Penny done? His mind was racing with possibilities, and none of them were good. Leo ordered the two patrol cars to wait at the bakery while he checked out Niño Aguilera. He drove down the street at a snail's pace, scanning both sides of the road for any signs of Penny's car. It was dark and unusually cloudy for an El Paso evening. The road was jammed with cars parked on both sides of the road. The streetlights were casting ghost-like figures between the vehicles, fueling Leo's frustration. Why hadn't he made it clear that Penny should not go off on her own? *What was she thinking?* This was his turf, and it was his job to find Rosa. His mind was jumping to the darkest of conclusions.

The thought that something might happen to her stirred a fear in Leo that he had not felt since Alejandra's death. It surprised him to realize he had feelings for Penny. He didn't want to lose her too. *God, where is she?*

Near the end of the street, Leo thought he saw the front bumper of Penny's green Saab pressed into the mud of an aqueduct with the hood open. He threw open his car door and ran. He looked inside the car and saw it was empty. He pointed his flashlight into the cavernous engine compartment, where he saw the yellow sticky note attached to the air cleaner. Penny was asking him to head to the blue cottage at the end of the lane on the right-hand side of the road.

*Why didn't she wait for me?*

Leo dashed down the road on foot. So far, he had seen no sign of Penny and no blue cottage. He began running up to each house. Nothing remotely looked like the blue house she had described. Finally, as he neared the end of the street, he saw a lane sheltered by large oak trees. As he ran down the lane, he could barely find his way, not wanting to use his flashlight for fear of drawing attention.

He stopped just short of slamming into the rear of a black SUV parked in the middle of the lane. The late-model black Cadillac Escalade stood out in this poor neighborhood like a baked potato in a Mexican buffet.

The windows were darkly tinted, so the sheriff could not see inside. The doors were locked. He moved past the Escalade and saw another vehicle parked in front of it. He risked a flick of his flashlight on the back of what turned out to be a Dodge van with a *3500* badge above its blue crumbled fender. He smeared his hands across the dusty windows of the van's tailgate, looking for signs of Rosa or Penny.

*Nothing!*

Leo realized everything Penny had seen was coming true. She had been right in spite of his department's hesitance to believe her. Why had he doubted her? Fear and fury raged inside him. He kicked the ground and drove his fist into the side of the van, denting its passenger door. *This is my fault!*

He leaned against the van and wiped the sweat from his face with his arm. Leo was driven by an intense desire to rescue Penny. He could think of nothing else. He had not been able to rescue Alejandra, but he should have had control over this situation. Shamefully, his need to rescue Penny even overrode his obligation to find Rosa. He reached for his revolver and wished he had the 9 mm automatic pistol his department had recommended. He had been stubborn and had stuck with his old .38 snub-nose revolver. It had been his father's and now seemed like a useless relic of law enforcement days gone by.

There was movement in the living room windows. Leo was sure he had seen Penny and a large man wrestling. But then, they seemed to fall away from view. Leo fought the urge to blow down the doors of the cottage, but good sense told him he would only place Penny, and maybe Rosa, in harm's way. He looked back at the van and then at the SUV. He was clearly outnumbered and probably outgunned too. Before he could do something foolish, Leo turned and ran to his car and drove back to the bakery.

The sheriff ordered all his officers to block the roadway with their cars from both directions on Niño Aguilera to prevent any escape attempt by the suspects. He asked them to get out of their cars and to seek cover between the neighbors' parked cars until he ordered them to move. Leo pulled his car into the middle of the road, halfway between the bakery and the cottage. Then he exited his car, leaned against the Mustang's hood, and unsnapped his holster. He opened the leather cartridge box on his belt and counted the bullets. There were twelve. He had five bullets in his gun, giving him a total of seventeen shots—not enough to make much of an impact, even in a surprise assault. He went to his trunk and pulled out an automatic rifle. He hated it and had never even fired it except at the range, but this situation called for major firepower.

On his command, Leo would have his men move on the cottage. From there, they would surprise the kidnapper and hopefully recover Penny and Rosa without harm to either. The presence of two vehicles in the driveway, however, made Leo reluctant to move too quickly. He tried not to think about what might be going on inside that house. He took a deep breath, adjusted his vest armor, and for a moment wondered if he should call Lieutenant Ontiveros and ask him to take the lead.

He opened his cell phone but hesitated. Sweat dripped from his forehead, and his right arm ached from an old bullet wound. This rescue had become personal, and he hated being in that position. It left him vulnerable to screw-ups.

*I need to make this right!*

Leo put his cell phone back in its case, holstered his revolver, and loaded the rifle with ammo. He put two other clips on his belt. He was now ready to take on these slugs. He just hoped he wasn't too late.

# CHAPTER 22

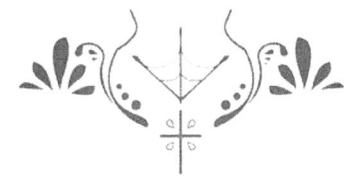

Donnie Harper was Penny's miracle. He walked into the living room from Rosa's bedroom just as Petya was trying to remove Penny's blouse. "Petya, I thought Andy said to leave her alone!"

Petya jumped up and charged at Harper, who reeled backward. The food tray fell to the floor, breaking the dinner plate and a drinking glass. "Get out of here, Diego! Mind your own business!"

Penny watched Harper slink off and knew she had to act quickly. "Please. I need to use the bathroom."

"No!" Petya said. "You go nowhere!" He unbuckled his belt and dropped his pants. Penny heard the coins in his pockets hitting the floor, followed by his leather belt with the brass buckle. Penny held her breath. These were ominous sounds to her, steps in a foreboding ritual she had hoped to avoid. Her hands trembled as she watched him flex his lily-white legs with their well-defined muscles—no doubt in anticipation of what came next.

This time, she protested loudly, hoping for Harper's return.

He did not reappear.

Petya walked over to her as if ready to pounce while adjusting the crotch of his boxer shorts. Without saying a word, he pulled Penny to her feet. It was clear he'd had a change of heart. The rope cinched tightly around her socks had rubbed her legs raw. She looked down at it. "Could you loosen the rope? It really hurts."

"Okay, okay. But let's make this quick!" Petya grumbled. He made a slight change in the rope, which allowed her to scuff her feet in a forward motion. He moved in behind her and placed his hands on her shoulders. His bare legs came into view as he pumped his knees against the back of Penny's, occasionally wrapping them around her thighs in a thrusting motion. Penny shuffled along, refusing to move in sync with him, knowing it was her only way of not succumbing to more foreplay. No doubt, Petya was enjoying his dominance over her because he leaned in and licked her ear. This sent a chill down Penny's backbone.

The duo finally made it to the bathroom, which was unbearably small. Penny was able to maneuver herself to the toilet that hadn't been cleaned in months. She realized she could not pull down her jeans without help because of Petya's tie wrapped around her wrists. He saw Penny's problem and began unsnapping her jeans and tugging them downward. It was then that Penny regretted having worn her bikini panties because her underwear was now the focus of his delight.

Petya reached for the elastic waistband and gently pulled them down to her knees while leaning perilously close to her. Penny feared he would do something dumb and make a scene and foil her plans. But instead, he simply helped her sit on the crusty toilet seat. Penny complained to him that it was still going to be difficult to use the toilet with her ankles bound.

"Yeah, yeah, yeah! What else do you need?" Petya shook his head and loosened the rope around her ankles, leaving a slipknot ready to be tightened again when Penny had finished. He moved over by the bathroom door and waited. He pulled out a cigarette and a lighter from his shirt pocket. He inhaled deeply and blew the smoke in the air. Penny watched it sinking slowly toward the floor. Another puff or two and it would reach her; she knew she would be choking.

"Speed it up!" Petya yelled. "I don't have all day!"

Thankfully, most women can pee on command, so it was not difficult for Penny to comply. She then indicated to Petya that she might have to do more. This notion seemed to embarrass him, but he continued to wait patiently for Penny to finish. He stubbed out his first cigarette and lit another.

When Penny was done, she told Petya she would need to use the toilet paper to clean herself, and she couldn't do so with her hands wrapped up with his tie. Even Petya did not relish wiping her, it seemed, so he leaned over her and undid his tie, tossing it over his shoulder. Hot ashes from his cigarette, which he held between his teeth, dropped onto Penny's bare leg.

"Ouch!" she cried. She could do nothing but let it continue to burn until her hands were free.

"You are lucky I don't put it out on your leg, you stupid bitch. I do that sometimes when my women don't go along." He brushed the ashes away himself, with a flick of his wrist. The ashes had left a small burn mark on her thigh, but that was the least of her worries now. She had to contain her anger and continue with her plan.

"Excuse me while I take care of myself." Penny pointed to the roll of toilet paper on the wall.

Petya resumed his stance against the doorframe and fiddled with his lighter, bringing up the flame and then shutting it off. He turned to her, holding the flame up and taunting her. He burned his thumb in his efforts to scare her, and the lighter fell to the floor. He left it there.

Penny slowly unrolled a considerable amount of toilet paper—a wad big enough to hide her hands as she reached in her pocket for the pepper spray. She pretended to wipe. Then she pulled out more toilet paper, covering her left-hand pocket, and secured the wrench in her left hand. To her amazement, Petya was leaning over to pick up his lighter and missing everything.

*This is your big mistake!* Penny flushed the toilet, hoping the noise would cover up her next move. When Petya stood, she sprayed him with pepper spray and hit him in the groin with her wrench.

Petya's hands went to his eyes, which were already chafed from the chilies, and then to his crotch. She took this opportunity to exit the bathroom, kicking off the rope and pulling up her jeans and undies with one hand. She ran through the living room on her way to the kitchen. As she threw herself out the screen door, the spring snapped, flying around the door like a striking snake. Penny hoped she was long gone before Petya could get his pants on and his eyesight back.

She made it around the house and ran past the cars in the driveway, then across the neighbors' front yards toward the Bonita Bakery, hoping she would once again find the baker and get help. She figured if she ran in the street, the kidnappers could more easily capture her in their SUV.

*Where is Leo?* She scanned the street and its jumble of parked cars. Penny's mind was racing, but fear was no longer icing her veins. Adrenaline took fear's place and propelled her forward at a furious pace. She had gone almost half a block before she stopped to catch her breath. She noticed that her car was still in the ditch. As she looked back over her shoulder, she was distressed to find that Donnie Harper was only a hundred feet behind her.

Even though her lungs ached and her mouth was dry, she forced herself to begin running again while keeping a close eye on Harper. With her attention diverted from what lay in front of her, she stumbled twice, once over a flowerbed and then a tricycle. The delay meant that Harper was gaining ground, and Penny knew he would overtake her at any moment. She let out a growl, pushing more air into her lungs, and charged onward.

The Bonita Bakery was still a block away, and now Harper was only twenty or thirty feet behind her. She decided that her best chance was to take him by surprise. Penny stopped suddenly and flipped around, jutting her hands forward, trying to diminish a frontal blow. Harper crashed headlong into her, but she was still able to hit him on the head with her wrench as she flew backward. Miraculously, she only fell onto one knee. She gripped her wrench, jumped up, and ran forward into Harper, who was still dazed. This time, she hit him between the eyes. He grabbed for her arm, but Penny twisted out of his grip. When she dealt him the third blow to the head, he cried out in agony.

"Damn it, lady!" He fell down, writhing in pain.

Penny stomped her right foot on his chest and threw a wrench-driven punch at his left ear. "Aghhh!" Harper cried out again. "Somebody help me!"

# CHAPTER 23

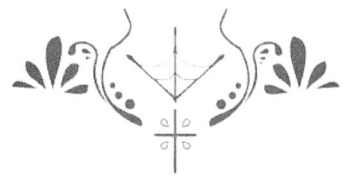

Penny held Donnie Harper on the ground by placing one foot on his chest. She leaned in, landed a blow to his chest, and was winding up for another when Leo grabbed her arm. "That's enough, Penny! We've got him."

Penny shrugged her shoulders and threw down her wrench. "All right. All right, you can have him—for now!"

She pulled away from Leo's grip on her arm, but then realized she was totally spent. She watched the deputies cuffing Harper as she fell onto the hood of one of the parked cars, where she slid to the ground. She was out of breath. Her hair was heavy with sweat, and her nose was running. She rubbed her hands across her face and tried to shake off the agitation that consumed her. The chilies, damn them, were now stinging her too.

Leo lifted Penny to her feet and handed her a package of tissues. She tried to inhale a breath of the chilly night air and wiped the tears from her face.

"I can't catch my breath." Penny's body crumpled, but Leo caught her and held her in his arms. The warmth of his chest against hers soothed her aching lungs, which were heaving from the race for her life.

They both watched as Leo's deputies read Donnie Harper his Miranda rights. As small as Harper was, it took two officers to throw him in the back of their patrol car. He shouted and pounded on the window as they shut the door. "Let me out of here!"

"Let me walk you to my car, Penny." Leo placed his hand on her shoulder, and she limped back to the Mustang, which was still parked in the middle of the street. She didn't have the strength to protest. It was all she could do to drop into the Mustang's bucket seat. The car was cold, and she began to shake uncontrollably. Leo ran to the trunk and pulled out a wool blanket, which he tucked around Penny's body. Her damp arms and chest pressed her clothes against her flesh.

"Stay here, and I'll drive you home when this is over." "What about my car?"

"I'll have a deputy drive it back to the station."

---

A pang of guilt shot through Leo's gut as he imagined what Penny might have endured in that cottage. He hoped he was the one who took these guys down. As he closed the door to the car, he heard the two deputies who had been stationed on the south side of Niño Aguilera shouting that two men were on the run from the cottage. He left Penny locked in his car and caught up with officers. One suspect was loading a child in the Escalade, and another was tossing in a case big enough for an automatic rifle.

Leo ordered his officers to hold their fire unless they were sure the child was not in harm's way.

Both suspects jumped into the SUV and backed out of the driveway. The driver spun his tires as he accelerated, apparently undeterred by the patrol car blocking its path. Harper was waving wildly from inside the patrol car, trying to get the SUV to stop. The driver swerved his Escalade around the police car and rolled onto the sidewalk, crushing the landscaping on neighboring lawns.

Two deputies, hidden just north of the roadblock, sprinted toward the Cadillac and opened fire, not having heard the sheriff's orders to stand down. The passenger window exploded. Blood gushed out of the shattered glass and poured down the side of the car. The Escalade was still moving. The officers watched as it bounced off the curb at the crossroads of Niño Aguilera Street and Buena Vista Lane, turned left, and disappeared in a flurry of dust that blew back on them.

All the deputies started running to their cars, but the sheriff called them off, knowing that a chase through this heavily populated neighborhood at night could endanger the residents. "Wait!" he yelled. Leo ran over to the patrol car where Donnie Harper was contained, realizing now that Harper had only been the hands and feet of a much larger operation. Leo opened the front passenger door and slammed his hand against the cage, startling Harper, who was slumped in the backseat with his eyes closed. His sweatshirt and jeans were filthy, and his face was covered with mud and scratches from his tangle with Penny. He sat straight up and ran his fingers through his sparse crop of hair, then leaned forward and spit on Leo.

"Harper, that isn't any way to start a relationship," Leo said as he wiped his sleeve with his hand. "You keep yelling that you want out of here. What if I could arrange for you to spend less time behind bars?"

"You are bullshitting me, Sheriff!"

"I need to know who those guys are who have Rosa Garcia and where they are going."

"Oh, please! Do you really think I would be that stupid? They would have me killed the minute I step in the jail."

"We can put you in protective custody and I can arrange for the DA to go easy on you. But you've only got ten seconds to give me what I need, or the deal is off."

Harper threw the weight of his body back against the seat and let out a breath. "These are dangerous guys, Sheriff. They kill and ask questions later."

"Your time is up. See ya!" Leo turned and slammed the car door. Harper began pounding on the window. "Stop! I'll tell you!"

Leo opened the door again. Harper was sweating through his shirt. "The ringleader is a guy named Andulov—Sergei Andulov. He's a Russian mobster who is into kids and black market vodka. He owns a restaurant in Oakland called Andy's and is never without Petya, his bodyguard. I don't know his last name, but he goes wherever Andulov goes."

"Where are they headed?"

"Andulov has a private plane waiting for him at the Santa Rosa airport. He has a buyer for Rosa somewhere. He didn't say."

"How do you know these jerks?" "I met them at a bar in Juárez."

Leo slammed the door on Harper, who yelled, "Don't forget about me!"

Leo headed toward the four deputies who were now clustered around the other patrol car. Because the Santa Rosa airport was in New Mexico, he would not have the jurisdiction to have his officers pursue them. He would have to leave his deputies behind, but he planned to call Ted Rodriguez, the sheriff of Doña Ana County, and ask for his help.

Leo ordered his officers to head back to the station and put Harper in a holding cell there.

"We'll deal with him later after we stop the others. I'm heading to Santa Rosa."

Leo ran back to his car and ordered Penny to buckle up.

"Are you heading to the airport? Andulov's flying to San Diego tonight," Penny said.

"How do you know that?"

"Petya told me. He said he had to stay behind to guard Andulov's vodka until he returns from San Diego. Something about importing illegal vodka into Russia disguised as window washer fluid."

"Where is this vodka?"

"I don't know except that he runs that business from the cottage's basement. I did hear Andulov on his cell phone, calling a pilot to ask him if he had room for one more."

Leo realized that the "one more" was probably Penny. He looked at the scratches on her face and her torn shirt and dirty jeans. He had underestimated her skills and her internal fortitude. He was proud of her for getting herself out of a dangerous situation. It would do little good to remind her that she had made a poor choice in checking out the cottage by herself. She had been punished enough.

"Penny, I think it is a good idea to have one of my officers take you home. You've been through a great ordeal, and you need to rest."

"Do you really think I'm going to take this abuse and not get Rosa's kidnappers?"

"I'm afraid you are operating on adrenaline right now, and soon, you might crash."

"I'll let you know if you need to call a babysitter, but right now, just let me chill out and get my wind back."

Leo thought better of it, but he decided to let her go with him. She was, after all, the reason he was here in the first place. And she might see something along the way that might prove helpful. He got back on the car radio and called dispatch. "I need you to contact Sheriff Ted Rodriguez in Doña Ana County and have him get a team over to the Santa Rosa Airport ASAP! Tell the sheriff there's a plane at the airport scheduled to fly tonight to San Diego. I'll call him once I'm on I-10 and have a better idea of my ETA. Don't let that plane take off!"

# CHAPTER 24

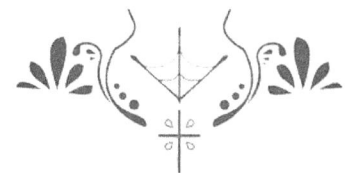

Dr. Jonathan Márquez leaned against a light pole near the Stanton Street International Bridge. The bridge carried thousands of cars and pedestrians each day in and out of Mexico and dumped them into the central part of El Paso. Traffic was heavy even though the evening was wearing thin. It was going on 8:00 p.m., and he was nervous. Andulov had promised to pick him up at 7:30.

*Where the hell is he?*

Exhaust from the cars streaming in from Juárez hung in the air. A street vendor walked up to him, waving a cheap pair of sunglasses. Márquez shook his head and sent him away. He was in no mood for the many vendors who were always hawking their wares near the bridges Márquez pulled a handkerchief from his pocket, coughed, and blew his nose. He pushed his black doctor's bag closer to his legs. There was not much chance anyone would try to steal it, but he had paid a handsome bribe to a US Customs agent to bring it over the border. It was brimming with pharmaceuticals, and he was taking no chances.

Andulov had been straight up about his reasons for wanting to work with him. He needed an investor who could also provide him with protection if he was going to do business in Mexico. Marquez's father-in-law, Jorge Fuentes, was a powerful member of the Chihuahua drug cartel in charge of the transportation of major drug shipments from Latin America and Mexico into the United States. Andulov needed someone to grease the skids and get his bootleg vodka on a boat out of Veracruz harbor. Márquez had told him that Fuentes was just the man to pull that off. In exchange, Andulov would give Márquez a piece of the action in his child-smuggling ring and cut Fuentes in on the profits from the sale of his vodka. It had all been done with a handshake. Márquez knew this was risky business, particularly in Mexico, but he was desperate to save up money to move as far away from his homeland as possible.

He had agreed to all of this before Guapo Chavez had come into the picture. Playing fast and loose with any drug cartel was really stupid, but it was particularly so with the major foe of his father-in-law. Márquez and his wife, Generosa, were considered a protected family by the Chihuahua cartel. If Márquez started mixing it up with the enemy, everything could turn deadly. He was sure his father-in-law wouldn't think twice about blowing his head off.

Last year, the Baja cartel had begun trying to muscle into his father-in-law's prized turf. The focus of the fight was a corridor running through the State of Chihuahua and across the border into El Paso. Jorge Fuentes considered this corridor the most profitable in the world and wasn't about to let it go to outsiders. Márquez's excruciating personal experience at the rehab center had convinced him that Andulov's deal was his best chance to move out of Mexico, but he was still wary of having anything to do with Chavez. For years, Los Betas cartel members had been the hired guns of Chavez and the Baja cartel. In fact, he was sure it was the Betas who had been after him at the rehab center. Who had ordered that hit? There were rumors they had broken off with Chavez, but still, Márquez might be walking into a trap. It was all confusing and downright scary. In the end, however, when Andulov had dangled the million bucks in front of him, it had been just too much to resist. He and Genie could buy the necessary papers for living in the United States and find a nice quiet town to call home.

---

Márquez saw the black SUV moving cautiously down the street. He waved at Andulov, who pulled to the curb. He was surprised to find the passenger-side window broken and a sticky liquid staining the side of the door. Márquez used his sleeve to grab the door handle, and he plopped down in the black leather seat. He dropped his medical case at his feet and slammed the door. Glass shards fell onto the street and into his lap.

"What the hell is up?" Márquez asked, brushing the glass off his pants.

"We had a little mix-up at the house. I will explain as we drive to the airport." Andulov moved forward, dodging some pedestrians heading back over the bridge, and took a right turn onto Paisano Drive.

Márquez felt something wet oozing between his legs. He reached down and found the same dark fluid on the side of the door also in a puddle on the seat. "Hey. Are you crazy, letting me sit in this stuff?" Márquez thought he knew what it was, but he hoped he was wrong.

"It's Petya's blood. The cops killed him as we tried to get away." Márquez was angry now, realizing Andulov had so little regard for him that he would let him drench his Italian slacks in another man's blood. He opened his bag and pulled out a towel, which he shoved under him as well as he could. Then he looked in the backseat, where he saw Petya slumped over, his deadweight lying half on the bench seat and half on the floor. The wounds were too many for Márquez to determine exactly what bullet had killed him.

"Where's the girl?" Márquez asked, hoping she was okay. "She's in the third-row seat, still out from that drug you asked Diego to give her." "Where is he?"

"Diego was snagged by the police." "What if he spills what he knows?"

"He will be smart and say nothing. Otherwise, I will arrange an accident in the El Paso jail. *No problem*."

Márquez knew Andulov had connections in the jail. He had told him lots of stuff over many beers at the bar. Andulov liked to brag when he was drinking, and Márquez worried his loose lips might come back to bite him. It was too late to worry about that now. Márquez was in this up to his ass—literally.

They were driving down a darkened portion of Paisano Drive, which ran along the Rio Grande. Just across the river was Juárez. They drove past two border patrol agents parked along the side of the road. Searchlights hit the Rio Grande and bounced into the windows of the Mexican houses nearby.

"Where can I dump Petya?" Andulov asked. "It looks crowded around here."

"There is a cement company a mile up the road. Let's try that." The Escalade headed down the long, poorly lit driveway to the cement company. The chuckholes in the road bounced Márquez around as he surveyed the area. The business was closed for the weekend, but two light poles illuminated the expanse of the property fairly well. Petya would be an eyesore, lying in the open when employees arrived on Monday morning. Márquez had to choose carefully where to dump him.

"There's a gravel pit to your left," Márquez said. "We can roll Petya into the water."

As the men carried Petya to the water's edge, Andulov stumbled over a cement block lying in the middle of the path. He rolled over his bodyguard's massive frame and fell into the pond.

Márquez had to use his flashlight to find Andulov, who was thrashing around in the muddy pit. "I can't swim!"

Márquez leaned forward and grabbed for Andulov, but the Russian slipped out of his grasp. Both of their hands were cold, and whatever was in the pit was more oil than water. Andulov was screaming profanities now. Márquez took a few steps into the pond. The water was up to his ankles. The muddy bank was slick, keeping his leather soles from gaining traction. Finally, Márquez got enough of a foothold in the shallow part of the pond to pull Andulov out of the muck. He fell forward onto the bank and cussed profusely. Márquez could hear the water squishing in Andulov's leather boots as he stamped off toward the SUV. "Damn it! You take care of Petya!"

Márquez found a rope hanging from Petya's belt and secured the cement block to his body. Then he shoved the block and the body a little at a time toward the edge of the water. Márquez's chest ached as he tried to shove the body forward. He hoped his heart would bear the brunt of this massive man. *He must weigh 300 pounds!* When he did finally manage to roll Petya into the pond, he barely made a splash in spite of his weight, disappearing immediately into the dark water. It would be days, months, or even years before he was found; even then, he would remain an unknown because, as Andulov had previously explained, men who worked for him had their fingerprints burned off.

"We're late!" Andulov shouted. "Come on!"

Márquez trudged back to the Escalade and climbed back into the bloody bucket seat.

"I promised I would meet Chavez at midnight at the San Diego airport. I just called the pilot, and your two girls from Palomas are already on the plane. He also said the guy you hired to snatch them told him he would be returning in less than an hour with two more. I don't want my pilot to have to deal with the girls if they wake up and start causing trouble. We need to hurry. I don't want to take a chance and have the pilot bolt on me."

The episode with Petya had cost them almost thirty minutes, and he knew time was running out, but Márquez was increasingly uncomfortable sitting in the congealing pool of blood with wet socks and shoes and having to endure the cold air rushing through the broken window. He suggested they get rid of the Escalade. "Won't the police be looking for your car?"

"Where can we get another one in this deserted place?" "Turn left on to Sunland Park Drive, and keep heading into New Mexico until you see the Rio Grande Race Track and Casino."

When they arrived, Márquez was grateful that the parking lot of the casino was jammed with cars. They had their choice of hundreds. Andulov smiled at Márquez. "I like your thinking." He pointed at his head, which was a mass of sweaty curls. His shirt and jeans were soaked with mud, but he hadn't complained any more.

Andulov pulled up behind a late-model Ford Explorer. In a few minutes, he backed the Explorer out of its parking spot. Márquez pulled the Escalade into the Explorer's place, and then the men moved a sleeping Rosa to the backseat, along with a long black case.

"My security blanket!" Andulov said, pointing to it. "Now that Petya is gone, I will need more than my Glock. Never leave home without your AK-47!" Andulov roared with laughter.

It comforted Márquez to know that if the police were hunting for them, they would not be looking for an Explorer, and he was happy Andulov had weapons. In Mexico, where guns were against the law, only outlaws owned them.

Márquez managed to relax some, now that they were on their way. Hopefully, no one was the wiser about their destination. He had hired his friend Don Koble to kidnap the girls in Palomas and Casas Grandes and fly them to Santa Rosa. Koble was a loose cannon but a great pilot, and Márquez knew the money he was paying Koble would keep him in line. He also had to pay dearly for the border patrol blimp to look the other way, but now all that was behind him. The girls were either there or on their way to Santa Rosa.

Andulov seemed to be more at ease too. He had calmed down after his near-drowning experience. "With the money from this first job, you will have enough to come to San Diego and sample the product for yourself, away from prying eyes—if you know what I mean." Andulov chuckled.

Márquez stifled an inward shudder and shifted in his seat. "This little girl is too young for my tastes."

"No, I don't mean little Rosa. She is spoken for. How about one of those teenagers you got me?"

Marquez stared straight at the windshield and did not answer. How was he going to politely refuse the offer of teenage sex? He loved his wife and had no desire to stray. Hopefully, a liaison with a young girl was not an initiation rite into the Russian mob. Losing his fingerprints would be punishment enough.

# CHAPTER 25

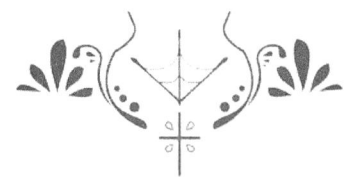

Sheriff Ted Rodriguez of Doña Ana County, New Mexico, called Leo to confirm he was headed to Santa Rosa. Leo asked him if he could blockade the entrance to the airport to keep the conflict away from any possible air traffic. Leo also knew there were large fuel storage tanks near the hangars, which could explode if a bullet hit them.

"We should be at the airport in forty minutes, and I would guess that the assailant is at least ten minutes ahead."

"Leo, I'll order my deputies to set up a road block on Palomino Road, a half-mile from the entrance to the airport. But while they're doing that, I want to check the outlying roads leading to the airport, just in case they come in from another direction."

Ted and Leo had been friends a long time, and Leo had every confidence that his friend would make the right decisions. It was almost as good as being there himself. He rolled down the window and placed a red flashing light on the top of his car. He jammed his foot on the accelerator and hurried through the tightly wound neighborhood streets of the Lower Valley as fast as he could safely go. He breathed a sigh of relief as he entered I-10 at Hawkins Street and headed west. He could make good time here, and chances were the Cadillac Escalade had taken side roads. It would be foolhardy for the driver to stay on the main highways with his window shot out and blood dripping down the passenger door. The sheriff thought maybe he had caught a break. "Hang on, Penny. We're going to make some pretty fast time down I-10!"

Leo looked at Penny, whose eyes were closed. *Did she hear me or not?* He knew she was still pretty shaken up.

"Penny, I said we are going to pick up speed on I-10, so make sure you are buckled up." Penny opened her eyes and appeared to have heard him because she checked her seat belt before closing her eyes again.

"I should have sent you home. You got quite a scare."

Penny bolted forward and glared at Leo. "I'm awake. I'm fine, and no, I'm not going home. I started this thing, and I'm going to be there when we grab this guy!"

---

Penny slumped in her seat and tried not to think about what might happen to Rosa if they didn't get to the airport in time. She pulled the blanket tightly around her body. The bulge on her right side reminded her that she still had her pepper spray in her windbreaker pocket. She would keep it there for now. Who knew what the rest of the night might bring?

She looked over at Leo. Something had been troubling her, and she thought this would be a good time to get it off her chest.

"Why did it take you so long to find the blue cottage?"

Leo looked insulted. This angered her. "I went looking for it as soon as I got your message."

"But you always answer your cell phone, and when I called you from the bakery, you let it go to voice mail."

Leo shifted in his seat. "I saw the unknown call, and I chose to take it later because we were just finishing our press conference. There were several reporters there with lots of questions."

"And then?"

"And then, I forgot about the call. I knew it had gone to voice mail, but I just forgot about it. I'm sorry." Leo brushed his hair out of his eyes and cleared his throat.

"I figured you were avoiding my calls."

"Why would I do that? And besides, I didn't know it was you!"

"I thought you were avoiding me."

Leo looked straight ahead. Perhaps the truth hurt. "Penny, let's just say that some of my deputies are not as enlightened as you and me. They look for facts and hard evidence to make an arrest. Our court cases depend on them. They think you are a psychic, and they can't convict someone on nothing but conjecture. I have repeatedly told them that remote viewing is right out of US Army protocols, but they refuse to believe me."

"I don't think you tried hard enough." Penny was a little uncertain about the wisdom of continuing on this road. She didn't want to mess up the opportunity to work with Leo again, but she barged right ahead. "You should have formally introduced me to your officers at the start of the investigation, explained how remote viewing can help in the search, and just what my role would be."

Leo had told Penny early on that he was going to pick and choose which viewings he would share with his investigators. He had said he wanted to protect her. That had certainly made her methods questionable in the eyes of his deputies, she had concluded. "Maybe that's why I couldn't see anything about Rosa right away."

"Oh, now you're blaming me for your inabilities."

Penny's body was cold to the touch. She felt as if he had slapped her. She rubbed her hands across her shoulders to warm them. She had no right to put the burden of her failure on him, but he was just plain cruel, talking to her this way.

"I'm just saying that not introducing me and not setting the ground rules up front was a bad way for me to start my relationship with your department."

Leo finally turned and looked at her. "I'm sorry I let you down. Truce?" He seemed sincere, but Penny couldn't be sure. In fact, she wasn't sure of anything anymore. She was too tired to fight with him any longer. She turned her body to the door and pulled the blanket over her head.

---

Leo's cell phone rang. Ted Rodriguez was calling back. "The patrol car working close to the airport reports that there is a Citation jet sitting on the tarmac. I called a buddy of mine at the Las Cruces airport who flies charters, and he believes that particular plane can hold seven passengers. Could there be more people planning to board that plane?"

"We can't be sure, but let's put it in our contingency plan and call in reinforcements. Is there any sign of a black Escalade?"

"Negative. I have two deputies staked out just to the north of the runway, and they say everything is quiet. The plane has only its interior lights on, and the engine is not running. The blockade is now in place, just east of the airport. I'm finishing my patrol around the back roads and should be arriving within five or ten minutes of you."

---

Penny had drifted off. She was dreaming that she was at the Santa Rosa airport and had climbed the steps to a fancy corporate jet. When she got inside, she was shocked to see two girls sitting in the back row of parchment-colored leather seats. Their heads hung down to their chests, and one of them was drooling. Penny panicked, thinking she was among those who had been taken.

*How can I get out of here?*

Her heart thumped in her chest. She grabbed the door handle of the jet, shaking it and trying to force it open. It was locked! *I'm trapped!*

She couldn't believe how stupid she had been to let herself be captured again. Suddenly, someone started pulling on her arm, trying to keep her from opening the airplane's door. She held on tight, knowing full well that to release her grip meant she was again in the kidnapper's clutches. Her knuckles grew stiff as she held on, and her fingers were pinched and sore, but she would never give up. The kidnapper would have to cut her hands off first. "Let go of me!" Penny yelled and tried to wrestle away from the stranger's cold, hard grip.

"Penny, wake up!" She heard the voice calling to her. She was confused and winded from screaming at the top of her lungs.

Was someone trying to save her? No! She had to save herself. She looked around the airplane and saw no one who could help her. She threw all of her weight against the door.

"Penny, wake up! It's okay." Leo kept shaking her and trying to get her to let go of the door handle. She had a firm grip on it, and he could see that her hands were red and swollen. Penny's cries were drowning out the roar of the Mustang's engine as he tried to steer the car and pull Penny away from the door at the same time. She had now managed to open it, and the sound of the road reverberated inside the car.

Leo exited the interstate, hanging onto her and calling out her name. He pulled onto the frontage road, but he had yet to find a place to park. "It's all right, Penny. You're safe."

She made one final lunge at the passenger door and fell halfway out. She was hung up by her seat belt, and she began thrashing around. Gravel from the roadway flew upward and struck Penny in the head and sprayed the passenger seat. Nothing seemed to wake her up.

"Penny!" Leo screamed at her this time and yanked her back in the car, causing the car to swerve and coast into a bank of grass, where it stopped. In desperation, Leo slapped her. Penny's eyes popped open, but she stared blankly at him. She blinked and raked her hands over her face, pushing her hair out of her eyes. "You've got to save the girls on the plane!" She threw her head forward and began to sob.

"What are you talking about?"

---

"It's Andulov!" Penny felt her pulse throbbing in her temple. "I'm never going to be rid of him!" Her chest hurt, and her whole body trembled as if it were broken. She felt for her pulse. *God, am I having a heart attack?* "There are two girls in the plane! They look like teenagers. I think they've been drugged." Penny exhaled and flexed her hands, which had curled into fists without her even noticing.

"My God, Penny, what are you saying? There can't be more!"
"We've got to save them."

Leo pulled back onto the interstate, joining other cars heading west. Penny noticed the billboards flying by as they picked up speed.

Thankfully, traffic was light. Maybe there was a chance they would arrive before Andulov.

"How long before we get there?"

"We're still thirty minutes away from Santa Rosa. Why don't you try to get more rest?"

"Rest? How can I rest?" Her head was on a pivot as she tracked the cars in front, to the side, and then behind them.

"Do you think we're making better time than Andulov?" Penny became increasingly more agitated.

"I'm hoping he took the back roads." She understood that Leo had to keep focused on his driving, but she would do her best to help him and maybe spot the ominous Escalade. It could be pulled off the side of the road, and she wanted to be the first to spot it. But the white line running down the center of the road was beating down on her pupils. She was blinking frequently, trying to keep her eyes open. Penny tried everything to stay awake. She lowered the window and let the night air blow through the car. It had been many hours since she had seen her king-sized bed. She was feeling disjointed and separated from reality. Her eyelids began to press against her face, and her breathing slowed. She couldn't fight sleep any longer nor did she want to. She yielded to the power of the inner workings of the subconscious. It was easier this way. Just give up. Just give in. She was floating now, and it felt good. She was moving effortlessly across the desert floor. She felt called to be a part of its essence, dry and forbidding—a thorn at every turn. There were no roads here, just a dusty track where the tires of a four-wheeler had left their mark. She could see the prickly pear and the Joshua trees rising from the sand.

On the horizon was a huge, sterile mountain range. Its cold, dark presence lay claim to everything in its shadow. She saw a tiny speck in the sand. As she glided closer, she realized that it was a small child. As she got nearer, she realized the child was standing in a garden rimmed with flowers. The garden seemed out of place in the middle of the desert.

As Penny circled over her, she tried to focus on the child's face. Finally, Penny's gray-green eyes met the child's dark brown ones and rested for a while. Penny knew her.

"Hello, Rosa." She was struck by how healthy and happy Rosa looked. She was wearing black patent leather shoes, pink socks, and a pink dress that reminded Penny of a frothy summer drink. In fact, Rosa was sipping something from a straw. As she came closer, she saw that Rosa was drinking from a carton that read "Santa Inez Milk Company."

Seeing Rosa looking so well confused her. She appeared as though she had grown! And what about the Santa Inez Milk? She thought that Rosa was being taken to San Diego and not to Santa Inez, which was up the California coast by several hundred miles.

"Rosa, what are you doing here?" Rosa moved away as if she hadn't heard her. Penny tried to touch her, but her arm ran right through the child's body. This startled Penny and jerked her awake. Rosa's viewing dissolved into the darkness, and Penny was thankful to find herself still in the Mustang. Leo was staring intently at the highway, his hands gripping the steering wheel, and he was still passing other cars at lightning speed.

"I just saw the strangest thing. Rosa was standing in a beautiful garden. She was wearing patent leather shoes and a dress that looked much more expensive than her family could ever afford. And she was drinking from a carton that said, 'Santa Inez Milk Company.'"

"What did you say she was drinking? Leo asked.

"It looked like a carton of milk, and I know it said, 'Santa Inez Milk' on it. It had a purple flower on the front."

"The Baja drug cartel runs the Santa Inez Cattle and Dairy Company in Culiacan, Mexico. The US government bans American importers from buying their products."

"Then, how could she be drinking that milk?" Penny asked. "It only means one thing. Rosa would be in Culiacan, but that is impossible. There would not be enough time for her to get there. It's a three-hour flight from San Diego."

Penny was perplexed. Maybe it was just wishful thinking on her part to see Rosa looking so well, or maybe this was where Rosa actually is, or maybe there was another tantalizing possibility.

"Leo, maybe this hasn't happened yet. Maybe that's where Rosa is headed once she arrives in San Diego. I've never viewed the future before, just things that happen in real time." Penny refused to consider herself psychic, and didn't psychics see the future? She remembered her run-in with Deputy Gómez and how he had made fun of her. She massaged the back of her neck with her fingertips, trying to banish the thought from her mind. But she couldn't push it away. Right from the start, Penny had figured there was more to Rosa's kidnapping. A lot of things didn't add up, and now here was one more thing that didn't make sense.

"Leo, maybe we are going to save Rosa after all!"

# CHAPTER 26

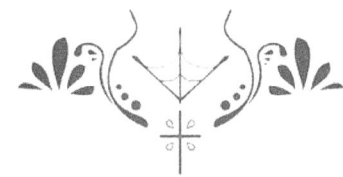

"So I'm thinking we should make quite a haul this evening," Andulov said. "You like this kind of money?"

Márquez did not answer. Andulov pounded him on the shoulder. "Hey, Doc! When we deliver Rosa, you will be a millionaire!"

Márquez looked over at Andulov, who wore a big grin. His dark hair, once soaked with pond water and now with sweat, had dried in frizzy curls, reminding the doctor of a bad perm. Hoping to divert the conversation from talk of his new profession, Márquez changed the subject. "When you get back to El Paso, we can throw a big party to celebrate!"

"I think I can spare a gallon of vodka—or two!" Andulov howled with laughter.

Márquez thought Andulov was laughing a little too loudly. Perhaps running from the law was getting to him too. Andulov pulled a cigarette out of his shirt pocket and lit up. Márquez hated secondhand smoke. He hit the automatic button to open his window. Once the tinted window was open, Márquez saw nothing that looked familiar. "Which way did you turn when we left the racetrack? I was still getting Rosa settled and didn't notice."

"I turned left."

"Andulov, you've gone the wrong way! Pull over, so I can get my bearings."

Andulov drove the car onto a wide spot where the shoulder was not too sandy and stopped. He left the engine running but turned off his headlights. The SUV's turn signal was still flashing, and Andulov appeared to be oblivious to it. The blinking irritated Márquez. He realized that this wrong turn could cost them valuable time. They had to get to the plane before anyone figured out where they were headed. Márquez had planned to drive the Explorer from the airport, leave it at the bridge, and walk back to Juárez, but now everything was at risk. They were lost.

Fortunately, it was a lonely stretch of road, lined with cotton fields, irrigation pumps, and an occasional cottonwood tree. Márquez saw nothing that helped him determine their location. A single car approached them from the rear. Márquez figured they could always ask for directions if they could get anyone to stop, but at this time of night, that was doubtful.

As the vehicle crawled by them, Márquez could see the Doña Ana County sheriff's seal on the side of a patrol car. Since the sky was cloudy and the moon was not visible, it would make it difficult for the officer to see inside their SUV. Márquez gritted his teeth and prayed the patrol car would keep moving. Luckily, it rolled by them without incident. Márquez let out an audible sigh. "What, you scared of some county sheriff?" Andulov slapped Márquez on the knee. "He wouldn't be so dumb to pull over on this dark road, asking questions."

But the men watched as the patrol car made a U-turn and drove by them again. Still, the officer did not stop. Now Márquez was anxious, but he tried not to show it. He did not want to let on that he was upset for fear that Andulov would do something stupid.

"I am sure he has seen plenty of people stopped on the side of the road," Márquez said as flipped on his flashlight and opened a dog-eared map of New Mexico he had found in the glove compartment. Without a point of reference, he knew there was no sense trying to find another way to the airport. Márquez laid the map in his lap and shook his head. "You're going to have to turn around and go back. I don't know if there is another way to the airport from here."

High beams from an oncoming car shot straight through their SUV, lighting up their faces. Márquez saw the red lights flashing and knew the sheriff had returned. Andulov squinted and reached for his pistol, which he pulled out of his holster.

"Calm down, Andulov. Let me handle this." Márquez was far from calm himself. He tried to hide his trembling hands. He was used to Mexico, and being parked on a rural road pricked his gut like spines on an agave. Mexican bandits, who wanted money for your right to be on the road, or worse, who wanted to steal your car, would think nothing of blowing you away if you didn't cooperate. "The sheriff is probably checking to see if we've had car trouble," Márquez said, trying not to agitate Andulov, who was now palming his pistol and checking his ammunition.

The sheriff, a tall, broad-shouldered man in his forties, walked slowly up to the Explorer, stopped in front of the driver's window, and leaned into the Explorer's open window. Shadows fell over the officer's face, making it difficult for the men to see his eyes.

"Can I see your driver's license and registration?" he asked. There was no indication in his voice that this was anything other than a routine stop.

"Is there a problem?" Andulov asked.

"No problem. I noticed your tail light is out. You'll need to get that fixed. It's a violation here in New Mexico."

"Thank you, Sheriff. We were just checking our map," Márquez said. "We are lost."

"Where were you headed?"

There was a stony silence. A slight breeze blew into the SUV, ruffling the frayed edges of the worn map. Márquez knew he would have to respond naturally and quickly.

"We were headed to Santa Rosa to visit friends." Márquez offered the sheriff his professional smile, the one he gave his patients when he entered the exam room.

"You're heading north toward Las Cruces," the sheriff said. "You need to turn around and head back eight miles to Country Club Road, and then make a right. Santa Rosa city limits are just a few miles west of that intersection."

Andulov handed his license to the sheriff, along with the registration Márquez had found in the glove box.

"Please wait right here."

Andulov looked at Márquez in anger and then leaned his head out of the car window. "Is this necessary, sir?"

The sheriff ignored Andulov and backed away from the Explorer, not taking his eyes off the SUV until he reached his patrol car. He reached in the car window and pulled out his radio. Andulov grabbed his gun and leaned out the window. Márquez tried to pull his arm down. "No, don't shoot him. Let's wait and see what—"

Andulov didn't let Márquez finish. He hit Márquez in the face with the pistol, causing blood to jet from his nose. The gun went off and blew a hole in the side of the Explorer's passenger door. Márquez was completely shaken by Andulov's anger toward him. He wiped the blood from his nose and snarled. He looked out the back window and saw the sheriff running toward the Explorer with his gun drawn. "Now he's coming for us!"

Andulov leaned out the window and fired his pistol, knocking the sheriff off his feet.

"What in the hell did you do?" Márquez screamed. "You are an idiot!"

Rosa stood up in the backseat and began screaming and pounding Andulov on the shoulders. He turned around and shoved Rosa back down in her seat. "I am not an idiot, *you* are. This guy knows who we are. I saw it in his eyes." Andulov hit the gas and roared up the road until he found a driveway, where he turned around and headed back toward Country Club Road. As they passed by, Márquez could see the sheriff lying just off the side of the road. His heart cried out for him. He wanted to save him but knew he could not. He was a criminal now, and criminals only help themselves. Márquez looked over at Andulov, whose eyes were on fire. He jammed his foot on the gas pedal. Márquez realized he was driving like a crazy man, and this could endanger them all. He could hear Rosa whimpering in the backseat. He didn't dare look at her. It would crush his will to continue.

The rapid speed made for a bumpy ride. Andulov threw his gun into Márquez's lap and smacked the steering wheel. "This is your fault. You were supposed to get me to the airport, and you failed."

Perhaps Andulov had forgotten that it was Márquez who now had the pistol in his lap. Was he testing him? Márquez thought for an instant about ordering Andulov to pull over and get out of the car. He could leave him on the side of the road and head straight for the border—just a few miles south. Then he remembered Rosa.

"I never signed up for murder," Márquez growled and turned his head away so Andulov could not see the look of despair on his face.

"What did you want me to do? Wait until he looked up our papers and saw my license and the registration didn't match?"

"But there was no reason to kill him!" "In my world, killing solves problems."

"This has only aggravated the problem. Now the sheriff's department has your driver's license. They know who you are."

"You think I gave him my actual driver's license? I have many licenses." Andulov's laugh was spiteful. He gave Márquez an evil once-over.

Márquez fingered the gun. He had sworn to save lives, not destroy them. And apparently Andulov knew this too. He had given him the gun, perhaps daring him to kill? Márquez regretted ever choosing to join Andulov. He felt filthy now. It was more than the dried blood on his hands and pants. He was nothing more than a mangy rat, scratching and clawing at everything good in his world.

The gun's metal grip was soaking up the warmth in his hands and making it hot to the touch. His fingertips brushed over the barrel and then found the trigger. Márquez traced the curve, the small indentation where his finger could rest until he was ready to squeeze. He was very angry now, mostly with himself, and could sense that the gun was now an extension of his arm. Was that how killers felt—totally justified in taking matters in their own deadly hands? The weight of the pistol was digging into his palm. It was heavier than he had imagined. His wrist ached as he lifted it and pointed it at his own head.

Andulov took a sharp turn, throwing Márquez against the passenger door and causing the gun to fall back into his lap. Andulov glanced over at him and laughed. Márquez knew Andulov was mocking him, knowing the gun was safe in his hands because Jonathan could not shoot anybody, not even himself. Márquez agreed. There were just some things he could not and would not compromise.

# CHAPTER 27

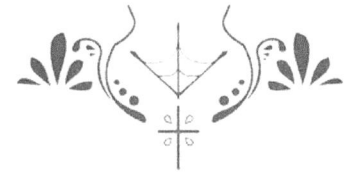

Andulov drove erratically down Old Ridge Road. The dark, poorly paved road was filled with blind curves and narrow stretches where only one car could pass. It was all Márquez could do to hold on as Andulov veered from one side of the road to the other. Márquez could see that the Russian was breathing too hard. He was probably hyperventilating, which could cause him to pass out behind the wheel. A pack of coyotes ran across the road, too late for Andulov to avoid them. He jammed on the brakes, but not before hitting one of the animals in the hindquarters. Rosa rolled forward and crashed into the back of Marquez's seat. The pistol fell to the floor. They watched the coyote limp off the road,

his back legs bloody and probably broken.

"Oooh!" Rosa cried. She sat up and looked out the window. "I see a doggy in the road. Is he hurt?"

"Rosa, lie back down. We're almost there," Márquez said. Rosa whimpered. "But the doggy *is* hurt."

Márquez assured her that this was not a dog, but rather a wild animal that didn't like little girls.

"Did I scare you?" Andulov asked. "I tried to!" He laughed and pounded the steering wheel.

Márquez tried to ignore Andulov and tucked his trembling hands between his legs until they finally reached Country Club Road and turned right. He blew the stale air out of his lungs. He had barely had a chance to take a deep breath since they'd left the sheriff on the side of the road. It was a straight shot to the airport, but it would be impossible for him to feel completely okay until Andulov was on his plane and taxiing down the runway. *God, please let this end well!*

Andulov's cell phone rang, piercing the darkness that hung between them. His Bluetooth was on a scratchy speaker. "Andulov, you got my merchandise?"

"Yes, Stefan, we have them, safe and sound. We are just a few minutes from the airport."

"Good, very good," Stefan replied. "What is your ETA?" "We should be in San Diego around 3:00 a.m."

"Did you fill my whole order?"

"Yes, Stefan. I've got four girls for you. The doctor came through for us."

"Don't be late. I have to put the girls on another plane tonight." "So far, so good, Stefan."

"When you arrive, look for a white van," Stefan said. "It has no windows and says, 'Martin's Plumbing and Air Conditioning' on the side."

"Good. I will see you in a few hours."

Andulov looked over at Márquez, who had remained quiet. "Why don't you come to San Diego tonight? We can celebrate. And you will be safe with me."

"Thanks, but I've got a couple of patients who need me tomorrow."

"It is too risky! They are killing doctors all over Juárez. I need you alive!"

"I know, but I need to—"

Andulov leaned over and slugged Márquez in the shoulder. "You don't need to do anything!"

Márquez was afraid to admit he wanted to include his wife in his plans to leave Mexico. It was something Andulov didn't need to know at this point. It was a fair trade after all. He was taking care of Rosa and using his contacts for kidnapping women in Mexico. And he had convinced his father-in-law to help Andulov move his vodka from the United States through Mexico to Russia. Certainly, Andulov didn't need a partner to party with him too.

"I still have two patients who are critically ill in the hospital. I need to make sure they get good care if I decide to leave Juárez."

"Decide to leave? I thought you were dying to get out of there."

"Well, yes, I am, but there are things you aren't aware of that I must handle before I leave Juárez for good."

"You think I don't know all about you? I checked you out before I agreed to do business."

Márquez was astounded to hear this. *What exactly does Andulov know?* He moved around in his seat and checked to see if his seat belt was still fastened. He had told him about his father-in-law and his ties to the Chihuahua drug cartel, but he had never mentioned his wife's name or anything about the rest of his family. Had he placed them all in danger? The Russian mob had long tentacles.

"I know all about your family. Your wife's name is Generosa. You call her Genie. Your father-in-law wants her protected at all times. He would be very angry if you took her away. He might find you and kill you."

"How would you know this?" "People talk for money."

Márquez was ready to scream. He did not want his wife harmed. "There is no reason to go back for your wife. You are a dead man if you try to take her away from her father. Why do you think I chose you as a partner? You have no reason to remain in Mexico. Genie is very beautiful, and her father will find her another husband."

The thought of losing his wife to another man crushed him. He wanted to punch Andulov in the face. He loved Genie and hoped to have children in a few years. They had made plans to build a home in a plush, gated *colonia*.

"You also have two sisters. And your parents live a few blocks from your home. I met your sister, Rosa, at a restaurant a few weeks ago. She is a stunning woman!"

"She is only a teenager," Márquez replied. He was furious Andulov had spied on him. Now, he was also alarmed that Andulov had his eyes on his sister. At seventeen, she wasn't much older than the girls they had kidnapped. Márquez looked squarely at Andulov. He could not contain his outrage. He kicked the pistol, which still lay on the floor.

Andulov looked irritated. "You keep close eyes on your sister!" Andulov jabbed two stubby fingers toward the doctor's blue-gray eyes. It was the first time Márquez noticed the snarl that turned one part of Andulov's lips upward. It had caused a permanent frown line in his sallow skin.

Márquez wanted to vomit. The thought of his sister becoming a victim of someone like Sergei Andulov was repulsive. Bile rose in his throat, causing him to pull his handkerchief out of his pocket and spit into it.

The yelling between the two men had apparently awakened Rosa. She was calling out for her mother. "Please help me, Mamá. I am lost!" She was standing and jumping up and down in the backseat.

"Do something with her!" Andulov demanded. "Pull over, so I can get into my bag."

Andulov lurched to the right and parked in front of a large stone house illuminated by a bright porch light. Márquez pulled a syringe out of his bag and loaded it with a vial of a clear liquid. He hoped the Benadryl would do the trick. He hated to mix Rohypnol with anything else. He hopped out of the car and opened the passenger door. Rosa had one of her legs hoisted over the top of the front seat. That made it easy for him to inject the serum into her tiny thigh right through her clothes.

"Ouch!" She jerked her leg back over the front seat and sat up, rubbing her leg and sobbing.

"It's okay, Rosa. You will be fine soon. Get your rest. Your fever has broken."

"Water! I am thirsty." Rosa began to sob.

Her cries made Márquez queasy. He offered a silent prayer for her safety. *Please, God, I am sorry. If there is any way to keep her from harm, please do help her.*

Márquez returned to his satchel for a bottle of water. He helped Rosa take several gulps, then wiped her tears with his handkerchief and lay her down on the seat. He wanted to make sure she was as comfortable as possible. He fastened a seat belt around her, just in case the SUV had to take some hard turns.

"I want my Mamá! I want to go home!" Rosa tried to get back up. Márquez gently held her in place. Realizing how cold the night air had become, Márquez covered her with the blanket and patted her hand. "You'll be home soon, Rosa. I promise." It disgusted him to lie to her, but he had to get her calmed down. Who knew what Andulov might do if he didn't.

Rosa continued to whimper and rub her thigh where he had injected her with the antihistamine. Márquez could see her eyelids were getting heavy, and her cheeks were red and swollen. Her body showed signs of complete exhaustion. He was concerned he had given her too much Rohypnol over the past two days, and that it might affect her cognitive function in the long term. There was no profit in delivering faulty merchandise, he knew. And he would be blamed for not giving her better medical care.

"What's taking you so long?" Andulov yelled.

"Give me a few minutes!" Márquez answered with a gruff voice that surprised him. He turned on his flashlight and examined Rosa's small frame. If she were really eleven years old, what had happened to make her so small for her age? Had she come into his office, he would have moved heaven and earth to find out why she hadn't grown. He picked up her hand. Her bony fingers wrapped around his index finger, like those of a newborn exploring the first dimensions of her world. The fingers lacked a youthful luster. For certain, Rosa appeared to be malnourished. But there was something more. He wished he had a lab where he could draw her blood and study it. That was no longer an option. In a few hours, Rosa was going to be somebody else's problem. He turned and looked at the stone house as the tears welled up in his eyes. No one should be living like this. He envied the owners of the home that looked so welcoming.

He climbed back in the front seat, and Andulov pulled back on the road. It was so dark that Andulov could not see his face, and for that, he was happy. His eyes were red from crying. The disgust Márquez was feeling for his partner was growing by the minute. Watching Rosa suffer got him thinking about the four teenagers he had arranged to be taken in Las Palomas and Casas Grandes. He had ordered their kidnapping with a simple phone call. He had never considered what their families might be going through, wondering where they were. Too many young women had already been murdered in Mexico, and he supposed they thought their daughters had met with the same fate. They would never know that they were alive somewhere, serving as sex slaves. He had been the cold, calculating thug who'd made this atrocity possible. Watching Rosa's inconsolable tears made him see how stupid his decision had been to join Andulov. No money or even threats to his life was worth the feeling of utter self-loathing that now permeated his soul. He had left the health of the four teenagers to the skills of a pilot who'd flown them to Santa Rosa from Mexico. Had Don Koble known how to give the Rohypnol properly? Would they still be alive when Andulov's plane arrived in San Diego tonight? He was so distracted with his worries that he failed to see the police car one hundred yards ahead.

Andulov saw the flashing lights first, reflecting against the dark sky, swollen with clouds. He drove his foot into the brake, and the SUV slid to a stop. "What the heck is going on ahead of us?"

Rosa screamed. The doctor, who had one hand against the dashboard, looked back at her and was thankful she was still buckled in. When he turned back to look at the stretch of road ahead of them, he thought he could make out two men standing in the middle of the highway, but he couldn't be sure. Why would they be there? He suspected the reason, but he did not want to rile up Andulov.

"Maybe there's an accident," Márquez said. "We can't just stop in the middle of the road. We'll draw attention. Drive slowly toward the police car."

Andulov shifted into first gear and then into second. As they got closer, their headlights revealed two police officers stretching wire fencing across the road.

"Damn!" Andulov shouted. "They're trying to block the road." "We should turn around and try and find another way into the airport," Márquez said.

Andulov pulled onto the berm, turned off his headlights, and threw his car in park. He reached behind his seat for the case lying on the floor. He opened it and hoisted an AK-47 over the back of the seat.

"I'm ready!"

"Don't be stupid!" Márquez knew Andulov had a hair-trigger temper, but shooting one cop was enough. Andulov revved the engine as if to aggravate him.

Márquez wondered if he could jump out of the car while he still had a chance of turning his life around. Andulov would probably shoot him in the back as he tried to run away. Márquez was once again trapped in a situation where there appeared to be no way out. Besides, he couldn't leave Rosa with this beast. He let out a loud sigh to show his disgust and looked away. He really didn't want to see what Andulov had planned.

Andulov touched his arm and spoke to him in a calmer voice. "Look. We have no choice. I have to be in California in three hours. You know that." Andulov shoved his rifle between his body and the driver's door. Then he pulled slowly back on the roadway with the headlights off. As the Explorer picked up speed, Márquez realized how rapidly his world was spiraling out of control.

"Sergei, don't do anything crazy! You are running right into a trap. They are waiting for us. Don't you see that?"

"I see nothing ahead I can't handle."

"I didn't sign on for killing cops. Pull over, so I can get out of the car!"

Andulov picked up his automatic weapon and slugged Márquez in the side of the head, dazing him. He slumped over in the seat, blood running from his mouth. His brain felt like a boat in a storm; giant waves were crashing against his skull. The pounding made it difficult to hear Andulov, who he now realized was yelling at him to sit up. He threw a pistol in Marquez's lap. "Earn your keep! You work for me now!"

Márquez fumbled in the dark for the gun, a revolver he had never seen before. It now lay heavily against his thigh. He unlatched the safety and stuck the gun between his legs.

Andulov moved slowly toward the fencing, which now stretched completely across the road. It was nothing more than chicken wire, but to the innocent, it would be cause enough to stop, Márquez thought. For Andulov, it would be nothing more than an irritation, like swatting a mosquito on his arm. When they were about twenty yards from the blockade, the deputies saw the SUV picking up speed and heading toward them. They pulled their guns, and one officer yelled in a bullhorn.

"Stop! Please, we are checking all cars."

Andulov acted as if he hadn't heard the warning. He didn't even slow down. He lowered both the driver and passenger windows. "Shoot when I tell you," he ordered Márquez. Andulov rested his rifle on the windowsill with his left hand while driving with his right.

The doctor's hand was shaking. He was a surgeon and had always had steady nerves, but now he couldn't get his hands to stop trembling. His eyes wouldn't focus, perhaps because they were filled with tears. The officers faded in and out of his range of vision. There was no way he would fire at a police officer.

"Do they think I am that stupid? I can get through a flimsy wire fence!" Andulov growled like a wild animal as he got closer and closer to the blockade. He suddenly gunned the accelerator. It was obvious that at this speed, the wire would not be a deterrent. The officer who was standing near the open door of his police car blasted the Explorer with ammunition from a 9 mm.

"For God's sake, stop the car! They will kill us!" Márquez was frantic. He pounded on Andulov's arm. Andulov responded by shoving Márquez away with a blow from his elbow and then spraying the officers with bullets from his rifle. A second officer, who had taken cover behind the hood of the car, ran toward the Explorer, firing first at the driver and then at Márquez. The bullet grazed the top of the doctor's head. Blood ran down his face and soaked his shirt. He put pressure on his wound, trying to stop the bleeding.

Andulov fired at the second officer. The deputy's body was blown back against the side of his car as blood shot out of his body like water from a spigot. Andulov roared through the fence, which was no match for two tons of steel, but the SUV caught the fencing under its wheels, causing the car to careen out of control. Márquez gripped the door, bracing for a crash. Andulov slammed on the brakes, bringing the SUV full circle and just inches from the deputy lying in the road. Rosa began screaming again and trying to get out of her seat belt. The smell of rubber permeated the air. Breathless, Andulov turned to Márquez. His eyes were wild. Looking at his scarred face and his shapeless nose,

Márquez recognized what he had refused to see before: Andulov was nothing more than a petty thug.

Andulov grabbed the revolver out of Márquez's hand and aimed it at his head. "This is where we part company, Doc! I don't have any use for you in this shape." He unbuckled the doctor's seat belt and leaned over and opened the passenger door. Rosa sat up and threw one leg over the back of the seat. Andulov reacted by shoving Rosa, trying to get her out of the way. Márquez knew this was his only chance to escape. He jumped from the car and rolled into an irrigation ditch that ran along the side of the road. Andulov fired his pistol twice. Márquez heard one bullet ricochet off the irrigation pumping station. The other hit his left arm. He could still hear Andulov screaming at Rosa as he shoved the SUV in gear.

"Lie back down, you little bitch!" She was mumbling something Márquez could not hear. He regretted doping her up. Now she couldn't defend herself.

Andulov spun his wheels, throwing a cloud of dust and gravel all over Márquez. The doctor pulled his head and shoulders as far out of the water as his weary arms could bear. He hated the thought of drowning. He would rather bleed to death. He rested his head on a patch of soft, damp grass and looked up at the murky sky. He was now losing blood from his head and his arm. Without help, he would eventually bleed out, but it might take hours. He would have to lie here in agony, regretting his stupidity. Dying at the hands of the drug cartels was more honorable than this. He was just happy he didn't have to watch Andulov load Rosa on the plane and fly away. Why Guapo Chavez insisted on owning someone like Rosa was still a mystery to him, but it was no longer his problem. The best part about dying would be not seeing Rosa's sad face haunting him forever.

Pain hit his chest like a hammer. He reached for his nitroglycerin in his pants pocket but remembered the meds would be soaking wet. He pulled out the paper sleeve that held them. The tiny white pills were dissolving into a thick paste. He took his index finger and rubbed it across the paper, then stuck his finger in his mouth.

The doctor felt his neck for his pulse and traced a shallow beat with his fingertips. He dropped his eyes from the clouds and breathed in deeply, thankful that the angina had subsided, at least for the moment. He looked out across the road. For a second, he thought he saw *La Santa Muerta*, Martín Ladera's saint of holy death, circling his body. How ironic would that be? He swore he could make out the glint of her amber medallion dangling before his eyes. Then he realized the glimmer wasn't from her amber necklace at all, but from the police car's flashing yellow lights.

# CHAPTER 28

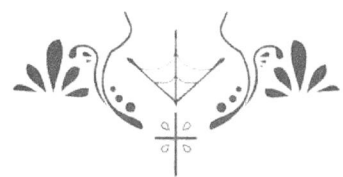

Leo and Penny exited the Interstate at Mesa Street and headed west on Country Club Drive. They had driven through an Upper Valley neighborhood, which was as rich as parts of the Mission Valley were poor. Posh homes encircled a marvelous golf course, and the landscape created an atmosphere of lushness and peace for its residents.

In short order, the Mustang crossed the bridge over the Rio Grande. They were now in New Mexico, and officially, the El Paso County Sheriff's Office had no jurisdiction. Leo shut off his flashing lights and slowed to the speed limit. He looked over at Penny and noticed that she looked pale and her eyes were glassy.

"Are you all right?" Leo asked.

"I feel really dizzy, and my eyes aren't focusing." "When was the last time you had something to eat?"

"Our peanut butter sandwiches come to mind." Penny ran her fingers through her hair and sighed.

Leo made a left hand turn into a small convenience store. He returned with two bottles of orange juice and a package of peanut butter crackers.

When he opened the car door, Leo saw that Penny was sitting up but staring blankly out the passenger window. "Here, Penny."

Penny took the bottles and put one in the beverage holder in the console. She nibbled on the crackers and took a slug of the juice.

"I think I waited too long to eat. My blood sugar is wacked out." "You a diabetic?"

"No, the doctor calls it hypoglycemia. I call it hell."

Penny hated it when her blood sugar went haywire. She had to watch everything she ate and eat in small portions at regular times.

Since she'd gotten involved with this case, nothing had been regular about her life. She finished off the crackers, hoping that would be enough to keep her from being overcome with drowsiness. As she drank the second bottle of orange juice, she could just imagine the sugar coursing through her bloodstream. For a few minutes, there would be celebration. Her body would thank her for the sugar, but it wouldn't be long before her blood sugar would fall, and she would have to sleep whether she wanted to or not. She yawned and stretched her hands toward the ceiling of the car.

"I'm sorry, Leo. I think I am going to have to sleep off this sugar rush."

"Not to worry. I'll wake you when we're almost there."

Penny gave in to the inevitable. If she didn't sleep, she would be of no help to Leo when they got to the airport. As things were going, he needed all the help he could get. She shut her eyes and let her body embrace the darkness.

Soon, Penny had the feeling she was floating again. The weightlessness made for a peaceful journey. She wasn't exactly sure where she was going, but she felt the wind rushing past her. She opened her eyes and found herself orbiting the earth, watching the beautiful blue ball from a distance. It was wonderful to be free of earthly cares.

Without warning, Penny began to spin out of control. She reached for something to stop her, but there was only thin air and nothing more all around her. The earth's topography was becoming more detailed as she spiraled closer. She was traveling faster and faster, the weight of her body aiding in the momentum. She was panting, and her throat ached. She tried to call out for help, but her voice was mute.

The earth was in full view now. It might have been a welcome sight, had she not been careening toward it at such a high speed.

The wind was stinging her face, arms, and legs. She brought her hands in front of her, trying to protect her eyes. A road no wider than the long mark of a pencil appeared on the horizon. It ran between a ridge of green trees and desolate sand. Her body was hurtling toward this ribbon of blacktop, and there appeared to be no way to stop the inevitable. Was this the way her life ended—a splat on a deserted highway?

Penny tried to brace herself for the landing, but at the speed she was traveling, she crashed into the pavement with a tremendous force. She had never felt such a massive impact. She tried to move, but she was writhing in pain. Was every bone in her body crushed? Before she could see how badly she was injured, her body began rolling down a small hill, stopping when she hit a speed bump in the road. She raised her right arm and touched the hump in the roadway, which was blistering hot. Not a tree was in view, and sand was blowing over her, landing in her hair and stinging her eyes.

Penny tried to breathe, but the fall had knocked the air out of her lungs. Or maybe she was dead. Everything was so surreal Penny couldn't separate death from life. She checked her arms and legs for any visible wounds and noticed that her jeans were torn and her legs were covered with a black ash. She ran her hands through the black powdery substance, which caked under her nails. Had she traveled through fire during reentry?

She rolled over and tried to sit up. The air rushed back into her lungs, and she gasped, grateful to be breathing again. Her heart was racing; she needed to get out of the middle of the road or she wouldn't be alive for long. A car speeding over the hill would not be able to stop in time. She wobbled a little as she stood and tried to take a few steps—to where, she was uncertain because nothing looked familiar. She struggled to stay on her feet, and she fell onto the pavement, skinning the palm of her hand. "I can fall thousands of feet with little injury, but slice up my hand when I fall just a few feet," she said out loud. She was very confused.

Once Penny got the hang of walking, she decided to follow the blacktop toward the setting sun. What other choice did she have? After several minutes of stumbling in that direction, she saw a sign that pointed her to the Santa Rosa airport. She walked down the long driveway. The sun was hitting her in the face as it moved toward a mountain range in the distance. She had no sunglasses, and she was burning up in her blue jeans and dusty shoes and socks. She wiped her sleeve across her sweating face and then realized she probably looked rather frightening to anyone she would meet along the way.

Finally, Penny saw a large metal building ahead and thought it might be a place where she could get some water. The heat was boiling now, and perspiration was soaking her clothes. She opened the double doors to what turned out to be the airport terminal, and the cool air came rushing over her. Before she could step inside, she saw her reflection in the glass door. She was a shadowy shape without a fully defined body. Seeing herself this way scared her. Would she really need water if it were going to run right through her? She looked around for a drinking fountain anyway. She encountered a man walking through the waiting room, dragging two teenage girls by their arms. One was fighting with him, and the other seemed as if she didn't know what was happening. Her eyes were watery, and her skin was pale.

Penny gave them room to pass through the terminal doors and out into the scorching sun. She followed them as they made slow, sloppy progress toward an airplane parked on the runway. One girl stumbled, and the man reached down to yank her back up onto her feet. *Maybe I can help!* When Penny got close enough to grab the man's arm, she panicked. *What if I can't subdue him?* Then she saw a gun strapped to his chest. One of the girls broke free. The man, dragging the other girl by the hand, chased after her.

Penny watched helplessly as the man caught up with the other teenager and wrapped his arm around her throat. "Don't try that again!" All three of them were now marching together with a common destination: the corporate jet.

When they got to the side of the plane, he dropped the two girls onto the tarmac and placed his foot on the chest of the girl who had tried to escape. Penny could see that his tight grip had bruised their bare shoulders. The one on the ground was whimpering, but the other appeared to be unconscious. He was holding her sagging body with his right arm, his muscles bulging out of his T-shirt.

The man yelled, "Open the door, John."

Another man, dressed in a pilot's uniform, looked out the door and scampered down the steps to the tarmac. He grabbed the arm of the unconscious teen, but she fell forward into his arms. He picked her up and carried her up the steps into the plane. The other man yanked the second young woman into a standing position. Penny could hear her crying. "*No, por favor.* Don't take me. Please!" He scooped her up in his arms and carried her into the plane.

Penny was able to watch as they guided the teenagers into the first row of leather seats in front of the two other girls, who were already seated in the second row and appeared to be unconscious. One of the new girls was staring at nothing. Her body was limp. She didn't even blink as she fell into the thick cushion. The other teen was screaming and kicking, as the man jammed her into the seat and buckled her in. The noise, which reverberated around the small plane, was difficult for Penny to endure.

Penny moved toward the girls, desperate to find a way to help. Could she comfort them in some way? It was stifling inside the plane because the engine was off, and Penny was surprised she wasn't even perspiring. The pilot had beads of sweat on his nose and his upper lip. He was snarling his disapproval at the newest arrivals. He shouted over the cries of the teenager. "Who are these girls? I only agreed to fly one girl, along with Sergei Andulov to San Diego!"

"Shut up and do as you are told. You are making enough money to keep you happy. Who cares how many girls there are?" The kidnapper, who had a fanny pack hooked to his waist, reached into it and pulled out a syringe filled with a clear liquid. He shot a little bit into the arm of the crying teenager. Then he threw the syringe out of the jet onto the runway. The girl seemed to give up. She was sniffling. A few tears still slipped down her face, but her sobs were low and cautious. Penny wished she could offer her a handkerchief.

"She'll calm down in a few minutes. Meanwhile, let's get this jet fired up. Sergei is on his way with his prized passenger."

Penny looked at all four girls who were slumped in their seats with their heads resting on their chests. It angered her that she could not help. She watched the kidnapper leave the plane. She leaned out the door and watched him run toward a large metal building about one hundred yards away, which she figured was an airplane hangar. *Does he have a plane in there? Is he going back for more?*

As Penny turned to follow him, she saw the pilot checking out the new girls. He felt their arms for a pulse and then went to the restroom at the back of the plane, moistened a towel, and wiped their foreheads. This stirred them somewhat, but they couldn't seem to remain that way. He still didn't give up. He unbuckled their seat belts and tried to get them to stand up, but they were so heavily sedated, Penny knew there was not much chance of them waking up.

*Is he trying to help them escape?*

The pilot appeared frustrated and afraid. He paced up and down the aisle, glancing at his four charges. He pulled out his cell phone, then seemed to change his mind as he headed for the cockpit. Penny could hear the roar of the engines. The inside of the plane began to cool down. She walked over to the girl who had been screaming for help. Penny tried to take a tissue clutched in the girl's hand and wipe her nose, but she could not. She also attempted to unbuckle the seat belt, but her hand moved through the belt like clouds through a starry night. She wasn't physically there, and there was nothing she could do to stop this flight from taking off.

# CHAPTER 29

Someone gripped Penny's shoulder and shook her. Her head was spinning and she felt disoriented. "Penny, wake up!" She blinked and took in the lights of a console. Was she still on the plane? Instead of the roar of the jet engines, she heard the sound of tires grinding against the ground. Was the plane taking off?

The hand that had been holding her shoulder was now pinching her arm. She lashed out. "I said, let me go!" She turned to hit the intruder but was shocked to find that it was Leo. With a sense of relief, she threw her head back against the headrest. She was still in the Mustang and had never left it. But it had all been so real.

"Please wake up and help me find Ted. We are almost to the airport, and I don't want to take on Andulov without his help. Every time I call him, it goes to voice mail. Can you keep calling him while I try to contact his dispatcher?"

Penny took a deep breath and exhaled. "Sorry. What did you say?"

Leo shoved his phone at Penny. "Just keep hitting redial."

Penny took the phone in her hands and turned it over and over, wondering what Leo wanted her to do. She listened as he made a call to the dispatcher, who also reported that Ted had not called in and she could not reach him on his car radio. Finally, Penny realized what Leo had asked of her. She opened Leo's phone and hit the redial button. The sheriff's voice mail clicked on. "This is Sheriff Ted Rodriguez. Please leave a message, and I'll get back with you as soon as possible."

Leo was yelling into his car radio. "Can you please send out an officer to find him? I don't like this."

"Of course, Sheriff. I'll get on it."

Penny sat up straight in her seat and placed her hand on Leo's arm. "Sorry, I checked out for a while." She waited for a response, but he appeared to be ignoring her.

"It doesn't make any sense. Ted said he was just going to make one more pass through the back roads before joining us." Leo looked at Penny and shook his head. "My only course is to keep heading to the airport."

They drove in silence for several minutes. When Penny saw the flashing lights a few hundred feet ahead, she hoped it was Ted's car, but as they got closer, she could see a tangle of wire fencing under the wheel of the patrol car.

"My God, is that Ted?" Penny screamed. She pointed to a man lying on the road next to the police car. Leo swerved to avoid the fencing and stopped short of the motionless man lying next to it. "It can't be Ted. He's more than six-foot-five. This guy is too short." Leo pulled to the side of the road and jumped out of the car. Penny was right behind him. Leo knelt down on the highway and felt for the officer's pulse. He leaned into the officer's chest and listened for a heartbeat. "This man is dead."

Penny shivered and took a few steps back. She had never seen anyone who had died from a gunshot. She had only watched her mother die in the hospital or watched actors die on television, which she knew was just make-believe. The blood had congealed around the officer's nose, and his eyes were glossy and empty. This man was really gone. Did he have a wife and kids? What would happen to them? What about his mother and father? Her hands felt numb. She began to choke up. She shouldn't cry. It would make her seem weak in front of Leo. When she turned away so that Leo couldn't see her in tears, she saw a second deputy on the side of the road. "Oh, God, not another one!" The patrol car's door was open and its interior lights spilled out onto the pool of blood that surrounded the officer. She hoped he wasn't dead too. Her hands were shaking as she pointed him out to Leo.

Leo could see that two bullets had penetrated both of the deputy's legs, but his body armor had deflected an otherwise deadly blow. His breathing was rapid, but he was conscious.

"You okay?" Leo asked.

"He isn't dead! Help my partner please!" The man's lips were gray, and his pupils were as large as nickels.

"Penny, stay with this officer and keep him talking!"

Leo jumped to his feet and ran toward the Mustang. As he pumped his legs forward, he could feel the blood coursing through his veins like gasoline pushing through a fuel rail on its way to the engine. It would only take a spark to fully combust his fury. He had to keep his rage under control. "What the heck is going on?" He opened his car door and grabbed for his radio.

Leo wondered who had broken this roadblock. It scared him to think that Sergei Andulov had made it past these officers, who had been expecting him. He found the casings from an automatic rifle scattered across the road. He needed more backup.

"I need help," Leo told the dispatcher. "One officer has been wounded, and the other is dead. Send an ambulance to the cross streets of Old Ridge Road and Palomino Drive."

"I was just going to call you, Sheriff," the dispatcher answered. "We've found Sheriff Rodriguez. He has been badly wounded. He was gunned down on Old Ridge Road, just three miles from the roadblock. He has lost a lot of blood, and he was refusing to go to the hospital. Deputy Rios had to handcuff him to get him into a helicopter. He's being life-lined to an El Paso hospital right now."

---

Penny stared at the carnage. There were bullet casings everywhere. *Is this Andulov's work?* Penny looked back at the wounded deputy, who was trying to get up off the pavement. She ran up to him and kept him on the ground, with a gentle hand on his shoulder. "Sir, please stay where you are. An ambulance is coming for you."

"I need to help him. He looks bad."

"Sheriff Tellez is taking care of him. You need to keep still."

The deputy began to cry. This upset Penny more than his wounds. She wasn't sure what she could say to make the situation better. "Sir, it will be okay, but you've got to remain down."

She noticed that the collar of his brown shirt was now stained with blood. Leo apparently hadn't seen it or the bleeding was fresh. She pulled back his collar and saw what appeared to be a line of burnt flesh with bubbles of blood piercing the skin.

Penny shuddered. She ran her hand through his hair. His scalp was embedded with gravel. She began to pick the rocks out one at a time. Then she noticed that the gunshot wound to his right leg was bleeding heavily. She took off her socks and covered the wound with one of them, applying as much pressure as she could. Tears welled up in her eyes. Was this what she would be doing if she agreed to take on other cases? She wasn't sure she could. Her heart went out to this man lying helpless on the ground, but she had never even taken a first-aid course.

She admired the officer. His first thought was for his partner, not for himself. You always had to have your partner's back. Would Leo always have hers, if she ever got another chance to work with him?

Her knees began to ache from using them as part of her improvised human tripod to keep the weight of her hand on the deputy's bleeding wound. She lifted her knees one at a time to relieve the pain of pressing them into the gravel.

Surprisingly, the officer began to sing softly in Spanish. Penny had never heard the tune before. He looked at her questioning eyes. "My mother used to sing it to us kids when we got hurt playing," he said. "Just thinking of her makes it not hurt so much."

"Where is your mother?" Penny asked.

"She's in heaven now, but maybe she will hear me singing and send an angel to keep me alive."

"Can you teach the song to me?" Penny asked.

He managed a smile and repeated the first verse for her several times. Penny tried to sing it, although her Spanish was not very good. Penny saw that Leo had retrieved a second flashlight and a large first-aid kit from the Mustang and was walking toward them. "Can you go get the blanket from the trunk? I forgot to pick it up."

Penny handed Leo her other sock to keep the pressure on the deputy's leg, but he waved a sterile bandage in front of her. "Good substitute though!" He smiled at her and threw the sock into a black trash bag.

Penny ran to the car to get a blanket from the trunk, which was standing open. As she groped around the darkened trunk, she heard a moan coming from the grassy bank that held the irrigation water back from the road. It caused her spine to tingle. She shuddered, then shook it off. It could be nothing more than a rusty pump working to distribute the water to nearby fields. She took the blanket to Leo. The officer was shaking now. She laid the blanket over him.

"You arrived just in time. He was going into shock." "Is he going to be okay?"

"His leg has almost stopped bleeding." Leo showed her the bandage he had been applying to his leg, and it held very little blood. "Thanks for your quick reaction! Using your sock was genius!"

"Did you see the wound at his neck?"

Leo had his flashlight pointed toward the officer. "I just noticed it. He is very lucky. A bullet actually burned the back of his neck. It got that close!"

Penny let the air out of her lungs and tried to make sense of it. One man was dead, and the other would live, just through pure luck. She looked up at the clouds, which were covering the quarter moon and making it difficult to for her to see Leo's face.

She was grateful he was a compassionate man, even in times of professional urgency.

She heard the moaning again. "Did you hear that?"

"No, what?" Leo was now kneeling in front of the deputy and had a stethoscope in his ears, listening for the officer's heartbeat.

The moaning had a rhythm to it now. Penny thought it was more human than animal.

"Hear it?"

Leo shook his head.

Penny walked carefully toward the sound.

"You probably should stay out of that grass," Leo called to her. "It could be a dying coyote in there."

Penny ignored Leo's warning. She still had her pepper spray. She pulled it out of her pocket and fingered the trigger. The moaning got louder, the closer she got to the side of the waterway. She could see nothing. It was almost pitch-black, with the clouds covering the only source of light. She parted the tall grass and planted her feet so far inside the ditch that the toes of her shoes touched the water's edge. The ground under her feet was spongy and slick.

She turned around and ran back to Leo. "Can I have a flashlight?"

Penny secured the pepper spray in her zipper pocket and returned to the ditch. She tried to be careful as she stepped downward, closer to the water, but her leather soles made it impossible to secure a foothold on the bank. She hadn't counted on that. She felt the water filling the insides of her leather shoes as she hit the bottom of the ditch. Without her socks, it made her toes icy cold, and her feet felt like lead. She moved the flashlight's beam back and forth across the ditch. The sandy bottom allowed her to stand in the stream of water. There was a lingering smell of decaying plants. She heard crickets rubbing their legs together. Penny looked back to see if Leo were coming to help her, but she was alone. She knew he had to stay with the officer. She held her breath, waiting for the sound to call to her again. This time, a cry pierced the night air. She jerked back, hitting her hand against a cement wall, dropping her flashlight in the canal. The light remained on, but it cast a weird halo across the water. It was time to get out of there. She reached her hand deep into the water and pulled out the flashlight, which was wedged in the sandy bottom. She scrambled and clawed her way back up the slippery trench. Maybe Leo had been right. If this were a wild animal, it might be ready to pounce on her. Penny was breathing out of her mouth, panting and coughing, in a desperate attempt to get away. Just as she got to the top of the ditch, she grabbed a handful of reeds, but they pulled free from the sandy soil. She lost one of her shoes when her foot caught on the root of a tree. She tumbled headfirst into the cold depths of the canal. She landed with a splat, but was unharmed. She pulled her head out of the water, and her wet hair drained its contents down her shirt. She was covered with muck, and a trailing vine was wrapped around her arm. Although the water was only a few feet deep, it was cold and forbidding. She was shaking uncontrollably as a ripple of water splashed against her arms. Icy fingers wrapped around her leg, pulling her backward. She let out a bloodcurdling scream. "Leo!"

# CHAPTER 30

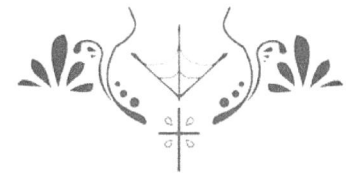

Márquez had been clinging to the bank of the aqueduct, partially hidden by a tall thicket of reeds for almost thirty minutes. The grass was slick with dew, causing him to shift his grasp from one patch of grass to another to keep from dropping into the canal. Exhausted, he had finally given up and let his body slide slowly into the water. He'd held his breath as he sank to the bottom, praying to God for a swift deliverance. The angel of deliverance had appeared almost immediately. Márquez had watched her hit the water, landing a foot or so from where he lay.

This was his savior. He had only to reach out and gently grasp her ankle, and he would live.

The glare of her flashlight assaulted his eyes as the angel grabbed his injured arm and tried to pull him out of the water. He was much too heavy for her to remove him from the canal, and her efforts to save him caused his arm to bleed. She did manage to get his face out of the water, and he gasped for air.

"Over here, Leo!" the woman shouted.

When Leo arrived, Márquez saw he was wearing an El Paso County Sheriff's badge. A wave of angst engulfed him. What was he doing in New Mexico? *Hunting for a cop-killer?*

"We need to check and see if he has any spinal injuries before we pull him any farther out of the water," the sheriff said. The officer checked Márquez while the woman pointed the flashlight at his wounded body. "He looks like he has a couple of gunshots. I think we'd better take the chance and move him."

The angel got blood on her sleeve as she cradled his head in her arms. They laid him on the roadway, close to a deputy who was strangely singing in Spanish. Márquez knew that tune from his childhood. It brought back memories of happier times. The flashing lights of the patrol car allowed Márquez to see that the officer had been shot in his lower extremities. He was thankful the man had his eyes shut for now. He hated lying so close to him. The proximity increased the likelihood that the officer would identify him as the passenger in the Explorer. Márquez squeezed his arms together and rolled on his side, away from the deputy's line of vision, should he open his eyes. The gunshot to his arm caused him to cry out, and the pain in his chest reared its head again. Márquez shoved his hand into the pocket of his slacks and felt for what he knew would be a paste of wet pills, but they had slipped deeper into his pocket. He moaned again. They were out of his reach.

The angel took off her coat and placed it over him. Her kindness brought tears to his eyes. *I don't deserve this!* He could see that she was beautiful and had lovely eyes. He was grateful for her courage to find him in the depths of the water.

The sheriff knelt down and tended to his head. He had an alcohol swab and was cleaning around the wound, quite expertly, the doctor thought. He had probably treated people on the roadside before. *Would he be so kind if he knew who I am?*

"Sir, the paramedics are on their way. I can't find any sign of the bullet in your head. It must have just creased your scalp. Your arm does have a bullet lodged near your elbow. Where were you when you were shot?"

Márquez did not answer. He was party to a cop killing, even if he hadn't pulled the trigger. He sighed, rolled his eyes toward his forehead, and winced in pain, hoping to delay the inevitable line of questioning. The sheriff rolled him on his back, reached into Márquez's drenched suit coat, and pulled out his soggy wallet. He would now know his name. He always carried his medical identification as well as his State of Chihuahua driver's license. This filled Márquez with shame. He had wanted to be a physician since high school, and now he was asking to be saved, instead of saving others.

"Penny, this man is a doctor from Juárez. Stay here while I radio the ambulance to make room for two. And keep him talking."

"Doctor, who shot you?"

It was a simple enough question, Márquez thought, but little did the woman know how complicated the answer was. He turned on his side once again, trying to avoid locking eyes with her. He coughed and started to wheeze. This time, he dug deeper into his pants pocket and finally was able to rub his fingertips across the pasty mixture of nitroglycerin. He touched his fingers to his mouth.

The woman's eyes widened. "What is that powder on your hands? Cocaine?"

"Nitro." He could barely form any words. He was going into shock and he knew it.

"Are you in pain?" She picked up his hand and rubbed it. Her warmth calmed him somewhat.

"Are you hurting?" she asked him again, but he could barely hear her now. He was fading in and out, and he could no longer focus on her beautiful face. He would have preferred to tell her the truth, but he was experiencing such grief that the words wouldn't come out of his throat. He couldn't tell her that he was an accessory to murder and a kidnapper. She would walk away and leave him to die on the road. He inhaled deeply, choking on his own bile. He could only speak one word, and that was a whisper. "Rosa."

The woman dropped his hand and stared at him. Her eyes were full of confusion and fear. She jumped up and ran toward the Mustang. "Leo! The doctor knows about Rosa!"

Márquez began to sob. His hands trembled as he tried to wipe his tears away before the woman returned. He felt cold. The road was a brittle bed for a wounded man. It was clear now that he and Andulov had not been fooling anyone. The police had been on their trail all along. The only question that remained was whether or not Andulov would get away before the El Paso County sheriff could stop him. Márquez prayed that the sheriff would win.

# CHAPTER 31

A chuckhole in the road threw Rosa off the backseat of the Explorer. Dr. John's black bag and Andulov's suitcase kept her from hitting the floor of the SUV. She had been sound asleep, and now she was groggy and sick to her stomach. She shoved Andulov's suitcase toward the door. Without any warning, she vomited.

"What's going on back there?" Andulov yelled.

Rosa began to cry. "I'm sick!" She rubbed her tummy, which hurt.

"I need you to shut up!" Rosa vomited again.

"For God's sake!" He pulled to the side of the road and slammed on the brakes. He hopped out of the car and opened the back door. "Did you get anything on my rifle case? You better not have!" He yanked her out of the car and shoved her toward a grassy spot a few feet off the road. "If you're going to be sick, do it out here!" Then he turned and picked up Rosa's blanket to clean up the mess. Andulov tossed the blanket onto the road.

Rosa threw up again. Her mouth tasted terrible. Her nose was running, and her eyes burned. She wiped her face on her shirtsleeve.

"Get back in the car!"

Rosa stumbled over some large stones on the side of the road. She fell into the gravel. Her bare feet were cold. *I wish I had my shoes!*

Andulov grabbed her by the back of her shirt and pulled her up. "Go on, now! Get in the car."

Rosa crawled into the backseat. She began to sob. "I said shut up!"

Rosa drove her face under her arm to hide the sound of her crying.

Andulov started the engine, spun his tires in the gravel, and raced down the road. This time, Rosa braced herself for the bumpy ride by hanging on to the edge of the seat. A sharp turn in the road, however, took her by surprise and slammed her against the window. She rubbed her forehead, where she felt a tiny bump. Dr. John had told her she would always feel better if she drank a lot of water. Maybe water would help her head. She groped in the darkness for her water bottle and drank until the bottle was empty.

*But my head still hurts! I need to drink more water!* Rosa felt guilty opening the clasp to the doctor's large black bag, but her mouth tasted yucky. She dug into it, hoping to find another bottle of water. Her fingers instead found a flashlight. It was big and heavy, but she managed to drag it out of the bag and lay it on the seat. A couple more searches of the bag didn't turn up any water, so she quietly closed it.

With Dr. John gone, Rosa felt completely alone. Now, she wondered if she would ever see her family again. Dr. John had promised her he was taking her home. She was worried about Andulov. He was mean, and he didn't care if he hurt her. She was pretty sure he had no plans to take her home.

Rosa started wondering how she could get away from him. She had seen a show on television where a woman blinded a man with a flashlight. She sat up and pulled the flashlight to her chest. She first thought of hitting Andulov on the head with the light, but that would only make him madder than he already was. She leaned toward him.

"Can I have some water? Please."

Andulov turned his head and looked back at her. "You idiot! Sit down. We're almost to the airport."

Rosa held the light tightly with both hands. She was very afraid now. Her little fingers barely wrapped around the flashlight. She wanted very badly to get away from him, but if she did try to shine the light in his eyes, it might not work. Maybe he would just laugh at her or stop the car and try to shoot her as he had shot Dr. John.

Rosa thought about her parents and her brother, Pedro. They were probably crying right now, wondering where she was. *I don't want them to cry anymore!*

Rosa pushed the button on the flashlight to test it. It was pretty bright. It made her blink when she shined it on her own eyes. Once she could see again, she stood up, right behind Andulov's head.

"I'm really thirsty!" she shouted in his ear.

This time, when he whipped his head around, Rosa was ready. She aimed the light right in his eyes. Andulov brought his hands to his face. Rosa watched him try to regain control of the steering wheel. The Explorer hit something so hard that she flew over the back of the seat and landed right next to him. She held on tightly to the flashlight. He grabbed her by the throat and began to squeeze.

"You brat! You trying to get me killed?"

Rosa gasped, trying to get her breath. She pushed the flashlight against his chest, but he wouldn't let go. She wanted to kick him, but she couldn't lift her legs. Andulov pitched her against the passenger door and pulled the flashlight out of her hands. Rosa's arm and elbow ached. She rubbed her arm, but it still hurt. Now, Andulov had Dr. John's flashlight. Rosa saw him rolling the flashlight around in his hands.

"Why did I ever agree to do this?" He pounded the flashlight into the palm of his other hand. Rosa swallowed hard. A wave of nausea came over her. She threw up all over the front seat and on Andulov's pants. "Oh, no!" Andulov dropped the flashlight and jumped out of the car. Rosa watched him wipe his hands on the ground and then walk to the back of the car.

"We've got a flat tire!" Andulov yelled. He pounded on the passenger window and opened the door. "It's your doing. Get out and help me!"

Rosa shivered. It was cold and dark. She had no coat and no shoes or socks. Her tiny feet felt like popsicles when she touched them. "I'm c-c-cold." Rosa's teeth were chattering. She felt as though she were going to throw up again. *That will make him very angry!* She brought her hand to her mouth and swallowed.

Andulov threw his hands in the air, slammed the door, and headed to the back of the SUV.

"Of course, you can stay in the car. You are of no use to me!"

Rosa crawled into the backseat and watched as he opened the tailgate and rummaged around for what turned out to be a spare tire and a jack. She had seen her uncle change a tire and knew it was hard work. She remembered how the car tipped a little once the jack got under the car to free the wheel from the road.

*Is this my chance to run?*

Rosa decided she would wait until just the right moment when Andulov was busy jacking up the car. Then she would jump out and run as fast as she could. At least she wanted to run. Could she? She was so tired and felt so sick, she wasn't sure she could run fast enough. But Rosa was smart. She knew better than to go in the same direction they had been traveling. She would head the opposite way, and she wouldn't stop until another car met her on the road. Just the thought of being free made her heart beat fast.

Rosa could hear Andulov pounding on something, and it seemed to be making him mad. Finally, the car's wheels rolled forward a little. Then the car began to tilt to the right, forcing Rosa against the door. With the racket of the jack pumping the car up off its left front wheel, Rosa sensed it was time to go. She opened the door to the cold night. She began to shake. She was wobbly and afraid, but she jumped out with both feet, landing in the gravel. A sharp rock cut into the bottom of her foot, and she wanted to cry. Rosa tried to take a step forward, but every time she tried to move, her chest hurt. This was her only chance. She started walking as fast as she could away from the car. She turned her head to see if Andulov was coming after her. He was walking around the car, carrying the flashlight.

*Does he know I'm gone?*

Rosa saw him kick the passenger door shut. Then he turned his flashlight right on her as she stood in the center of the highway. Stunned, she stopped and just stared at him. She felt like the little mouse her Mamá had caught one time when she had turned on the kitchen lights.

"I see you!" Andulov began moving toward her.

Like the mouse, Rosa scurried away as fast as she could. She knew he would try to catch her. She just had to be quicker. The mouse had escaped into a hole in the wall. Rosa didn't have any place to hide. Andulov was getting closer and shining the light directly on her as she ran. What chance did she have when he could see her?

His shoes stirred up the gravel, creating a cloud of dust on the dry road. That made him cough, and it slowed him down. Rosa could smell the dust also. She coughed too as the dust reached her throat.

"Rosa! Come here."

His dirty hands were almost touching her. She remembered how she had won the big race at school. She gave it one more try and lunged away from his hands, which were inches from her neck.

Andulov grabbed for her. When he fell down, he made a lot of noise. Rosa heard him cussing and shouting at her. "When I get a hold of you, I'll beat you with this flashlight."

Rosa started walking fast again. It hurt too much to run. He was rolling around on the ground and rubbing his leg. Without the flashlight pointed right at her, she could find a place to hide. She rushed over to some big trees on the side of the road and hid behind one of the largest ones. She peeked around the trunk of the tree and watched him try to stand up. He was having a hard time. It looked as if his leg was hurt. He would stand and then fall down again.

Rosa slid down the side of the tree. Her behind hit the cold ground. She heard water running near her and crawled toward it. She found a ditch full of water hidden in the tall grass. It was like the ditch where Andulov had thrown Dr. John. Remembering that he had been shot made her want to bawl, but she didn't dare make a sound. She wondered if he was still alive. When she got back home, she would tell her parents how Dr. John had made her fever go away.

Rosa had hunkered down in the tall reeds, and when she looked up, she realized Andulov was standing just a few feet from her. He waved the flashlight around him in a circle. She lay completely flat against the ground. The light flickered over the very place where she was hidden.

She heard Andulov's legs moving through the tall grass. His feet crunched against the dry leaves. If he came any closer, he would trip over her. She could hear him breathing fast and remembered his bad breath. Rosa shuddered.

"Rosa! Come on out! If you do, I'll forgive you and take you home to your parents."

Rosa stayed put. He had promised her this before. She wasn't going to ever believe Andulov again.

She always won the game of hide-and-seek with Ana and Pedro because she could lie very still and make herself invisible. It was her very own magic trick. She was hoping it would work now. *I'm wishing myself invisible!*

Rosa saw Andulov lean over the very place where she was lying. His stubby hands parted the grass, folding it over the spot where she lay flattened against the ground. The light shot right over her and found its home in the ditch. When the light hit the water, it shot right back into her eyes. She closed them, figuring if she couldn't see the light, it couldn't see her. Finally, after holding her breath for what seemed like forever, Andulov stood, turned, and started walking away.

"I'm leaving you behind, Rosa! The rattlesnakes will find you soon. I saw one in the ditch!" Andulov laughed and clapped his hands. "Come on out, little snake. Rosa is waiting for you!"

Rosa's whole body shook. *I hate snakes!* She had to make a choice, and she chose the rattlesnake over Andulov. She heard his foot dragging in the gravel on the side of the road. He seemed to be waiting for her to show herself and run for her life. But she did not.

It wasn't long after that, Rosa heard Andulov open the door to the SUV, start it up, and drive away. She could hardly believe he was gone. Maybe he would be right back. She lay in the grass for several more minutes before she even dared to open her eyes. All she could hear was the water running through the ditch and the wind stirring in the grass.

Finally, after what seemed like forever, Rosa tried to stand. Her right arm hurt so badly it made her want to lie down again. But she knew she had to find a way home. It was hard for her to see anything now. There were no lights from the SUV to guide her. She took a few careful steps toward the road. She stepped on a thorn from a cactus. "Ouch!" It was too dark to pull the thorn out of her foot, so she would just have to hop along the best she could.

When she felt the gravel between her toes, she started walking the opposite way from where Andulov had gone. Rosa had never been so scared. Her legs ached. Her left foot was cut up from the rocks and pierced by the thorn. She couldn't bend her right arm. To keep it from hurting, she had to hold on to it with her left. But somehow, this didn't matter. She was brave and she was free.

Rosa tried to think of something happy. She remembered her friends Ana and Pedro. They made her smile. Thoughts of seeing them again kept her from feeling sorry for herself. It was lucky that Andulov had gone away because she didn't think she could run from him again. She was feeling very sick.

Rosa got braver and moved to the middle of the highway. How else would anybody find her if she was on the side of the road where the grass was tall and it was dark?

The headlights rushed up behind her so quickly she didn't have a chance to jump out of the way. Would the driver hit her? Thankfully, the driver saw her and stopped just in time to keep from hitting her. Rosa was happy she didn't get run over. A man jumped out of the car and ran to her. He had a flashlight, just like Andulov's. It was Andulov!

"Do you really think I'm so stupid to just leave you out here? I knew if I waited long enough, you'd show yourself."

Rosa tried to breathe, but it seemed as if there was no air. Andulov sucked it all up as he loomed over her. Her legs and arms felt numb. She had no fight left in her. Andulov picked her up and carried her to the SUV. There was nothing else she could do but go with him. A few tears rolled down her cheeks, but there was no use even crying about it. She was never going home.

# CHAPTER 32

Penny and Leo were back on the highway and just ten minutes from the airport. The delay at the broken roadblock and the attention to the wounded deputy, doctor, and the dead deputy had cost them valuable time. Leo figured they were too late to rescue Rosa. She was probably heading to San Diego by now. And the other women Penny thought she saw on the plane? What about them? *We don't even know who they are.* He dreaded arriving at Santa Rosa and finding the tarmac empty.

A feeling of heaviness covered him. He felt alone, even though Penny was at his side. The despair pressed against his chest. He looked out the windshield; the road ahead was a dark canvas broken only by the white ribbon that divided the highway. He reached for his radio and contacted the dispatcher for an update. He listened to several minutes of static over the airway before the dispatcher returned. "Sheriff, the deputies report that all is quiet at the airport. The Citation jet is still parked on the tarmac with its wing lights on."

Leo looked over at Penny, who was also pensive. She rubbed the side of her face and then pulled out a tissue. He watched her wipe her eyes, then stare out the passenger window. He cleared his throat, and that brought Penny's attention away from the window. "I thought Andulov would be there by now. I hope he wasn't using that plane as a decoy."

"You think he went to another airport?"

"I feel in my gut we've got the right one, but something's slowed him down."

"Could he have taken another road?"

"There are no turnoffs between here and the airport. He would have broken down on the side of the road or have been at the airport by now."

"Do you think Rosa is still alive?" Penny shifted in her seat as she zipped up her windbreaker. Leo saw her shiver, and he turned on the heater.

"I hate to say this, but she is better to him alive. It's one thing we've got working in our favor." The fan kicked on, and the heat began to permeate the car.

"I can't imagine what she has gone through." Penny said. Leo could see that her eyes were tearing up. He reached over and touched her gently on the arm.

"I wish I could tell you everything is going to be okay, but in cases like these, it's sometimes a matter of luck. And so far, we're not getting much of a break."

"What will happen when we get to the airport if the plane is gone?"

"The FBI will have to follow up at private airports in the San Diego area and hopefully apprehend him on the other end."

"I thought the FBI didn't want to help you."

"Now that Andulov has taken Rosa across state lines, they have no choice."

"Are they on their way?"

"I don't know. I had trouble getting a message to Agent Brooks, but his aide promised he would tell him we are on the way to the Santa Rosa airport." Leo didn't want to worry Penny, but he wasn't sure the FBI would come. Not talking directly to Brooks made him feel uneasy.

Leo returned his focus to the road ahead. He had an iron grip on the steering wheel, and his shoulders were bent toward the windshield, causing his back to ache. He looked down at the speedometer, and it read eighty-five miles per hour. He let up on the accelerator. There was still a sense of urgency, but with Andulov still not at the airport, it worried him. He knew worry and speed didn't mix.

Leo was so tense that the voice of the Doña Ana County dispatcher, slicing through the silence, made him jump. "Sheriff, I checked again, and there is still no sign of the Cadillac SUV or any other vehicle at the airport. Is that plane a decoy?"

The dispatcher had wondered the same thing. Leo thought they were heading to the right location, but nothing was making sense right now. He just had to rely on his gut instinct.

"Tell your deputies not to move out of position. I'll be there in less than ten minutes, and we can decide what to do next. Also, tell them the FBI has been notified."

"I wonder what could have happened to Andulov and Rosa?" Penny asked. Leo knew Penny wasn't going to let up on her questions. She was worried, and she had a right to talk it through with him. He just hated to give her suppositions. Assuming things never got him anywhere.

"I'm not sure what's up, but keep an eye out for anything unusual. Maybe Andulov's car broke down or a gunshot created a slow leak in a tire. He might even be waiting to ambush the police, if he thinks they are on his tail."

As soon as he said it, he regretted even bringing up the possibility of Andulov lying in wait for the police. Penny looked a little pale now. He could tell she didn't like thinking about Andulov firing at them.

"I think it is highly unlikely he would take on the police without provocation," Leo said. "I'm sorry I suggested that, but he's got to be around here somewhere." Leo flipped on his flashers. At sixty miles an hour, he guessed he would be at the airport entrance in less than seven minutes. That was still good time.

The Mustang's tires pounded the road, matching the cadence of his heartbeat. The car was outracing its headlights, and this made it almost impossible to guess where the road led next. Leo flicked on his bright lights as the Mustang moved into a long narrow curve. The headlights spread like a beacon over a broad swath of the highway and illuminated the large cottonwood trees growing on both sides of the road. The tree limbs were swaying to the rhythm of the wind. It was all very distracting, even to an excellent driver like Leo. He tried to adjust his hold on the steering wheel, but perspiration was running down his arms.

He entered the curve with the precision of a racecar driver and looked for a disabled SUV at every turn, but the highway appeared to be empty. As he pulled out of the curve, he let out a sigh and wiped his sweaty hands on his uniform. He knew that a long stretch of straight highway lay before them. They would make excellent time now.

Leo saw that Penny was sitting up, her right hand pressed against the dashboard. She was scanning every crevice where the car's headlights landed. He was sorry he had worried her.

After several miles, Penny looked as though her back was hurting too. She rubbed it and started to sit back in the seat, but then bolted forward. "Stop! I see something in the road!"

Leo saw nothing, but he lightly pumped his brakes. The high speed caused the wheels to vibrate anyway, and then the whole car began to shake. He could smell burning rubber.

"Darn it!" he yelled. "Hang on!" Leo swerved left to avoid the dark blob, which he now spotted in the middle of the road. The Mustang's rear end bounced off of the large trunk of a tree. He rolled down the window and pointed his flashlight at the area where Penny had seen the looming shape. She jumped out of the car and ran to the center of the road where she picked something up.

"It's a stinky old blanket!" Penny said. She held her left hand over her nose as she carried it to Leo and showed him her mistake. "Sorry. I am so nervous about finding Rosa, I overreacted."

"It stinks like vomit! Get rid of it."

Penny slung the blanket into the ditch and climbed back in the car. She was panting and her face was flushed. "Now I wish I had a bottle of water to wash my hands. We should have thought about picking some up at the convenience store."

Leo ignored her and jumped out of the car to check for damages. Fortunately, there was only a minor dent in his left rear fender, but his left taillight was history. Leo tried to control his frustration. *God, another delay!* He didn't say that out loud, but he wanted to. It would only make Penny feel worse. He thought he could smell the vomit on Penny's hands. It was making him sick too.

It took a few minutes for the Mustang to get back up to making good time. Thankfully, it was a direct shot to the airport. Nothing would hold them back now.

---

Penny was feeling like an idiot for making Leo nearly wreck the car. Maybe she should just shut her eyes and keep quiet until they arrived. Leo had kicked on the flashers and turned on the siren again. Penny knew the siren wasn't getting them there any faster, but maybe it made Leo feel like it. Cars, which seemed unlikely in this rural area, would certainly pull over if they heard and saw them approaching well past the speed limit.

Penny studied him. If Leo was angry with her, it didn't show. He was forever the gentleman, she thought. He had even been kind to Dr. Márquez as he'd listened to the doctor's confession and placed him under arrest. Now, Leo was staring intently at the highway. His eyes didn't even blink. She considered how much resolve and concentration it took to be in law enforcement. Was she up to it? It had shaken her to see the dead officer and the blood rushing out of the wounded deputy. But she knew she could handle that part of the job. It was the frustration of seeing a target and watching a crime taking place and not being able to do anything to prevent it. That's what drove her crazy. *What good does it do for me to see if I can't help?*

"We'll be at the airport in a few minutes," Leo said as he looked over at her. She saw a smile on his face and sensed his relief. "I'm going to have to ask you to stay in the car when we get there. There will only be the two deputies and me to take on Andulov and the pilot. I requested a helicopter from the FBI, but I don't know if they will actually send it. I never received any confirmation."

Penny nodded her head. She wanted to help Leo, but she had no intention of taking on Andulov.

The Mustang was picking up speed again. Maybe Leo didn't even notice it, but to Penny, it seemed as though they were going faster than they had gone before. She didn't dare look at the speedometer.

But then again, maybe it was just her nerves. She was exhausted from everything and wanted it to be over. Penny decided her time would still be best spent keeping her eyes on the road. It would distract her from worrying about what they might find at the airport. She braced her body with her hand on the dash again and peered at the dark highway. Every waving tree branch caused little palpitations in her chest. The combination of the speed and her anxiety about possibly seeing Andulov again was rattling her resolve to stay the course.

When she saw the small form moving in the road, it caught her off guard. *Could it be Rosa?* She started to yell at Leo to stop, but then she saw a frightened red fox, caught momentarily in the beams of the headlights. Thankfully, it scampered out of harm's way.

Penny was flustered and furious with herself. Now she was overreacting to everything that moved. She threw her head against the bucket seat. She could only hold out hope that Leo was right about Rosa. Andulov had every reason to keep her alive. She could not be so hopeful, however, that Rosa would not endure something in Andulov's care that would scar her for life. The thought of Rosa being sexually molested filled her with rage. She squeezed her hands into fists until her nails pierced her palms. The flashing red lights rippled through the car and bounced off the windows, creating a sinister atmosphere that brought goose bumps to Penny's arms. *If Andulov isn't at the airport*, she wondered, *and he isn't on the side of the road, where could he be?* A wave of panic enveloped her when she thought of a third possibility. "Leo, what if we are right behind Andulov? We could run into the back of him, going this fast!"

# CHAPTER 33

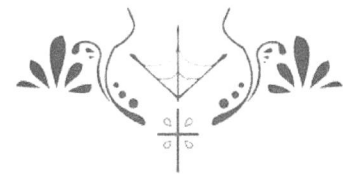

The rest of the way to the airport, Leo and Penny saw nothing out of the ordinary. They passed only an old pickup truck, which pulled over to let them pass. Leo turned into the driveway of the Santa Rosa Airport and called the dispatcher to announce his arrival. "What frequency are your deputies on?" "Channel 10."

"Can you break one-zero for me? My cell phone is running out of power."

"Yes, sir. I'll clear the channel for your use."

"Tell them I'm here, and I'll communicate with them by my hand radio from now on. And could you alert the state police to monitor the channel? If the FBI isn't on their way, I may request their help."

"Will do, and good luck, Sheriff."

Leo turned to Penny, who still looked agitated. There was fear in her eyes, and he didn't know how to change that. He tucked the Mustang behind the terminal, which held only one other car, a late model Ford Explorer. He presumed it belonged to the air traffic controller.

"Penny, I'm going to check things out on the tarmac. Stay low, and keep the doors locked."

"I want to go too!" She opened the car door and started to exit. "Let me check the jet out first. I'll call you to let you know if it's safe for you to join me."

"But I thought your cell phone was dead!"

"I've still got a couple of bars. I'll hold them just for you." Leo reached under his seat and pulled out a .38 snub-nose revolver. "Can you shoot?"

"My father taught me with a gun just about like that." She grabbed for it and checked to see if it was loaded.

"You only have five shells out of six." "I hope I don't have to use it."

"I'll leave the keys in the car, just in case." Leo pointed his flashlight into the SUV parked next to them. It looked harmless enough. He opened the trunk of his car and pulled out his automatic rifle. He still had ammunition clipped to his belt, so he was all set.

He walked around the terminal, which was nothing more than an abandoned metal airplane hangar, with a back door that led to a Dumpster and a front door facing east. The lights were on in the waiting room as Leo passed by, but he could not see anyone milling around there. He knew the air traffic controller's perch was on the north side of the building. He wondered for a moment if he should check in with him to see about the status of the Citation. Then, he figured it would be faster to check it out for himself.

There were two light poles one hundred feet apart on the tarmac, which provided limited visibility at night. As far as Leo could tell, there was no sign of the Escalade, but in the distance, he could see lights on the wingtips of the Citation jet. He pulled out his radio and told the two deputies he was on his way. "Meet me behind the refueling shed to the north of the jet."

# CHAPTER 34

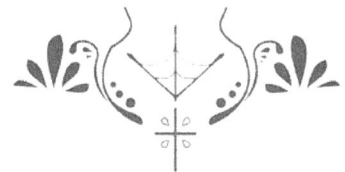

Rosa could hear Sergei talking on his cell phone as he stood outside of her bathroom stall. She was barely holding on to the toilet seat. Her stomach hurt. Every time she leaned forward, she felt dizzy, as if she had just got off the merry-go-round at the park. She was about to wet her pants when they had arrived at the airport, and she had begged him to let her go. She could tell he wasn't happy about it, but he had parked the car behind a big building, and they'd entered through the back door.

"Yes, but why do I have to change airports?"

Rosa hated the sound of his voice, and she drowned it out by flushing the toilet. She slowly opened the door to the stall. Andulov's loud voice was bouncing off the bathroom walls and hurting her ears. When he saw her, he turned his back on her and continued to talk on the phone. She moved to the sink to wash her hands.

"The FBI did what? Okay. Okay. I'll tell my pilot to file another flight plan."

He slammed his hand against the bathroom wall. Rosa was bending over the bathroom sink, splashing water on her face. "Come on!" He yanked Rosa away and pushed her out the door into the long, dark hallway. Rosa could hear him on his cell phone again. Why did his voice make her feel sick?

"George, we've got to file another flight plan. We're heading to Hayward, California, instead of San Diego. Seems the FBI is already there. Stefan said they are crawling all over the place. Yep. I'm here and am heading to the jet now."

Rosa watched as Sergei threw his hands in the air and then frowned at her. "Stay close to me!" She followed him down the hall as he talked to someone else. "Yes, Guapo, she's here and we're all set. I'll see you shortly in Hayward."

The corridor had a small light that created dark shapes on the walls. Rosa jumped as she walked by a big shadow that looked like a monster. She began to shake again. It was cold in the hall. She rubbed her arms, but it didn't help. The only good thing was she didn't feel like she would throw up again. In the car, she hadn't been able to think straight, and her eyes had been fuzzy. Now things looked clearer, but Rosa didn't like what she saw. She followed Andulov out of the building, like a puppy trailing after her mother. She had seen puppies do that. She wasn't much more than a dog now. She walked by the place where the airport threw their trash. It smelled bad. When they turned the corner around the big Dumpster, Andulov stopped so fast that she ran into the back of his legs and fell down. She didn't think she could stand up by herself. Her legs were shaky.

He grabbed her by the arm and pulled her to his side. He took Dr. John's flashlight and shined it into another car that was parked right next to his. It had not been there when they'd gone to the bathroom.

---

Penny placed the revolver in the right-hand pocket of her windbreaker and zipped it closed. She couldn't let her fear of Andulov keep her from giving Leo some backup. She did a quick check of the other pocket to make sure that her pepper spray was also still secure. With the gun and the pepper spray, she felt safe enough to move to Leo's location, but she had to hurry. Her hand was on the door handle of the car when a bright light bounced off her eyelids. She placed her hands over her eyes, waiting for her pupils to adjust. *What the heck is going on?*

Someone started pounding on her window. When the light flew from her eyes to theirs, she could see a man and a child standing outside the car. She reached her hand inside her pocket, fingered the revolver, and turned the safety off. She considered lowering the window to ask them what they wanted, but when the light fell on the child's face, she recognized Rosa. Penny tried to scream, but fear sucked the sound from her throat. Was this really happening, or was it another remote viewing? It was the gun that gave up Andulov's identity. Penny had already seen his pistol up close, and she would never forget it. The tan grip was oily from the grit of his hands—filthy hands. He had the gun pointed right at her. This was no dream.

Penny sat paralyzed in the passenger seat. Even if she could shoot at Sergei, she was unsure of her aim, and she might hit Rosa.

"Open the door!" Andulov yelled. Penny did not move.

"Open the door, or I'll kill you!" Penny knew he meant it. She couldn't see Rosa's face, but knew she was petrified. The last thing Rosa needed was seeing Penny take a bullet. She waited another beat, just hoping he would give up and go away. He didn't.

Penny opened the door slowly. Andulov jerked her out of the car. She stumbled forward and fell into him.

"Ah, we meet again!" The flashlight gave Andulov a grisly look. He gave her a big smile. His horrid breath made her tremble. She reared back from his face, but he pulled her close again.

"So you are mine after all!" He breathed in deeply and pushed the gun into her shoulder blades. Penny hoped that by staying calm, Andulov wouldn't check to see if she was armed. Why should she be?

Rosa began to cry and pull away from Andulov. He dropped his hand from Penny's waist and yanked Rosa backward. "You are not going anywhere!" Rosa cried louder, and he yelled, "Shut up!" Rosa stopped whimpering, but tears were still tumbling down her face. Penny saw that Rosa's eyes were pinched, as if she had seen more than her share of bad things. Penny wanted to tear into Andulov and make him pay for his cruelty, but she knew better. She dropped her head and let her hair fall over her face. There was no hiding from Andulov, but at least now, he could not see her eyes.

Andulov pulled her hair so hard that it felt like it was coming out at the roots. "I want to see your eyes!"

Penny moved toward him, trying to relieve the discomfort. Andulov forced her head upright and gouged his pistol into her ribs. She inhaled and cried out. "No!"

Andulov growled. "You had it coming. Take Rosa's hand. You can start earning your keep." He laughed and pushed them over to his SUV.

Penny wondered if she would ever take a full breath again. Tears poured down her face. Rosa looked up at her and threw her arms around her legs. Andulov withdrew the pistol from Penny's body long enough to remove an automatic rifle from the floor of the backseat. "We might as well walk the rest of the way. I like my odds with the two of you in front of me."

He shoved Penny forward with the butt of the rifle. "I said walk!" Rosa tugged on Penny's arm as they both limped along. She could see Rosa was barely holding on. She had to drag Rosa, whose feet were bleeding. "Please don't take me with you. I want to go home!" Rosa pulled hard on Penny's arm, resisting her.

"Let's go! We've got to be airborne in ten minutes," Andulov growled.

Penny was sure if he thrust the gun into her body one more time, it would go off. She turned and looked at his eyes, which she could barely see in the glow of the tarmac lights. His pupils were virulent and as dark as the night sky. She bent down and touched Rosa's face. "Please. We've got to go with him." She helped Rosa take a few steps until she was sure she could walk on her own. Penny wished she could sweep her up in her arms and protect her from experiencing any more horror, but she guessed that their nightmare was just beginning. When they rounded the corner of the terminal, she saw the plane's lights flashing and heard its engine idling on the tarmac. She was afraid even to wonder where Leo was. She looked all around but could see nothing but the sliver of Andulov's flashlight pointing toward their unknown future. She could only hope Leo was hiding behind the row of trees just north of the runway as he had planned. She felt the heavy weight of the revolver on her right side and hoped she didn't have to use it.

# CHAPTER 35

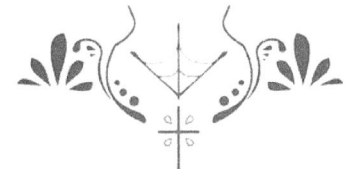

Leo met the two deputies behind a small refueling shed. It was situated conveniently at the end of the tarmac, out of sight of both the pilot and anyone else approaching the plane. The aircraft's engine had just fired up, which Leo figured indicated the pilot was planning to move toward the runway. He wouldn't let that happen, but he hesitated to ground it without any sign of Andulov.

"Are you sure you didn't see anyone boarding the plane?" Leo asked the deputies again, even though he knew the answer.

"Yes, sir. It's been totally quiet for the past two hours."

He knew it was impossible for Andulov to get Rosa on that plane without the deputies noticing. *Where could he be?* Leo didn't have to wonder very long. He saw a shaft of light spreading across the blacktop. Leo observed three people approaching the jet. "We've got company!"

He recognized the shape and size of one of them, even in the murky light. It was Penny! *Why did I leave her alone?* He moved quickly to brief the officers. "One of them is a member of our department, Penny Larkin. She is holding the child's hand. I think that's Rosa Garcia. The man, I believe, is Sergei Andulov, Rosa's kidnapper."

Leo was devastated by his stupidity. In his hurry to stop the plane from taking off, he had placed Penny in danger. His hands were sweating. When he brought the automatic rifle up even with his chin, he saw that his hands were also trembling. He dropped his hands and let the butt of the rifle rest on the tarmac.

"Unless you have a clear shot of the suspect, don't fire." Leo cautioned. "Let's monitor the situation for a few minutes before we move in."

As the trio got closer, Leo could see that Rosa was limping and hanging on to Penny's hand. Andulov was bunched up behind them.

Rosa looked up at Penny, and Penny leaned down and gave Rosa a comforting pat on the shoulder.

Leo's mind raced. His decided to have the deputies, on command, run in opposite arcs around Andulov, Rosa, and Penny, while he ran straight toward them, trying to draw Andulov's gunfire. He hoped this would allow the officers to grab Rosa and Penny while he distracted Andulov. Leo was on the verge of ordering the officers to move when he noticed another man creeping up behind Andulov. It was too dark to see who it was, but he could hear the conversation clearly.

"Hey, Andulov! Where do you think you're going?" A slim thirty-something man stepped into the path of Andulov's flashlight. Andulov whipped his body around, causing Penny and Rosa to stumble. The newcomer's body cast a gangly shadow across the asphalt. He had a handgun pointed straight at Andulov's head. Andulov pulled the females up from the tarmac and wrapped his arms around them.

*Coward!* Leo knew Andulov would make Rosa or Penny take a bullet before he did. Leo motioned to the officers to hold up.

"Koble! You surprised me!" If Andulov was worried, Leo didn't think he showed it.

"Surprised? Did you forget that you owe me for delivering four girls to your jet?" The man waved his pistol in the air.

"Márquez made that deal with you, not me," Andulov shouted over Rosa's cries.

"Where is the doc then?"

"He had an unfortunate accident and won't be going with us this evening."

"I want my money now."

Rosa was now making a racket, and it was difficult for Leo to hear. It frustrated him, but he knew that Andulov must have been having trouble hearing too because he clamped his hand over Rosa's mouth and yelled. "I don't have any cash on me. What can I do to make this okay?"

"If you get on that plane, I don't have any guarantee I'll ever see you again."

"You saw all that vodka in the hangar! Take as much as you want!"

"Thanks, but no."

"Look, I'll be back in El Paso in two weeks. Put a padlock on the hangar, and you can keep it as collateral until I get back."

The man moved closer to Andulov. "I'm no fool!"

"That vodka is worth a quarter of a million! I'll split the profits with you."

Leo had heard and seen enough. He motioned for the two officers to circle left and right while he stepped into Andulov's line of fire. "Hold it right there!" Leo ran headlong toward Andulov, Penny, and Rosa.

---

Andulov released his hold on Penny and aimed his gun at Leo. Penny yanked the revolver from her pocket and fired point-blank at Sergei. A spray of blood from Andulov's chest blew back on her jacket. Penny watched in horror as Andulov, instead of trying to take her down, raised his gun again, still determined to shoot Leo. Before he could fire, his large frame buckled and dropped like a rock onto the pavement. He fell against Rosa, who began screaming and kicking as she tried to get out from under him. Leo ran toward Andulov and rolled him off Rosa. Penny watched as Leo checked to see if Andulov was breathing. Distracted, she did not see Koble move toward her. He grabbed her gun and pulled her close to his chest. Deputy Rogers approached Koble from his left side, but Koble whipped around so quickly that Penny was now in the line of fire. The deputy pulled back.

"Hold your fire!" Leo yelled.

Rosa scrambled away from Leo and ran toward Penny. "Don't leave me!"

"No, Rosa. Stay away."

Penny knew that Rosa was too confused and tired to go forward. She fell back onto the tarmac, and it appeared she had fainted. Deputy Rogers ran to Rosa, scooped her up, and carried her away from the conflict.

Leo charged toward the man holding Penny. "No, Leo, stop!" "Do what the lady says, Sheriff, and no one will get hurt."

---

Leo watched helplessly as the man named Koble jammed his gun into the side of Penny's neck and dragged her by her hair, backpedaling toward a hangar whose double doors were wide open. He had stripped Penny of her revolver, but apparently couldn't juggle both weapons. He threw her gun on the ground, causing a wayward bullet to ricochet across the tarmac. Leo and Officer Manigeras followed them and took cover to the right of the doorway to the hangar. Leo leaned around the side of the entrance and peered inside, hoping to see where the gunman and Penny had gone. All he could see was a black hole, but the pungent smell of aircraft fuel dropped over him like a spider's web. He was caught. Firing a gun in this environment could cause a flashpoint explosion.

"We can't make a move just yet," Leo said. He looked over at the deputy for confirmation that he understood. Leo wondered if Koble had a plane in the hangar or if he was just trying to hold them off. The dismal lighting of the tarmac was of no help. He had to find out what was happening inside that building. He took a chance and flicked on his flashlight, then moved it in concentric circles around the cavernous interior, hoping the man would not shoot at him or, even worse, shoot Penny. The beam finally found the glint of a metal propeller. Leo heard an engine turn over, and then he heard what he dreaded most: a propeller spinning, faster and faster. He guessed that Penny was on the plane because there had been no gunfire. "Be ready to take out the pilot when the plane exits the hangar!" Leo was angry over the situation in which he had placed Penny. If anything happened to her, he would never forgive himself.

Leo and Officer Manigeras had their guns pointed at the double doors as the roar of the engine came closer. Leo's hands were shaking, and he hoped the deputy wouldn't notice. When the nose of the aircraft punched out of the hangar, Koble surprised them and fired, hitting Manigeras and bringing him to his knees. Leo returned fire, but not before Koble slammed the plane's door shut and roared past him on his way to the tarmac. On the run, Leo shot at the tires, hoping to hobble the plane that way.

He couldn't contain his rage. "Damn it! I can't stop him!" The plane was picking up speed. Leo ran behind it, firing recklessly at the wheels. In the darkness, the rifle had missed, and now the wheels were lifting off the runway. *I've lost her! Please, God, no!*

Leo looked back and saw Manigeras attempting to stand. "I'm okay, Sheriff. My Kevlar saved me."

Leo heard the sound of a helicopter in the distance. The FBI had arrived after all, but it was too late! He had no idea who this Koble was or where he was headed, but he was pretty sure Penny had gone with him, and he was going to do whatever he could to get her back.

# CHAPTER 36

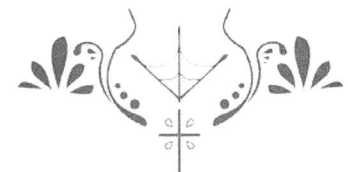

Don Koble kicked Penny in the legs, and she fell forward into the only row of seats. He yanked her to her feet and shoved her toward the back of the plane. Penny managed to crawl in between the two passenger seats and stuff herself in the tail. She rubbed her right leg, which was red and swollen, and rolled onto a pile of canvas bags. A smell of kerosene caught in her nose and throat, making her wheeze and cough. Penny had no time to worry about what was in those bags. Koble had fired up the engine, and the propeller was shaking the whole plane. Then the floor began to vibrate. The plane was moving! Penny watched out the rear window as they exited the hangar, turned left, and picked up speed. She couldn't see anyone trying to stop them from taking off. *Where is Leo?*

Penny grabbed hold of the metal bracing on the rear seat, trying to keep from being thrown about. Then she heard what sounded like bullets flying under the fuselage. *Doesn't he know I'm in here?* The gunfire under the belly of the airplane made her angry. She shook all over. But her anger also emboldened her to act. *I'm going to have to stop this guy myself!*

When Penny saw the aircraft tilt toward the dark sky, she made her move. Her only chance was the pepper spray in her windbreaker pocket. She ran to the front of the plane and leapt onto the pilot's back. She tried to douse his eyes, but the fall in the ditch must have ruined it.

"You bitch!" He lunged for her, but she pulled free. "I should have killed you when I had the chance."

Penny could feel the plane's wings tipping back and forth as Koble tried to regain control of the rudder. Penny crawled to the back of the plane and hung on to the metal legs of the passenger seat, tucking her head under it. When the aircraft hit the runway, the tires blew out. The aircraft lurched to the left, and she could hear a wing scraping on the side of the asphalt. An explosion threw her out of the plane. When she landed on the ground, she tried to move away from the crash site, but her right leg and her back hurt so badly, she could only whisper for help. "Leo!" But there was no one to hear her.

Orange flames were gnawing on the plane's wings, and the air reeked of gasoline and melting plastic. Penny managed to turn her head away from the intense heat and close her eyes. There was nothing left for her to see anyway. The tarmac warmed her like a blanket. She could hear the hissing of the fire as it closed in on her.

# CHAPTER 37

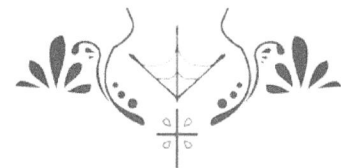

Leo gazed at the single-engine aircraft rising a few hundred feet above the runway. The plane was so small that only tiny points of light danced around the dark sky. Then, he watched as the lights began streaking toward the earth. He held his breath in anticipation of the crash.

When the plane hit the ground, its left wing tore off as it rammed the refueling shed where Leo and the deputies had first formulated their plans to rescue Rosa and Penny. A fireball blew a hole in the dark clouds. Leo threw his jacket over his head and started running toward the flames. He could not have Penny burn up inside that plane! His heart ached, and his chest heaved as he reached the airplane's small door and saw it mangled shut. Its hinges were shoved into the fuselage. Leo used his bare hands to pry away the sharp pieces of crumpled metal. They cut his fingers, and blood fell on his shirt. Somehow, the metal yielded to his will, and he climbed inside the plane. "Penny!" He called her name several times, but there was no answer. He saw the pilot wedged between the rudder and the instrument panel. Steam was rising from his body, and blood was gushing from his mouth and ears. The pilot opened his eyes and stared vacantly at him. Leo could tell flames would soon engulf the interior of the plane. Thankfully, it didn't take him long to realize that Penny was not on board! *Was she in the hangar all along? Did Koble kill her?* He had to make a judgment call. Would he rescue the pilot or go find Penny?

Rage hotter than the fire blazing around him coursed through Leo's veins. He forced his body through the door again, this time cutting up his legs and shredding his uniform. *Could she have been thrown out of the plane?* Leo bent down as low as he could, still protected by his jacket, and ran north beyond the fuel shed, calling her name. "Penny! Penny! Penny!" Sirens from a fire truck were drowning out his voice now. He shouted louder and louder, but there was no response.

He turned around and retraced his steps. In front of him, he saw a pool of gasoline and jogged left to avoid it. He tripped over Penny's body and fell to his knees. His hands touched the tarmac. The asphalt was sticky and blistering hot! The airplane fuel burst into flames, surrounding them. It licked at his arms. He jerked his hands off the ground, but not before he felt the sting of burning hair on his knuckles.

There was no time to find her pulse. He scooped Penny up, using his jacket to protect her, and ran through the flames. He looked back to see the fire swallow up the airplane's interior. He felt a twinge of remorse for not pulling the pilot out. He was sure he was dying, but it still filled him with regret.

The sweat was pouring off Leo's body as he navigated the runway, sidestepping burning embers of the scattered plane. Penny wasn't heavy. It was his arms that were slowing him down. He saw they were smoking. He was on fire! But he didn't stop until he reached the FBI helicopter that had just landed on a pad nearby.

FBI paramedics offered to take Penny from his arms, but Leo was reluctant to give her up. "Sir, your arms are smoldering!" He let Penny go and fell on the ground, rolling to douse any flames. An EMT threw a fire repellent on him, covering his arms and face with white powder.

Leo looked up at the EMT. He was afraid to ask the question, but he had to know. "Is she alive?"

"She's being loaded on the helicopter now."

Leo shamelessly burst into tears. When he wiped his eyes, they began to sting from the chalky substance that covered him. He looked back at the medic, pleading for answers.

"I asked, is she alive?" The medic ignored his question.

"Sir, we recommend you go with us to the hospital. Your arms need attention, and with burns, the sooner the better."

"But Rosa and the other girls!" Leo tried to stand up, but fell back on the pavement.

"The FBI has that covered, sir. Please, we need to go!" "Where is Special Agent Brooks?" Leo scanned the tarmac for him.

"He didn't join us, sir. Please, we need you to go with us now!" Leo finally gave in and let the EMT help him to his feet and walk him to the helicopter. He wanted to be with Penny more than anything anyway. The propeller was beating the air like an angry animal and causing ash from the explosion to float aimlessly into the air. The smoke had permeated everything and had even spread inside the helicopter. It was difficult to see as Leo climbed on board. He looked around for Penny. He saw a slender shape lying on a stretcher at the back of the plane, covered by a white sheet. Leo's heart crashed in his chest. Tears rolled down his cheeks. *Please, God. She can't be dead.* He cried out so loudly that the pilot turned to see what had happened to the sheriff.

A paramedic stripped off Leo's jacket and wrapped a damp gauze bandage loosely around his arms. He guided him to a passenger seat at the front of the helicopter, but Leo refused. He threw the gauze pack onto the floor and shoved his way back to the stretcher. He crouched opposite the medic, whom he could now see through all the smoke. He was preparing an IV. *She's alive?*

"We are trying to keep the smoke out of her lungs, Sheriff," the medic said, apparently reading Leo's mind. He had made the sheet into a kind of tent to shelter Penny from the billowing smoke that surrounded them all. The medic lifted the sheet so Leo could see that Penny was breathing on her own. She moaned and tried to open her eyes. Leo's own lungs filled with the transient air as he gasped for joy. He didn't care that he was choking on the smoke or that the hair on his arms was burned away. He was consumed with happiness.

"Sheriff, she has been calling for Leo. Would that be you?"

Leo did not answer him. He turned his head away so that the medic wouldn't see that his eyes were filled with tearful gratitude. God had answered his prayers. He felt the helicopter lifting off its pad. As they got airborne, Leo felt buoyant too, as if a heavy yoke of sorrow had lifted off his shoulders. He gazed out the window as the chopper climbed above the low-hanging clouds on its journey to University Medical Center. He dreaded hospitals. His luck there had been dismal, but Leo knew he wouldn't want to be anywhere else right now. No matter how long it took, Leo wanted to be there to help Penny get well.

# CHAPTER 38

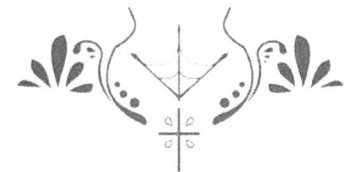

It was 5:16 a.m. on Saturday, and Leo sat in the waiting room outside of the intensive care unit, longing for information on Penny's condition. His arms and hands were bandaged, with only his fingertips available to do anything but press speed dial on his cell phone. He'd called his office and reported that Rosa Garcia and four Mexican teenagers were in the hands of the FBI. He told them he was waiting for word about Penny Larkin and explained how valuable she had been in solving this case. Without her, he said, he was sure Rosa would have been on her way to San Diego. He wanted to pace up and down, but the emergency room doctor had told him to remain quiet for the next few hours and let the medicines he had injected do their work. A racing heartbeat or even walking fast could slow down the healing process. The nurse had covered the slices in his calves with antibacterial ointment. Thank God for his cowboy boots, which had deflected most of the damage to his legs. He would be left with scars, but that was a small price to pay for finding Penny.

The emergency room orderly had sent him into the showers to wash off the zinc borate powder and to clean his arms thoroughly. He had first-degree burns on his right arm and considerable redness on his left, but both would heal in a few weeks without anything other than antibiotics, salves, and patience.

Patience was not Leo's strong suit however, and as the night broke into a new day, he was still sitting there alone with his concerns for Penny, dressed in a set of the orderly's scrubs and a pair of his small tennis shoes in which Leo had shoved his large feet.

"Sheriff?" A man stood in the doorway of the waiting room. He was dressed in street clothes, but he had a stethoscope around his neck. His expression was serious.

"Yes!" Leo stood, a little too rapidly. He was light-headed, and his back hurt from sitting for so long. He grabbed the back of his chair and steadied himself.

"I'm Dr. Morton."

Leo's heart swelled with panic. Was he bringing news about Penny? His body felt like a balloon that held too much air. A tiny prick of bad news would cause his world to explode. He took a few steps toward the doctor.

"I've just come from seeing Dr. Jonathan Márquez. I called your office, and they told me you were in the ICU waiting room. Dr. Márquez would like to talk with you."

"How is he?" A mixture of relief and worry blew through him. "It is touch-and-go because the wound to his head is infected, probably from lying in the irrigation ditch. We removed the bullet from his arm, but he has a very high fever and a bad heart.

He is coherent and keeps mumbling your name." "Where is he?"

"Let me take you to him."

Leo walked out of the ICU waiting room and looked for the charge nurse. He asked her to call him if any report came back on Penny. He would return as soon as he could. Then he turned and followed Dr. Morton down a long, dimly lit hallway.

The hospital had placed Jonathan Márquez in a corner room set away from the general population. A uniformed El Paso police officer sat just outside of his door. Leo nodded to the guard, and then he entered the hospital room alone. Márquez's head was bandaged as was his right arm. His face was red; drops of sweat had puddled around his eyes and nose.

Leo found a clean washcloth in the private bathroom and used the tips of his fingers to soak the cloth in a basin of cool water. As he wiped it across the doctor's face, water trickled inside his bandaged arms.

"Thank you." The doctor tried to raise his hand but apparently thought better of it.

"Dr. Morton said you wanted to see me." "Did you get Andulov?"

"Andulov is dead." Leo watched carefully to see how Márquez would react. Márquez rolled his eyes back and shut them. Then he opened them again. "Good." That news seemed to relax him a little. Leo saw his eyes brighten. "Is Rosa okay?"

"Yes. Right about now, she should be arriving back home with her parents."

For some reason, this information did not please Márquez. He frowned. His heart monitor recorded a faster beat.

"I have a favor to ask you." "Go on."

"Could you contact my wife, Generosa, and tell her where I am?"

"Yes, of course."

"I want to make up for the big mistakes I made. Can you help me?"

"In the United States, kidnapping is a federal offense. It is out of my hands now. You would have to make a deal with the FBI."

"I'm not sure I trust the FBI." "Why not?"

Márquez began taking quick, shallow breaths. "They're on the take."

"I find your statement incredulous."

"You might want to check on the whereabouts of that special agent, Brown." The doctor was coughing now, and the sweat had reappeared on his brow. Leo lifted the towel and gently cleaned his face.

"You mean Brooks?"

"I don't remember his name. Just know he's dirty." He began to have spasms in his chest, and Leo heard his heart monitor speeding up.

A floor nurse popped her head in to check on Márquez. "Everything okay, Dr. Márquez?"

"Yeah, sure."

The nurse seemed satisfied, and she left as quickly as she had appeared.

"If you could just promise me…" The doctor put his hand on his chest and let it rest there. "I could give you some very helpful information about Rosa Garcia."

Leo pondered the request. If there were more to this crime, it would fill in many holes in the case that had nagged both him and Penny. After all, how many kids got kidnapped twice?

Márquez took in a shallow breath, raised his head slightly off the pillow, and wheezed into it. His cough was deep and dry. Leo brought a water glass with a straw to his lips. Márquez sipped from the straw, then licked his mouth, which still looked parched. His eyes were beginning to look vacant and dim.

"You know who Guapo Chavez is?" Márquez was whispering now, and Leo had to lean in closer to hear him.

"Yes, of course. He's the Baja cartel boss."

Márquez turned silent. He stared at the lone window in the room for several minutes. Streaks of morning light were punctuating a restless sky and casting shadows on the tile floor.

Thinking that Márquez was not going to say anything more, Leo turned to leave the room. He needed to get back to Penny. The doctor grabbed his chest. "My nitro!" Márquez pointed to a cup of small white pills on his bedside tray. Leo placed the nitroglycerin under Márquez's tongue and waited for him to recover. Leo could tell the doctor was experiencing considerable pain. Tears fell from his eyes.

"Chavez is Rosa Garcia's father." "What did you say?"

"Chavez. Rosa's father."Márquez was wheezing uncontrollably now, and his face was beet-red.

Leo retreated from the hospital bed as if the words Márquez had spoken were poisonous. "Do you have the strength to tell me how you know this?"

"Chavez knew Marvela Garcia when she was a teenager—in Torreon. By the time he found out she was pregnant with his child, she had married Manuel Garcia and moved to the United States. Chavez left things as they were until Rosa was about five. He had his men check on her, and they reported that Rosa did not look well. She was very small, too small for her age." Márquez's voice grew hoarse and raspy.

Leo helped him take another sip of water. Márquez's skin was gray. The blood had drained from his face, and perspiration had filled the creases in his forehead. He asked for another pill. Leo offered to swab his face again, but Márquez shook his head.

"Chavez arranged a kidnapping of Rosa, but it went bad. The man who agreed to grab her turned out to be mentally unstable. He hid her from Chavez's men, and that's when you found her under the bridge."

Leo remembered Penny's dream about seeing Rosa drinking Santa Inez Milk. Everyone in law enforcement knew the company belonged to Chavez.

"About six months ago, Chavez sent another man to check on Rosa. They took photos of her playing in the park. Chavez was alarmed. To him, Rosa looked emaciated. That's when he set a plan in motion that included Donnie Harper snatching her and Sergei Andulov directing her transport to Mexico. Andulov hired me to tend to her medical care. I was to take care of her until she boarded the plane to San Diego where Chavez would take care of getting her over the border."

"So you are saying that Marvela Garcia knew that it was Chavez who was paying her for the child?"

"Yeah." Márquez broke into a fit of coughing and struggled to continue. "She was to tell her husband a story about a family in California wanting Rosa to help them around the house."

"And Marvela accepted $50,000 for giving Rosa up?"

"Yes, but there was to be more, if she continued to keep her mouth shut."

This information totally disgusted Leo. He had actually felt empathy for Marvela, and she had been playing him all along. Leo felt a wrenching in his stomach. He thought he might vomit. The room was beginning to spin, so he found his way back to the bathroom. So much for keeping himself calm. He rested his injured arms on the basin and leaned over the toilet. Sweat dripped off his chin and onto his tennis shoes. He swallowed hard and breathed in deeply. After several minutes, the panic abated, and he stood upright. When he glanced in the mirror above the sink, he was shocked at what he saw. A disheveled and disillusioned man was standing there. He looked sallow and old against his borrowed green scrubs. Leo ran water over his face, ignoring the massive bandages on his arms. They were now soaking wet. The air conditioning kicked on and blew a torrent of chilled air over him. He began to shake.

Leo heard Márquez crying out for his nitroglycerin again, and his heart monitor was beeping erratically. He rushed out of the bathroom just as an aide and a nurse entered from the hallway. The nurse ordered the aide to get help as she set up the defibrillator paddles, but before they were in place, Márquez's heart monitor flatlined.

Leo heard a Code Blue call on the hospital's P.A. system. A team of doctors and a respiratory therapist, and a couple of med students shoved their way into the room. Confusion reigned, and fear swelled in Leo's heart, reminding him of Alejandra, as he watched the frantic work to save Márquez. He hated hospitals. No amount of shocking or pounding on his chest made any difference. The doctor's face was flushed from trying to save Márquez. Finally, he looked at the team, their scrubs soaked with sweat, and turned up his palms and shook his head. The aide pulled the paddles off Márquez's chest. The heart monitor continued its lifeless hum until the nurse silenced it. Jonathon Márquez was gone.

# CHAPTER 39

Penny was lying in the hospital bed with her eyes shut. Her pupils were slow in adjusting to the glaring lights that hung from the ceiling. Dr. Rogers had promised her that her eyesight would come back within hours. The heat from the fire had upset her optic nerves, but it was only temporary. Her eyesight was the least of her worries. She was pinned down in the bed so that she could not turn on her right side. Her left leg, which had two fractures, wasn't hurting right now, thank God, because the pain in her right hip was excruciating. The only thing she could do was sleep, but no amount of rest helped her remember what had happened. Instead, every time she drifted off, she would see targets she had already viewed. They kept cycling through her brain, like bad reruns. This time she was on a dusty street she knew all too well. She found their dirty brown house with the messy paint job and the decaying wood steps that led up to their front door. She walked inside, uninvited. Penny heard a clatter of dishes in the kitchen and fully expected to find the Garcia family gathered around the kitchen table. Instead, she found a strange woman rummaging through the kitchen cabinets. Penny watched as the woman took down one of Marvela's dishes and wrapped it in paper. She placed it in a box that sat on the counter. Then she took a white tube, which reminded Penny of a large Q-tip, and swabbed the skinned-up wallboard. The paint, the dullest of greens, was peeling off in the woman's hands. She cleaned her fingers with a wipe from a packet in her bag.

*What is she doing?* She wished she could ask her, but Penny knew she couldn't insert herself into the physical realm nor speak in the spiritual one. The woman took out her cell phone. "Doc, I got a high lead reading on the kitchen wall. This whole place is a lead dumping ground. I fully expect those Mexican pottery dishes to come out high too."

A sheriff's deputy walked in the room. The woman put her cell phone back in her purse. "The social worker has taken Pedro and Rosa to a foster home. Are you about done?"

"I'm done. Let's get this report to the health department, pronto!"

---

Penny woke up when a hospital aide, who had brought her a Sierra Mist, called her name and offered to help her sip some of it from a straw. The aide's figure was a blob of gray. She felt her soft hands guide Penny to a position where she could take a drink. She was grateful for the help. It was impossible to sit up, and she had to lean over the left edge of the bed to drink from the aluminum can. The cold drink burned like lava as it moved down her throat.

"Ooooh! My throat kills!"

"Sorry, miss. Sometimes, when a tube gets stuck in your throat during surgery, it rubs it raw."

Penny took another sip and rolled back onto her pillow. "That takes too much effort! But thanks." She closed her eyes, feeling sorry for herself.

The aide turned on the television. "This might help take your mind off things."

The sun was breaking through the windows. "Could you please close the curtains?" She kept her eyes tightly shut until she heard the drapes sliding shut. Someone touched her shoulder, and her eyes popped open. What she saw at first was a Picasso-like blur. As her eyes began to focus, she could make out the image of a man wearing green scrubs. She braced herself for a blood draw, but the man reached over and placed the tips of his fingers on her face. Slowly, her eyes made an adjustment, and she could tell his arms were covered with white gauze, like a mummy. His fingers began tracing her lips and then her cheeks. She looked into his eyes and saw a good and kind man. "Leo!" Penny's eyes filled with tears, which spilled on to her face. Leo wiped each one away with his fingertips.

"What happened to me?" Penny blinked and tried to get a better look at him. He appeared to have been injured. "No one is telling me anything about how I got here."

"You don't remember?"

"No. The last thing I recall was sitting in your Mustang. Everything else is blank!"

"You were in an airplane, and it crashed. You were thrown out before it exploded."

Penny grabbed onto the white sheet and pulled it over her shoulders. She was suddenly cold, though a few minutes before she had been too warm. This was way too much to take in right now in her weakened state. "How did I get here?"

"I saw you lying on the ground, and…" Leo hesitated. "I carried you to the FBI helicopter."

Penny was overwhelmed with gratitude. She was lucky to be alive. Even Dr. Rogers had indicated that, but he wouldn't fill her in on the details. "Wait until you are feeling stronger," he had cautioned.

"What happened to the pilot?" Penny needed to know that too.
"He was killed."

She began to shiver under the sheet. Leo found a blanket on a chair and covered her up. It didn't seem to help. She was so cold, she was certain she would never get warm again. Her teeth began to chatter. "I-I-I am freezing."

Leo left the room and got a nurse. Penny watched as the nurse plugged in a heating pad and placed it under her blanket. "Thank you." Slowly, the heat began to permeate her body, and the shaking subsided. Her breathing transitioned into a gentle, reaffirming rhythm that assured her that life would continue, and she would perhaps heal in time. Penny could see Leo pretty well now. She saw his injured arms, wrapped in white. Had he been burned when he'd carried her from the crash site? Her heart melted at the very thought of him picking her up off the tarmac and carrying her to safety. No one risked life and limb without caring. She saw him staring out the window. "What about Rosa?"

He turned back and looked concerned. "We've run into a complication with that."

"Is she okay?"

"Rosa and her brother, Pedro, are in foster care." "Is it lead poisoning?"

"How did you know that?"

"I was just dreaming about a woman who was testing the Garcias' kitchen. She said it was filled with lead."

"There are so many things going on there, I don't know where to begin. Maybe after you get home, we can talk about it."

"No, we need to talk about it now! I am wedged into this bed and can't move much. It's driving me batty. Please tell me."

Leo took a nearby armchair and pulled it close to Penny's bed. "First, I want you to know that Jonathan Márquez is dead. He died of a heart attack this morning in this hospital."

"I'm sorry for him. He was trying to save his family." This news made Penny feel very sad. She understood that he was tied in with Sergei Andulov, but she could relate somehow.

"If you are going to stay in this business, you have to separate yourself from your feelings. Criminals are criminals, even if they seem to be nice guys."

Did this mean Leo would ask her help again? Penny turned her head away from his gaze. She knew her emotions would be the worst challenge of serving law enforcement.

"The second piece of news is that Manuel Garcia is not Rosa's real father."

"What?" Penny turned back in disbelief. "Manuel is a wonderful father. It's Marvela who needs a good shaking."

"Dr. Márquez told me Rosa's father is Guapo Chavez, the head of the Baja cartel. He has been trying to get Rosa out of Marvela's hands for several years, suspecting that something was wrong since Rosa never seemed to grow."

"Hence, the two kidnappings!" "Yep!"

"Was that why Dr. Márquez was involved?"

"Precisely. Chavez was worried about Rosa's health and wanted to make sure she was under the care of a doctor until he got her to Mexico."

"But he failed." Penny said.

"Thanks to you, Penny. We couldn't have saved her without you."

Penny smiled, even though it hurt a little to do so. She had a hard time thinking Marvela Garcia was so cold as to sell her little girl to a drug cartel. "Are you sure Marvela was in on Rosa's kidnapping?"

"Márquez said she knew who the money was coming from, and if she kept her mouth shut, Chavez would send more."

"And what about Manuel Garcia? How was he involved?" "We're not sure, but we believe Manuel was duped into thinking Rosa was his real daughter and that he knew nothing about Marvela's plan to sell Rosa to help her mother with her cancer treatments."

Penny tried to reach for her can of soda but failed. Leo helped her lean over the side of the bed and take a few sips. "Thank you." Penny looked in Leo's eyes. She could see them clearly now. Her muddled vision was healing quickly. She noted there was no sign of wistfulness that had prevailed when she'd first met him two days ago in her driveway. She rested there in the serenity of his pupils. Leo stood and began pacing around the room. "Now we've got a bigger problem. Trying to protect Rosa from a drug cartel won't be easy."

"As crazy as it sounds, Guapo Chavez sounds like he might be the better parent."

"Chavez is one of the most wanted men in the world. That doesn't exactly qualify him for father of the year."

# CHAPTER 40

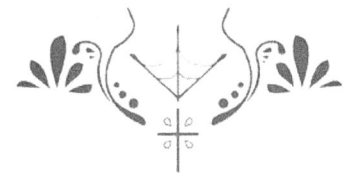

It had been forty-eight hours since Penny was admitted to the hospital. She was restless, and begged her doctor to discharge her, but he had said "no." She could sit up with the help of the electronic controls on the bed, and was reading the *El Paso Daily Sun,* when Zarn knocked on her open door and walked right into the room, without waiting for permission to enter. He was carrying a large bouquet of multi-colored balloons, one of which read, "Seeing is believing!"

"Hey there!" Penny laughed as Zarn wrestled with the helium balloons and tied them to a chair. They danced around in the sunlight that streamed into the hospital room. She had forgotten how Zarn's presence always brightened up her world, making her feel she could do anything and be anything.

His khaki shorts and golf shirt had been replaced with a pair of Levis and a denim button down shirt. His light brown hair had been contained with a little extra hair gel, having taken more time in front of the mirror. He brought so much good energy into the room that Penny felt as though she could jump out of bed and give him a hug. A twinge of pain raced through her right hip when she leaned toward him. She dropped her head back on the pillow and grimaced.

Zarn pulled a chair closer to the bed, and took her hand. "I am so proud of you, Penny. I placed you in a very tough situation, forcing you to prove yourself under an immense amount of pressure."

"I thought I couldn't do it. And I couldn't at first, but in the end, saving Rosa was all I could think of. I was driven to find her."

"And look what you accomplished."

"You mean killing a man?"

"The way I heard it, you probably saved Leo's life."

Penny was silent for a few moments. Her mind traveled back to the tarmac where she had been forced to kill Andulov at short range. She shivered, and pulled the blanket over her shoulders.

"Penny, you have to remember that you have a gift—a God-given skill—and you have an obligation to help others by using it for good. Sure, you sometimes can't help what you see, but you do have a choice in what you do about it."

---

Penny spent several more days in the hospital before being dismissed with the proviso that she have help 24-7 in her home. She hired a visiting nurse service, which sent her a lovely widowed woman in her mid-fifties. Clara was a blessing right from the beginning of their relationship. She made sure Penny followed her doctor's orders, even though Penny tried to bypass them often. Clara also drove her to physical therapy three times a week. For the first time in months, Penny was also enjoying home- cooked meals. Not since Porter's departure had she eaten so well. Three weeks after returning home from the hospital, Penny was well enough to move around the kitchen—with the help of a cane and a walking leg cast—to make coffee just the way she liked it. Clara was good at a lot of things, but making coffee was not one of them. She was sitting at the table in the bay window, enjoying the morning sun that rested on her shoulders, with her cup and reading the newspaper while Clara went to the grocery. It felt good to be home alone with her thoughts. Thankfully, she had picked up a couple of writing assignments, which helped her through the month, but in days to come, she wasn't sure just how she would manage.

A week after she had arrived home from the hospital, the news media was still reporting in about Rosa's amazing rescue and the discovery of four teenagers who had been kidnapped from Mexico. No mention had been made of Guapo Chavez, which wasn't surprising to Penny. No good could come of it. Nor was she surprised when she read the story of Rosa's rescue after the plane crash at Santa Rosa. The FBI had taken most of the credit for breaking up the child-trafficking ring that the Russian mafia had tried to launch along the border.

There was a small mention of Penny's injury during the plane crash, but she had been spared phone calls from reporters about her ordeal. The El Paso County Sheriff's Office had been given a small nod for aiding the FBI, but the press was abuzz about the agency's fine work, and even the president had called the agency to congratulate it. Leo, to whom she talked quite a bit over the phone, had never mentioned that any of this distressed him. Such was the life of a county law enforcement officer, he had told her.

Today, there was news of Donnie Harper. He had appeared before a judge on arraignment. Harper had been charged with Rosa's kidnapping and was facing life in prison, if found guilty. The article also mentioned Marvela Garcia, who was facing an additional charge of accessory to kidnapping. She had already pleaded guilty to failure to protect a child.

In a second story, Penny read a report from the El Paso County Health Department that the Garcias' house was found to have lead contaminants everywhere, including in the dishes the family ate on every night. The county health officer determined that both Rosa and Pedro were seriously malnourished and had been continually exposed to lead over their short lifetimes. They were to receive chelating therapy immediately. The health officer added, "I expect to dispel the lead from their bodies in about a year, but both children will always be smaller in size than their peers." He went on to say that it had been a miracle that both children had avoided any permanent damage to their internal organs, particularly their kidneys. Penny was relieved to learn Pedro and Rosa would be okay, realizing that kidney failure at such young ages could lead to early death. She also knew their whereabouts would remain a highly guarded secret to keep Rosa from being kidnapped again. Whether Pedro would ever return to his family was still unknown.

Penny was deep in thought about Rosa and her future, when the phone on the kitchen wall rang. She hobbled across the room to answer it. She recognized the voice and laughed.

"Zarn, it's so good to talk with you!"

"I heard the good news that Rosa is in a safe place—thanks to you."

"I have to admit, it feels great. Even though I almost got myself killed, I would like to do more remote viewing, if I ever get the chance."

"Well, that's why I called. Is there any way you could join me in training new converts to remote viewing? I hold classes for about two weeks every quarter."

"Are you serious? I would love to!"

"When can you start? I've got a class coming up in about a month."

"They had me on training wheels—chained to a walker— but I can now make it around with a cane. Yeah, I think I could manage it."

"I'll call you back in a couple of weeks, and see how you're feeling. You're a hero in my book, Penny. Thank you."

"I should be thanking you for not giving up on me. I sure did pitch a fit in your class!"

"Yeah, but it was worth pitching! Talk to you soon."

Penny hung up the phone, and leaned against the kitchen counter. *Who knew I could make a living at this?*

As she poured herself a second cup of coffee, the doorbell rang. In her usual uniform of khaki shorts and a black T-shirt, Penny limped to the front door. She could only imagine how she looked with her left leg in a cast and a cane to take the weight off her right hip. It still hurt, but the hairline fracture was healing. Heck, she was just lucky to be alive!

Leo stepped into the house without a single word of greeting and wrapped his right arm around Penny's shoulders. Although his left arm was still bandaged from his burns, he managed to maneuver two *machaca burritos* up to Penny's face.

"I thought I had better make sure you were eating well, now that you are charged with cooking on your own," Leo said.

"I'm not exactly cooking yet. I asked Clara to stay on with me.

She needed a place to live, and I needed the companionship." Penny got out two placemats and silverware.

"Let me help you!" Leo said. He rushed over to the kitchen cabinet where Penny stored the plates, then quickly set the table. It reminded her of the morning Leo had first sought her help on the kidnapping of Rosa. They had sat in silence, eating peanut butter sandwiches and gulping down coffee. They didn't know each other then. Now, they were laughing as Leo ceremoniously placed a burrito on her plate, scooped up some *pico de gallo*, and served her. He bowed like a headwaiter.

One month ago, the atmosphere between them had been tentative and filled with questions Leo was hoping Penny could answer. Today, those riddles had been solved, and Penny had more than proved her skill as a remote viewer. Now she and Leo were good friends, and there was the promise of something more. Leo reached across the table and took Penny's hand.

"I have something for you." He handed Penny a plain white envelope.

She looked at the formal stationery, then winked at him. "You are sending me a bill?" Penny laughed, and then her eyes widened. There was a check to her from the FBI for $100,000.

"What is this?" Penny was stunned. This was more money than she made in a couple of years.

"There was a reward offered by the FBI for Sergei Andulov. You brought down the ring leader of this Russian syndicate operating out of his Oakland restaurant, and the money is yours." "You mean, I killed him," Penny said. She had honestly not had time to deal with her shooting of Andulov to protect Leo.

She had been concentrating on her own physical healing, but now it was rearing its ugly head. A man was dead because of her. It stung.

"I have another bit of news. The Juárez police found Agent Brooks lying in a vacant lot off Avenue de Lincoln. He had been shot more than twenty times."

"What happened? " Penny was alarmed at hearing this. "The police chief said it looked like a drug cartel payback." "Wow! That is a shocker."

"It might explain why he gave me such a hard time about helping us find Rosa in the first place."

"We probably won't ever know why he was killed, will we?" "Actually, Donnie Harper is crying now for a better deal than his life in prison. He says he has information about the FBI." "Do you think you can believe him?"

"Lieutenant Ontiveros is at the jail now, questioning him. We will know soon enough."

Penny poured Leo more coffee, and both sat quietly for a few moments, watching the birds in the backyard. A screeching grackle was trying to drown out the singing of a pair of purple finches, who were flirting with each other on the rock wall. Leo got up from the table and walked to the window. Penny joined him, and they stood side by side, enjoying the simple pleasures of just being alive.

"What would you think if I gave some of this FBI windfall to Marvela's mother to help her with her cancer treatments? She is, after all, Rosa's grandmother, and Rosa may need her in the years to come."

"I would expect nothing less of you, Penny. But that is up to you. It's yours to keep. Do what you want with it." Leo walked back to the table where he had laid a black leather portfolio. "Would you believe I have two job possibilities for you to consider?"

"What are you talking about?"

"I got a call from Immigration and Customs. They were so impressed with your work on the sex trafficking case that they called me and asked if I thought you would consider working on contract when similar cases came along."

"And the other offer?"

"Oh, yes. The US Marshals office also got wind of your fine detective work. They've got more than 500 warrants out for federal suspects in El Paso that they can't locate. They asked if you might help with that too."

Penny shoved a burst of air out of her lungs. "Wow! Both of those sound very promising, as long as I don't have to put myself in harm's way, of course!"

"We can't promise you that a case won't place you in danger. You know that."

"I know. I just hope I can avoid falling out of airplanes!" Penny laughed, then got up, and limped to the kitchen sink with the dishes.

Leo laughed too and then walked up behind her and whispered in her ear. "I just hope you'll reserve a little time for cases with the Sheriff's Department. You've proven your worth to everyone. Even Deputy Gómez came up to me and apologized."

Leo gently leaned into her body and placed his arms around her. Penny laid the dishes carefully in the sink. Her hands were dripping with hot water. She was looking for a dishtowel to dry them when Leo turned her around and drew her in close to his face. His warm breath tickled the hair on her neck. Her eyes moistened, but this time, she was crying happy tears. She looked into his brown eyes, which were filled with admiration. He kissed her softly on the lips.

Penny laid her head on his chest. He rubbed her back, then leaned over and kissed her neck. What Penny was feeling for Leo was very different than what she'd felt for Porter. There was a sense of security with this man whose career was anything but secure. He placed himself in danger every time he put his gun in his holster and got into his patrol car. But none of that mattered to Penny. She wanted to get to know Leo better, and she believed he felt the same way about her.

The phone on the wall in her kitchen jangled loudly, startling them both. Penny left the comfort of Leo's arms and went to answer it.

"Porter?" Penny said in disbelief. "Where are you?" The connection was so close it sounded as if he was next door, and she heard no delay in the conversation. She turned her head away from Leo, who was standing there staring at her. Penny saw that she had tightened her grip on the phone. How could this be happening now?

Penny remained quiet as Porter continued to talk. It had always been that way. She seldom got a word in when Porter called. He was all business when it came to what he needed and expected out of his relationship with her or with anyone for that matter. Today was no different.

"I can't pick you up from the airport. I had an accident." She turned back to look at Leo, who was scowling.

"You will have to take a taxi here," she said. "I'm sorry, but that is just the way it is." She leaned against the wall as Porter continued talking. Her hip was killing her. "But, Porter." He kept insisting that he was on his way home, and he simply would not listen to anything Penny had to say. She knew better than to protest. "Okay. Fine! Good-bye."

Penny hung up the phone just as Leo was walking out of the kitchen and making a beeline for the front door.

"Wait!" she called out, but Leo ignored her and walked even faster. "Don't go, please."

By the time she made it to the front door and opened it, Leo's patrol car was pulling out of her driveway. She tried to get his attention, but he was looking straight ahead.

Hobbled by her broken leg and fragile hip, Penny could only make it to her living room sofa where she collapsed in tears. It drained her body of what little energy she had left after the long grueling month of healing. Why didn't she tell Porter to leave her alone?

Finally, Penny dragged herself from the couch and headed to her bedroom where she rummaged in her dresser drawer for the pearls Porter had given her. She fastened them to her neck and ran her hands across them, once again impressed with how they dressed up her old clothes. She went into her master bath, ran cold water over her face, and dried it with a hand towel. Somewhere under the sink, she had a jar of face cream. She retrieved it from a small basket of herbal oils and perfumes and rubbed it roughly on her face and neck. Penny looked at herself in the mirror. Was she the same person that Porter had left behind four months ago? She wondered if she had really changed or whether the same old Penny was hiding somewhere inside.

How could she feel so strongly about a man she had known for only a month when she had known Porter for many years? The doorbell rang. Porter must have been standing at the baggage claim when he'd called her because he had made it from the airport in record time. She threw the towel in the bathroom sink and walked at a snail's pace to the front door. A jolt of pain surged through her hip and down her leg. *There is no need to hurry. Porter can wait for me this time.*

She stood a few feet from the door, reluctant to walk any closer. It would take a great deal of effort to force her lips into a smile, but she had to. Porter had meant everything to her for many years. Perhaps he could again. Fortunately, her experiences with Leo had transformed the way she looked at life, and now she had a better understanding of what was important to her and what was not.

Porter would have to make some changes of his own if he wanted to stay in a relationship with her, even from a million miles away. She dragged her broken heart to the front door and reached for the doorknob, turning it slowly. She could see the familiar face in the beveled glass. Her body relaxed. She breathed in deeply and smiled. The sunlight was bouncing off his sheriff's badge. Leo stood patiently, waiting for Penny to open the door.

www.ingramcontent.com/pod-product-compliance
Lightning Source LLC
LaVergne TN
LVHW010317070526
838199LV00065B/5588